ELMHURST PUBLIC LIBRARY
3 1135 01857 6022
W9-BSC-542

WATCH YOUR STEP

DON'T MISS OUT ON ANY OF THE MISCHIEF!

THE BAD APPLE

A WORLD OF TROUBLE

WATCH YOUR STEP

Merits of Mischief

#3

WATCH YOUR STEP

T. R. BURNS

ALADDIN

NEW YORK LONDON TORONTO SYDNEY NEW DELHI

ALADDIN
An imprint of Simon & Schuster Children's Publishing Division
1230 Avenue of the Americas, New York, NY 10020
First Aladdin hardcover edition August 2014

Jacket designed by Jessica Handelman
Interior designed by Mike Rosamilia
The text of this book was set in Bembo.
Manufactured in the United States of America 0714 FFG
2 4 6 8 10 9 7 5 3 1
Full CIP data is available from the Library of Congress.
ISBN 978-1-4424-4035-7 (hc)
ISBN 978-1-4424-4037-1 (eBook)

For Aunt Lorraine

ACKNOWLEDGMENTS

With special thanks to Rebecca Sherman, Liesa Abrams, Alyson Heller, the wonderful teams at Writers House and Aladdin, and my friends and family.

WATCH
YOUR STEP

Chapter 1

It's funny. Once upon a time, summer was my favorite season. Come June there was no school or homework, no alarm clocks or early bedtimes. There was only three whole months to do whatever I wanted, whenever I wanted. All year long I counted down to that stretch of freedom.

But this summer? I wouldn't mind skipping it. Because there's what I want to do . . . and there's what I *have* to do. And those are two very different things.

"What can I get you, Seamus? Fish-stick pancakes? Fish-stick waffles? Fish-stick bacon? Fish-stick home fries? A bagel with cream cheese and fish sticks?"

It's the first day of vacation. Mom's spiraling around the kitchen like a tornado in a cornfield. Dad and I are sitting at the table. He's reading the newspaper and drinking coffee—the only breakfast item not featuring my favorite food.

I'm waiting.

Mom gasps. Spins toward the table. Waves a spatula like it's a hundred degrees in here and she's trying to keep me cool.

"I know," she says. "How about . . . a fish-stick *omelet*?"

"Sure," I say. "Thanks."

"Believe me." Mom spins toward the stove. "It's my pleasure."

I bet it is.

"So, son." Dad folds the newspaper and places it on the table. "Your first day off. Three free months ahead of you. Have you thought about how you'd like to spend them?"

"Well, they're not totally free. We'll still have weekly homework."

Dad sits back like I've just sneezed without covering my nose. "But it's summer vacation."

"And a great opportunity to sharpen our skills." I sneak a

peek at Mom. She stills at "skills," then cracks another egg over a bowl. "It's okay. I don't have any other plans."

"Then we should make some. How about a few rounds at the Cloudview Putt-n-Play this weekend? Some quality father-son time? Just like the old days?"

Dad gives me a small, hopeful smile. Behind his thick black-framed glasses, his eyes are bright. So much has happened since the old days, it's hard to imagine going back. But Dad didn't do anything. None of it was his fault.

"Okay," I say. "Sounds fun."

"Wonderful! I'll call when I get to the office and reserve a cart."

"You're leaving?" Mom asks as Dad brings his dishes to the sink. "Already?"

"The numbers won't crunch themselves," Dad says proudly.

"It's Seamus's first morning home. Can't you go in a little later?"

"Sorry, my dear. But I'll be back soon, and we'll have a great night. Together. As a family."

I've just taken a bite of omelet and now force it down my throat. Not because it tastes bad—although I must say, despite being made with my favorite food, it's not my favorite dish—but because the thought of Mom, Dad, and I as a family, the kind that talks and laughs and plays board games, is so strange and unexpected that I almost choke.

Dad kisses her cheek, then comes over and gives me a hug. When he's gone, Mom catches my eye, quickly turns away, and continues cooking.

This is it. We're alone. For the first time since Christmas morning, when I found her in the attic, surrounded by boxes of—

My K-Pak buzzes. I take the handheld computer from my shorts pocket and press the K-Mail icon.

TO: shinkle@kilteracademy.org
FROM: loliver@kilteracademy.org
SUBJECT: hey

S—
Happy to be home. You?
—L

I smile at the five-word e-mail. This is typical Lemon. The only thing my roommate uses less than syllables is exclamation points.

I press reply.

"Errands."

I look up.

"I just remembered," Mom says, emptying the frying pan. "I need to go to the dry cleaners. And the post office. And the grocery store. And the vet."

"We don't have a pet," I say.

She drops the spatula. It lands on the floor with a *thwack*. "I think I read that they're having adoptions today. Wouldn't that be nice? To welcome an adorable puppy or kitten into our family?"

Our family. It sounds even stranger coming from her.

She steps over the spatula and places a plate of mushy eggs and seafood onto the table before me. "Don't worry about the mess. I'll take care of it when I get back."

My chin drops. This is easily the weirdest thing she's said since she and Dad picked me up yesterday afternoon. Before I left Cloudview Middle School for Kilter Academy for Troubled Youth—or was yanked out of one and left at the other—I had a list of daily chores that needed to be completed before I did anything else, including homework. The first item on that list was making my bed. The second was cleaning the kitchen after breakfast. Skipping either was never an option. One time I was up late playing video games, overslept, and had eight minutes to get ready for school—and I still swept the kitchen floor and loaded the dishwasher, even though my breakfast was a handful of granola that I gulped down while sprinting to the bus, which I almost missed. Another time, Mom found crumbs because I forgot to wipe the table, and I lost TV privileges for a month. After that I didn't want to find out what she'd do if I skipped the task entirely.

So why the sudden rule change? Like the morning fish-stick overload, is it meant to butter me up? Or distract me? Or make me forget what she did?

Hearing her hurry around upstairs, I return to my K-Pak.

TO: loliver@kilteracademy.org
FROM: shinkle@kilteracademy.org
SUBJECT: RE: Hey

Hi, Lemon!

So great to hear from you. I can't believe it's been less than 24 hours since we left Kilter. It already feels

> like 24 days since you made Abe, Gabby, and me our last black-bean breakfast burritos of the semester.
>
> How are your parents? And your little brother? He must be really happy you're home.
>
> Everything's okay here. Different, but I guess that's normal since I was away for so long. My dad and I already have some fun things planned, so that's good. I missed him.
>
> But it's still a little weird. I bet—

There's a loud bang upstairs. It's so loud I jump in my chair. My thumbs shoot across the K-Pak screen. I accidentally send Lemon's unfinished note. The sound's followed by several smaller, quieter thumps. When I land back in my seat, I register where they're coming from.

The attic.

Mom's cell phone rings. It's on the counter, next to her purse and car keys. I hurry over to it, glance at Dad's smiling face on the phone screen, and tap the red rectangle to ignore the call. The ringing stops. The screen goes black.

"Sorry," I say.

And I am. For sending Dad to voicemail before Mom can hear her phone and rush downstairs. For doing what I'm about to do, which is something I never would've done eight months ago—or anytime before I found Mom huddled in the attic, surrounded by Kilter Academy boxes.

Most of all, I'm sorry for having that reason to do what I'm about to do.

Taking Mom's keys from the counter, I slide the key ring onto a dish towel. I hold both ends of the towel so that the keys slip to the middle, raise my arm, and start making small, slow circles. Then I lift my arm higher and make bigger, faster circles. Soon the towel is whipping above my head like a lasso.

As my eyes look for a target, my head fills with other images. I see the Cloudview Middle School cafeteria. A shiny red apple flying toward a cluster of fighting kids. Miss Parsippany, my substitute teacher, collapsing to the floor. A big, open field. A line of apple-headed mannequins defenseless against the archery arrows headed their way. An ancient school bus flying through the desert. Flaming paper airplanes.

Me, throwing the shiny red apple. Firing archery arrows. Hurling flaming paper airplanes.

And then I select my current target. And the other images disappear.

I spin the keys again, then snap my wrist. The key ring slips from the dish towel, sails through the air across the kitchen, and descends in a perfect arc toward the stove.

Where it lands with a plop into a pot of fish-stick oatmeal.

I put the dish towel back on the counter, then return to my chair and pick up my K-Pak. I'm reading about Kilter's plans to expand the Kommissary, the school store, when Mom enters the kitchen a few minutes later.

"Well, that's strange," she says.

"What?" I ask, not looking up.

"My car keys were right here."

"Where?"

"On the counter. Between my cell phone and pocketbook."

"Are you sure?"

"Yes. That's where I always put them."

"You must've put them somewhere else."

"I didn't. I distinctly remember placing them here when we got home."

"Oh, well," I say. "Guess you can't do your errands now."

I peer over my K-Pak and watch her rummage through her purse. She turns the bag upside down and dumps its contents onto the counter. Her fingers tremble as she sifts through tissues and breath mints, loose change and coupons.

"We can spend all day together," I add. "Won't that be nice?"

Her hands freeze. They thaw a second later, and she throws everything that's on the counter back into her purse.

"No problem," she says. "I'll walk."

"Town's four miles away."

"The exercise will do me good."

Taking her bag, she flies from the kitchen. The front door opens and slams shut.

Still in my hand, the K-Pak buzzes.

TO: shinkle@kilteracademy.org
FROM: loliver@kilteracademy.org
SUBJECT: RE: RE: hey

Different how?

Weird in what way?

—L

I press reply, start typing.

TO: loliver@kilteracademy.org
FROM: shinkle@kilteracademy.org
SUBJECT: RE: RE: RE: hey

You don't want to know. Trust me.
I wish I didn't.

Chapter 2

DEMERITS: 300
GOLD STARS: 50

Relax your grip. Stand up straight. Shake it out. Spit."

Dad pushes his enormous black sunglasses, which remind me of the helmet face shield I wore during my first real-world Kilter combat mission, up the bridge of his nose. It's ninety degrees out and we've been standing under the blazing hot sun for an hour, so the instant he pushes them up, sweat sends them sliding right back down.

"Spit?" I ask. "Like, at the ball?"

"There." Up go the sunglasses. "Or anywhere." Down they go. "It's a good release."

I'm so thirsty I want to dunk my head and gulp the hole's water trap dry, but I do as he says. I relax my grip on the miniature golf club. Stand up straight. Shake out my sweaty arms and legs. Swipe my dry mouth with my dry tongue, aim for a nearby patch of real grass, and spit.

"Good." Dad paces behind me, analyzing the shot from every angle. "Now, just stay calm. Hold steady. Don't overthink. *Feel* the motion."

I try to hide my smile. Little does he know that this is kind of my specialty. Kilter students are divided by troublemaking talent into six groups. Because I was sent to Kilter for accidentally taking down my substitute teacher in a crowded cafeteria with a single apple, I was assigned to the marksmen group. That means that in addition to attending classes and doing regular homework (if you call burping the alphabet homework), I meet with Ike, an upper level marksman and my troublemaking tutor, who helps me improve my aim and technique. Compared to some of his assignments, putting a yellow ball down a patch of fake grass, through a fake polar bear's jaws, and into a small hole is like brushing my teeth. So easy I could do it with my eyes closed. Which I often do, because it takes me a while to wake up in the morning.

But Dad doesn't know this. And he never can.

I curl my fingers around the club and survey the course. Once again, the hole-in-one route's obvious. I need to whack the ball left.

"That's it," Dad says quietly from the sidelines. "You can do it, son."

Son.

I tap the ball right. When it stalls on the fake grass six inches away from the fake polar bear's mouth, I clap one hand to my forehead and groan.

"Hey, hey!" Dad says. "Don't be hard on yourself. That was a fantastic shot! And you'll just make up the strokes on the next hole."

Which is what he said after I finished each of the sixteen holes before this one. That's why I keep playing badly. He's always so nice, he deserves to win.

Dad finishes the hole in five strokes, plus a one-stroke penalty for his ball bouncing off course and into a bush. I finish in six strokes, plus a three-stroke penalty for hitting my ball into a bush, a sand pit, and a little boy's ice cream cone.

"Chin up," Dad says as he records our scores. "We still have one to go!"

The last hole is where you return your balls. There are no fountains or fake animals. There's only a narrow plank that inclines up toward the hole. All your ball has to do is make it up the plank without rolling off and dropping into the pit below. It looks like the surest, easiest shot of the entire course, but it's actually the hardest. Probably because whoever makes it wins a free game and two hot dogs.

Dad goes first. And misses.

I go next. And make it in.

Above the hole, a red light bulb flashes. A siren sounds. Dad throws up both hands, sending the scorecard and tiny pencil flying.

"Seamus! How did you—? What did you—?" He looks around, motions to nearby putters. "See that? That's my boy!"

I don't hide my smile now. "Can we come back tomorrow?"

"*Can* we!" He puts one arm around my shoulders and gives me a squeeze. "Have I told you lately how proud I am of you?"

For a split second, my smile disappears. My stomach turns. I'm tempted to tell him everything, only so I can apologize and swear I'll never do any of it again.

But then I remind myself that what he doesn't know can't hurt him. And say yes when he asks if I'd like a celebratory snow cone for the road.

The drive home is fun. I eat my treat. Dad sings along to the oldies on the radio. Every now and then I sing too, which makes Dad so happy he laughs and claps and swerves into the next lane. I try to think of somewhere else to go to prolong the trip. Before I can, my K-Pak buzzes with a new message.

I start to turn off the computer without checking my K-Mail. I'm sure it can wait, and I want to focus on having fun with Dad. But then I glimpse the sender's name. And my fingertip hits the digital envelope.

TO: shinkle@kilteracademy.org
FROM: enorris@kilteracademy.org
SUBJECT: Hi

Hi, Seamus,

How are you? Happy to be home? Having fun with your parents?

I'm great! Okay, maybe not great. But really

good. Definitely fine. The desert's a hundred and twelve degrees and the pools are still filled with snakes instead of water, but Mom hasn't thrown me into any of them yet. That's something, right?

Anyway, I just wanted to say hi and see how you were. Also, I know it's only been a few days . . . but I miss you.

Anyway, I'm sure you're really busy, but if you have a minute to write back, please do. I'd love to hear from you.

From,

Elinor

"Everything okay?"

My head snaps up. The K-Pak hits my chest.

"Your face is the same color as your mouth," he adds.

I lower the visor and check the mirror. The cherry snow cone stained my lips red. And Dad's right. My face matches them perfectly.

"Everything's fine." I flip up the visor.

"She must be special."

"She? Who said anything about . . ." My voice trails off. If he were anyone else, I'd totally deny his assumption. But he's Dad. So, "Yeah. She is."

His eyes are hidden behind the enormous black sunglasses, but I know he winks at me. Then he returns his attention to the road, cranks up the radio, and starts whistling.

I return my attention to Elinor's note. My eyes stick on "I miss you" and "I'd love to hear from you." Since leaving Kilter, an hour hasn't gone by that I haven't wanted to write her, but I've been waiting. After Lemon, Abe, Gabby, and I rescued her from her mother's strange secret school in Arizona and brought her back to Kilter last semester, Elinor and I hung out a lot. Usually in a group, but sometimes just us. By the end of the semester we were really good friends. So checking in after saying good-bye for the summer probably wouldn't have seemed like a big deal. But I didn't want to be pushy, just in case. Also, I wanted to see if she'd write me if I didn't write her.

And she did. Which makes a great day even better.

My K-Pak buzzes again. I open the new message.

TO: shinkle@kilteracademy.org
FROM: kommissary@kilteracademy.org
SUBJECT: Nice work!

> Hey, Seamus!
>
> After your impressive first-year performance we shouldn't be surprised by your stellar summer shenanigans—but we are! That trick with the laundry basket this morning? When you hid behind the vacuum and chucked in dirty socks every time your mom turned to the washing machine, so that the basket never emptied? Priceless!
>
> Know what's not priceless? The Kilter Bubble Blaster 3000.

A movie-reel icon appears. I make sure the K-Pak's on mute, then tap the icon. A video starts. In the demo clip, a kid my age empties a bottle of laundry detergent, then refills it with purple liquid. He takes a long, thin tube and places one end into the bottle. The other end holds a small wand that looks like the ones that come with toy bubbles, except it's silver. The kid raises the wand near his mouth, smiles at the camera, and purses his lips. He puffs once, like the wand's a birthday candle on a cupcake, and disappears. So does the entire room he's standing in. Everything in the camera's shot is swallowed by a thick cloud of white foam. In the next instant, the foam gives way to thousands of clear bubbles. The bubbles pop all at once, and the kid reappears. The room looks as it did before he blew into the wand.

The video ends. I return to the e-mail.

> With a 25-foot firing range and an automatic cleanup feature, the Kilter Bubble Blaster is the best in its class. If your mom thought doing the wash was a chore before, she'll wear the same skirt forever to avoid it now!
>
> This one-of-a-kind toy can be yours for 200 credits. Your dirty-sock toss this morning earned you 150 credits. Add that to the other ones you've earned since being home, and you have more than enough credits to make the KBB 3000 your own!
>
> And don't worry—shipping's on us. If you place an order, we'll overnight the KBB 3000 free of charge!
>
> Keep up the good work!
>
> At Your Service,
>
> The Kommissary Krew
>
> P.S. To make sure you keep making trouble at

> home, starting today you'll earn 50 gold stars a day, no matter what! And we don't have to remind you that you get 1 credit for every demerit you earn—and lose 1 credit for every gold star you earn!

When I finish reading, a thought occurs to me.

At Kilter, the school store's always e-mailing with credit updates and weapons suggestions. But that's because Annika, teachers, and even other students are always watching and reporting our troublemaking tactics. It's how they monitor our progress and keep us on our toes.

But I'm home now. Hundreds of miles away from Kilter.

So how does anyone there know what I'm doing here?

I'm still trying to figure it out when we turn onto our street. Then, not wanting the fun with Dad to end already, I decide to worry about it later.

"Want to play Scrabble?" I ask. This is his favorite game.

"Sure." He shifts in his seat. Loosens the collar of his yellow polo shirt. Checks the rearview mirror like we're being followed. "I just . . . have to do something first? Like, for work? Yes, definitely for work. It's extremely urgent."

"Okay." Wondering why he's acting so weird, I watch his neck turn pink. "Whenever you're ready."

We pull into the driveway. Dad turns off the car, throws open his door, and hurries toward the house.

I follow after him. By the time I reach the front foyer, he's already in his office with the door closed. Still hot from our game, I go to the kitchen for a glass of water.

"You're back!" Mom's sitting at the table with an open book before her. As I enter the room, she snaps the cover shut. "How was it?"

Once again I'm reminded of how different this summer is from other summers. Because this time last year, I would've gotten a nice glass of iced tea, sat at the table with Mom, and told her all about miniature golf. Part of me still wants to do that now. But the way she closed the book when I came into the room? She's definitely hiding something. And before I do anything else this summer, I *have* to figure out what that is.

"Un-fay-ay," I say, and head for the cabinets.

"Un-fay-ay?" she asks. "What does that mean?"

Exactly what I said: fun. Only I said it in pig French, which I learned at Kilter, and which is like pig Latin but with an extra "ay" at the end of each word. This is how I've been speaking to Mom for forty-eight hours. If I'd pulled this a few months ago, she would've banished me to my room until I promised to speak properly. Now she just grits her teeth and forces a smile, like she's amused by my language artistry.

When I don't answer, she gets up, taking the book with her, and flees the kitchen. "Time to weed!" she calls back. "See you soon!"

I gulp down a glass of water. Then I go upstairs, pass my room, and start up another flight of stairs . . . to the attic.

It's cold. Dark. Somewhere I rarely go. I'm going now because Mom's been acting nervous around me. And I want to make sure she's no longer doing what I found her doing when I was home for Christmas.

Holding my breath, I flick on the overhead lightbulb. And then I exhale, relieved. They're gone. All of the Kilter Academy boxes—filled with top secret troublemaking tools and weapons that no one off campus should ever know about, but that Mom somehow did *and* was able to get her hands on—are gone. All that remains are regular boxes filled with old clothes and holiday decorations.

Satisfied, I start toward the staircase.

Halfway there, my foot hits something hard. I stumble forward, then stoop down to pick up whatever tripped me.

And I almost fall over again.

Because I just walked into a brand-new Kilter Boomaree with night-vision technology. That Mom must've missed when cleaning out the other evidence.

Heart thumping, I grab the Boomaree and run down the attic stairs. I dart into my room and head for the open windows.

She's still there. Yanking weeds from the dirt and tossing them into a wheelbarrow. She's on her hands and knees with her back to me, so this could be the easiest trouble I ever make.

I'm still not sure I want to be the kind of kid who takes advantage of such opportunities . . . but Mom obviously wanted me to be. Why else would she have sent me away to a fake reform school? That she knew was actually a top secret troublemaking training facility?

I can't think of another reason. So I'll give her what she asked for, one more time.

The Boomaree's part boomerang, part Frisbee. With the help of a small control box, you throw it like a disc and it circles back to you like a boomerang. I haven't used one since the Ultimate

Troublemaking Task at the end of my first semester at Kilter. That's when Lemon, Gabby, Abe, Elinor, and I successfully completed the mission by making Annika, the school's director, cry by setting the merry-go-round on fire at the old dilapidated amusement park her father built for her.

Fortunately, it turns out that throwing a Boomaree is like riding a bicycle. The technique comes back the second I pull it back to fling it forward. The Boomaree flies so fast you don't see it, only hear it buzz as it whizzes past. Common target reaction is to bat at it like it's a pesky bug.

Which Mom does when I throw it again. And again. With every launch, her reaction gets better. Soon she jumps to her feet and shakes out her hair. Rushes to the opposite end of the vegetable patch. Hops between lettuce heads to get to the other side.

When I think she's had enough, I stop. After several days of similar tricks, we can call it even. Mom must've had her reasons for doing what she did, and maybe someday she'll tell me what they were. But for now, we can activate a silent truce and try to enjoy the rest of the summer.

I hide the Boomaree under my bed, then leave my room and

head for the bathroom. Our house is old and doesn't have air-conditioning, so the best way to deal with the sweltering summer heat is to take lots of cold showers. I was already burning up after miniature golf, and messing with Mom has made it worse. I can't wait to read Elinor's note again and write her back, but I don't want to be distracted by sweat dripping onto my K-Pak screen when I do.

Inside the bathroom I close and lock the door. Already imagining how great the ice-cold water will feel, I get undressed, step into the tub, turn the faucet—and scream.

The water's not ice-cold. It's molten-lava hot.

I leap out of the tub. Shake out my arms and legs. Jump from one foot to the other, like the tile floor is an active volcano crater. When I cool down enough to think straight, I turn off the water, then turn it on again, careful to keep the temperature pointer on the coldest position possible.

Steam billows around me as the water burns hotter.

I go to the sink and spin the cold knob as far as it'll go. When only hot water gushes from the faucet, I throw on my shorts, grab the rest of my stuff, and dash downstairs. The same thing happens with the sink in the kitchen and in the first-floor bathroom.

I'm now melting. Officially. But despite our silent truce, I don't want to ask Mom for help. Dad's still in his office, so I don't want to ask him either. Too hot to think of other options, I grab ice cubes from the refrigerator freezer, go to my bedroom, and collapse onto the bed.

I'm sucking on ice and pretending my mattress is a glacier, when my K-Pak buzzes with another message from the Kommissary. Congratulating me on my recent Boomaree performance and the one hundred credits it earned, and suggesting that I might like the brand-new Boomketball.

A movie-reel icon is at the end of the message. Instead of pressing it for a video demo, I hit reply.

TO: kommissary@kilteracademy.org
FROM: shinkle@kilteracademy.org
SUBJECT: RE: Nice work!

Hi,

Thanks for telling me about this! The Boomketball sounds like a lot of fun.

But quick question. Since I'm home and not at

school, how do you know what kind of trouble I'm making?

Sincerely,

Seamus

I send the message. Two seconds later, I get an answer.

TO: shinkle@kilteracademy.org
FROM: kommissary@kilteracademy.org
SUBJECT: RE: RE: Nice work!

Hey, Seamus!

We have no idea what you're doing at home. But somehow, someway, someone else does. And you can probably guess who that someone is!

I sure can. Because now that I think about it, I know only one person has that kind of sneaky superpower.

Annika.

Chapter 3

DEMERITS: 375
GOLD STARS: 100

First, fold the paper in half. Then unfold it. Next fold it in half the other way. Then unfold it. Now you have four perfect squares. See?"

I do. But I don't quite believe it.

"Lemon, no offense . . . but where did this new hobby come from?"

We're talking via our K-Paks' video-chat feature, which was magically remotely installed on our devices last night. This would be a shocking high-tech achievement back at Cloudview

Middle School, where notes are still taken with paper and pencils, but I learned fast that Kilter's ahead of the technological curve. So when I woke up this morning to Lemon staring at me from my nightstand, where I'd put my K-Pak before going to sleep, I was only slightly freaked out. After I blinked and he was still there, I put two and two together—and was just really excited to see him.

"Why would I be offended?" Lemon asks.

"You wouldn't be," I say. "Or shouldn't be. This . . . just seems a little unlike you. That's all."

His eyes hold mine. Then his head turns slowly, stopping only when his neck won't twist anymore. Several strings criss-cross the wall behind him. Hanging from them are dozens of brightly colored paper shapes. There are red paper dogs. Purple paper hats. Blue paper airplanes. Pink paper hearts. All of which Lemon made himself.

He turns back. "It's origami. The traditional Japanese art of paper folding."

"I know."

"Japan's cool."

"It is. And paper's awesome." I don't have strong feelings one way or the other about this nearly extinct material, but if folding it makes Lemon happy, it makes me happy too. "You just never did it at Kilter. Or ever said anything about it."

The corners of his lips turn down. Then they lift and his mouth settles into an even line. "I made a shark out of a piece of tinfoil the other day and gave it to my little brother. He really liked it, so I went online to find out how to make other things. That's how I learned about origami. You need special square paper to do it, so my mom and I went to the craft store."

Before I can say anything, there's a knock on his bedroom door.

"Enter," Lemon says.

The door opens. A shorter, skinnier version of my best friend hurries into the room and holds up a giant matchstick.

"Look what I found!"

Lemon peers over his shoulder. Then he drops the piece of paper he's been folding and jumps up. "Finn. Where'd you get that?"

"The garbage," Lemon's little brother says. "It's yours, right?"

"It *was* mine. Before I threw it out."

"But it still works. See?" Finn presses a button. An orange

flame appears at the top of the long lighter. "If you don't want it, can I—"

Lemon dashes across the room and snatches away the fire starter. "Play with these instead." He thrusts a stack of paper at Finn, ushers him out of the room, and closes the door. Then he returns to his desk, picks up the paper he dropped, and continues folding. "Sorry about that."

"No problem," I say.

"Anyway. You wouldn't believe how many different kinds of paper there are. All colors. All sizes. Some are shiny. Some even have glitter."

"It seems like a fun hobby. And you're obviously great at it. But—"

"Son!"

I jump. Dad knocks on my bedroom door.

"I'm off to work! And your mother's already left for her spa day with the girls. We'll both be back around five. Have fun! See you later!"

"Scrabble rematch tonight?" I call back.

He doesn't answer. All I hear are his usually slow footsteps racing down the hallway.

"Something wrong?" Lemon asks.

I frown at the closed door. "Don't know."

Because Dad usually won't leave for work until he gives me a hug. If I'm in the shower or getting dressed, he'll wait for me to come downstairs so we can go through our morning routine before he leaves. Even if it means getting to work late.

I'm about to run this by Lemon when my K-Pak beeps.

"It's Abe," I say, reading the name in the notification box now covering Lemon's nose. "Should I answer?"

Lemon analyzes his paper work in progress. Taking this as permission to proceed, I tap the notification box. The K-Pak screen splits as the face of our fellow Capital T alliance member appears next to Lemon's.

"Hey," Abe says.

"Hi." I smile. Abe and I aren't as close as Lemon and I are, but we still went through a lot together over the past year. It's nice to see him. "How's it going?"

"Great! I mean, fine." He tilts his chin toward where Lemon must be on his K-Pak screen. "Fancy finger work, L-Dog."

"How's your summer?" I ask before Abe can annoy Lemon.

"Busy," he says. "But I just wanted to check up on—I mean

in with—you guys. See what you've been doing. If you've been practicing anything we learned at school."

"I've been trying a few things," I say, intentionally vague. Abe's ultra competitive and is always trying to be the best Troublemaker in our class, so not knowing exactly what I've been doing will bother him—and entertain me.

His eyes narrow, but he doesn't press. "Lemon? Set any mailboxes on fire lately?

Lemon's hands freeze. It's a reasonable question, but he obviously doesn't like it. Fortunately, my K-Pak beeps again.

"Gabby," I say as her name pops up on the screen. "Should I answer?"

"No," Abe says.

"Yes," Lemon says.

I tap the box. Lemon's and Abe's faces shrink as the K-Pak screen divides into thirds and Capital T's fourth member appears.

"Oh my goodness!" Gabby squeals. "You *guys*! There you *are*! I've missed you *so* much! How *are* you? Tell me everything!"

"Did you just kiss your K-Pak camera?" Abe asks.

She did. At least that's what it looked like when her face got really big, disappeared behind a shiny pink mouth, and reappeared again after she rubbed lip-gloss film from the camera lens.

But Gabby doesn't confirm this. Instead, her blue eyes widen until they seem to take up half her head. They aim at Abe, who looks away to avoid becoming trapped in her powerful death stare.

"We're good," I offer. "How about you?"

Gabby's eyes return to their normal size. "Great! Especially now that we can talk to and see each other, like, all the time!"

A loud knock comes through the K-Pak speaker.

"Busy!" Abe calls out.

Abe's bedroom door opens. A man—I assume his dad—appears behind him.

"Even for a little sports action before work?" Mr. Hansen holds up both hands. A football is in one, a baseball in the other.

"Yes," Abe says.

"But you can pick the sport!" Mr. Hansen exclaims.

"Then I pick none," Abe says.

"Oh, come on! A little friendly competition is great for—"

Mr. Hansen stops when Abe swivels around in his chair. I can only see the back of his head so don't know what kind of look he gives his dad, but it must be pretty serious. Because his dad frowns and leaves the room without another word.

Abe swivels backs. “So. Gabby. Have you been making trouble?”

Gabby pauses, and I know she wants to ask about what just happened. But she answers his question instead. “Maybe a little. But only because I had to!”

“Why’d you have to?” I ask.

“Flora? My older sister? She’s out of control! She was *so* sweet when I first got home, but now? It’s like she’s doing everything she can to get rid of me. Like, she took my favorite stuffed monkey slippers without asking. Then when she gave them back, they were covered in grass stains. And—”

“Hey! Dorkus!”

Gabby’s mouth snaps shut. Her bedroom door swings open. A teenager with long blond hair bursts inside and flies around the room.

“Mom and I are going to the mall. I need a jacket. Where’s your denim one? With the crystal buttons? And flower patches? And . . .”

The girl, who I assume is Flora, Gabby’s sister, keeps

rambling as she opens drawers and flings around clothes, but I stop listening. I focus only on Gabby, who looks down and says nothing. *Nothing.* Gabby. Who always has *something* to say.

"Aha!" Flora pops out of a closet and holds up the jacket. "Have fun with your books. Oh, and don't wait on us for lunch. We'll probably eat out. Later, Geek Girl!"

Flora leaves. Gabby's still and silent for another second. Then, carrying her K-Pak, she gets up, closes the door her sister leaves open, and sits back down.

"So," she says. "Like I was saying, she got grass stains on my slippers. And who wears slippers, especially beautiful ones like that, outside? Then she ate all of my yogurt-covered raisins, which she hates and knows Mom only buys for me. Then—"

"Gabby," Abe says, and I think he's going to ask what that was about, why she let Flora just barge in and take her jacket, how come she didn't go to the mall too. But he returns the favor she paid him instead. By ignoring the incident entirely.

"What?" Gabby asks.

"Get to the point," he says. "What have you been practicing?"

I only half listen as she talks about glow-in-the-dark contact lenses, X-Ray sunglasses, and other tools she's been using to

get back at her sister. Gabby's in the Biohazard group at Kilter because of her ability to manipulate her gaze to get anyone to do anything she wants, and it seems she's been keeping up on those skills while home.

I'm still half listening when Abe—who for his talent in drawing, painting, and otherwise creating confusing, occasionally scary works of art, is a member of Les Artistes at Kilter—hints at what he's been up to. Clearly wanting to keep a troublemaking edge, he admits only to working on an outdoor wall mural in the dark of night. When completed, the masterpiece will supposedly turn his entire neighborhood upside down.

While they're talking, I focus mostly on Lemon. He folds and unfolds the same square sheet of paper over and over again. He doesn't pay any attention to Gabby and Abe. The only time he looks up is when there's a knock on his bedroom door. Then he puts down the paper and stares into the K-Pak camera.

"Later," he says, right before his third of my K-Pak screen goes dark.

"What's his problem?" Abe asks.

"*He* doesn't have a problem," Gabby says. "He's just being Lemon. What's your excuse?"

My stomach grumbles, reminding me that I haven't eaten breakfast. "I should go too, guys. V-chat later?"

They agree. We say good-bye and hang up. As I climb out of bed and shuffle across the room, I think about Lemon and his strange new hobby. Did something happen? Are his parents giving him a hard time about his old hobby, the one that made them send him to Kilter? The super-exclusive reform school for the worst kids in the country?

I pause with one hand on the doorknob. It's so weird to think that that's what parents—minus Mom, of course—believe Kilter is. A great place to turn bad kids into good ones. Its real purpose, to turn naturally talented amateur troublemakers into professional ones, is known only by Annika, Kilter staff members, and, shortly after their arrival, Kilter students.

"Crazy," I say, and turn the knob.

It doesn't move.

I twist the other way. Then back again. I make sure the door's unlocked. I twist and turn some more. I squeeze the knob and lean all of my weight back until I'm standing at a forty-five degree angle.

It won't budge.

My heart races. My palms grow slick.

"Don't panic," I say.

And I don't. At least not right away. First I take a sock from my dresser and the Rubik's cube from my desk. I hold the sock's ends in one fist and load the cube into the loop. Then I pull back the sock like it's a slingshot and let the cube fly. It nails the knob and drops to the floor.

Hoping to break the knob off the door, I do this three more times. Then I dart across the room and jiggle the knob.

Nothing. It's like it's superglued in place.

I start to panic. Just a little. Because nobody's home. It's only ten o'clock. Mom and Dad won't be back for hours. There's no phone in here, so I can't call and ask them to come let me out. I haven't been to the bathroom yet today. My empty stomach's growling. It's already hot in here, and once the sun's all the way up, the room will begin to boil. Then my skin will ooze off my body, my bones will splinter and crumble, and all that'll remain of the sometimes-bad-but-mostly-good kid formerly known as Seamus Hinkle is a messy mound of hair, green pajama pants, and a Kilter Academy T-shirt.

My K-Pak buzzes then, saving me from a premature

meltdown. Hoping it's an e-mail from one of my parents, even though that's impossible since the K-Pak can't receive messages from non-Kilter e-mail addresses, I rush to the nightstand.

The note's not from Mom or Dad. It's from Miss Parsippany. My former substitute teacher, accidental apple casualty, and current pen pal. Who's also the only exception to the no-non-Kilter-e-mail rule. (We've chalked it up to a glitch in the Kilter system.) I haven't heard from her in weeks.

TO: shinkle@kilteracademy.org
FROM: parsippany@cloudviewschools.net
SUBJECT: Happy Summer!

Dear Seamus,

Hello! How are you? Happy to be home? Enjoying your summer break?

I'm sorry I haven't written in a while. As I mentioned in my last note, I was doing some traveling. And I learned that when you're deep in the Appalachian wilderness, or lost among the Utah red rocks, or exploring a remote island fifty miles off the Floridian coast, Internet service can be hard to find. By the way, have you ever had a coconut? A real one, right off the palm tree? If not, I highly recommend it.

Anyway, I just wanted to say hello. Also, I was wondering if you'd seen Bartholomew John since you've been home. If so, how is he? Still starting fights? And getting into trouble? Have you visited with other kids from Cloudview? Or from around your neighborhood? Have you encountered any other local troublemakers? You're such an expert now I bet you can spot the real ones before they even fire a spitball—or throw an apple! ;)

My helicopter's about to take off so I should wrap this up. Please write when you can. I'd love to hear from you.

With Kind Regards,

Miss Parsippany

A few things in this note stand out. First, Miss Parsippany doesn't say what she was doing in all of those interesting locations.

Is she on a long vacation? But she mentioned traveling during the school year, too . . . so is she on a *really* long vacation? And why's she asking me about my archnemesis, Bartholomew John? Why does she want to know if I've met other local troublemakers? And most people fly by plane, so what's she doing in a helicopter?

These are all things to think about. But I can't. Not now. Because one thing in her note has made it impossible to think about anything else.

Coconuts. They remind me that I'm starving.

Vowing to write her back as soon as I'm free, I put the K-Pak back on the nightstand and go to the window.

"It's ten inches," I lie. Because my room's on the second floor. I hate heights. Trying to convince myself that the ground is much closer is the only way I'll be able to reach it.

I keep my gaze level with the trees as I sit on the window ledge. Holding my breath, I lift one leg up and through the open space.

At which point a swarm of bloodthirsty bats lunge at my face. Or two butterflies flutter past. It's hard to be sure since whatever it is makes me fly back through the window and land hard on the bedroom floor.

"Elinor's waiting in the backyard," I say, picking myself up. Unfortunately, this too is a lie. But pretending it's true helps me come up with another plan of attack.

I pull the top sheet from the bed and knot one corner around one leg of my desk. Then I toss the rest of it out the open window so that it hangs like a rope down the side of the house. I grab my K-Pak from the nightstand and stick it in the waistband of my pajama pants. If I fall and break my legs, I can always e-mail or V-chat Lemon and ask him to call 9-1-1.

Then I sit on the window ledge. Move my legs into the open air. Squeeze the sheet in both hands. Take a deep breath. And push off the ledge.

It works. My awkward slip-stop-shimmy technique probably wouldn't earn a standing ovation from Tarzan, but that's okay. All that matters is that five minutes after leaving my bedroom, my feet touch grass. Which, dropping to my hands and knees, I kiss before sprinting to the back door.

I find the spare key under Mom's favorite concrete turtle, unlock the door, and burst inside the house. I smile and wave to the couch, call out hello to the washing machine, feeling like I was this-close to never seeing them again.

I hit the bathroom first, then run to the kitchen.

"Fish sticks," I gasp. "Must . . . have . . . fish sticks."

I stumble toward the refrigerator. Throwing open the freezer, I relish the icy blast to my face, then thrust one hand inside.

They're not there. The freezer has held an endless supply of fish sticks since I've been home . . . but now there's none. Where bags and bags of my favorite food should be, there's only a half-empty ice cube tray and a box of frozen spinach.

Thinking they must be thawing out for tonight's dinner, I check the refrigerator. But there are none in there, either.

Mom's up to something. I'm as sure of this as I am that Lemon's new origami hobby is strange. I don't know what, exactly—but I'm going to find out.

Starting with the book she tried to cover up the other day.

I eat a bagel as I check cabinets and drawers. Finding nothing, I head for the laundry room. Since Mom's the only one who hangs out in there, she probably thought it'd make a great hiding place.

I'm halfway down the hall when something stops me. One hand clamps to my mouth, the other to my stomach. My breakfast sloshes around, threatens to shoot back out the way it just went in. My eyes water. My nostrils burn.

It's a smell. A *stench*. Of something dying. Decaying. Rotting.

The odor's bad. So bad, it's taking all my strength and concentration to keep the bagel down the hatch.

And it's coming from Dad's office.

Chapter 4

DEMERITS: 400
GOLD STARS: 100

Let me get this straight. Your mom was reading in the kitchen. You had no cold water. You got locked in your room. Your gross fish sticks were thrown out." Abe pauses. "Is that everything?"

I review my mental checklist. "Yes."

"You think your parents turned off the cold water?" Gabby asks. "Like, on purpose? And locked you in your room? And suddenly threw out your favorite food that they'd been making for you since you got home?"

"I do." It's the only explanation I can come up with.

"Why would they do all those things?" Gabby asks.

"No idea," I admit.

"Have your parents called a plumber?" Abe asks.

"Yes, but—"

"Has the lock on your bedroom door ever gotten stuck before?"

"Maybe, but—"

"Did you check the expiration date on the bag of fake fish?"

"No, but—"

"Then I don't get why you called an emergency alliance meeting," Abe says.

I'm talking to Capital T on my K-Pak behind a rose bush in the front yard. Eight hours have passed since I discovered hundreds of fish sticks decomposing in a large trash can in Dad's office. My parents got home two hours ago. Both looked surprised to find me sitting on the couch, but I couldn't tell if that was because they expected to be the ones to release me, or because I'd entered the living room without automatically turning on the TV. Dinner was fairly normal, but that could've been because Mom picked up a vegan pizza on her way home, so there was no need to address the fish-stick disappearance. If either of them noticed the stench coming from Dad's office, they didn't say so. When my stomach stopped spinning long enough for me to say I was going for a quick bike ride, they told me to have fun.

And then I came out here. I didn't want to be in the house during this meeting because I didn't want my parents eaves-dropping.

"Those are just examples," I say. "But they've been acting weird in general. Mom's been too nice. Dad's been as nice as he always is, but something else too. Like when we got home after our last miniature-golf game, he said he had work to do and went right into his office and closed the door."

"Wow," Abe says. "Your dad . . . went to his office . . . to work. Alert the FBI."

"Abraham." Lemon holds up a green paper monkey, adjusts its tail. "Seamus called an emergency meeting. That means something's wrong."

"What about your parents?" I ask before Abe can argue. "Have any of them been acting weird?"

"Actually . . . ," Abe says, to my surprise. "Maybe."

My heart skips. "What do you mean?"

He glances at his bedroom door, then leans closer to his K-Pak. "My supplies disappeared."

"What supplies?" Gabby whispers.

"Spray paint. Pastels. Watercolors. I keep art materials in every room for easy access when inspiration strikes. But the other day I couldn't find any of them. Not for eighteen hours."

"What happened then?" I ask.

"My dad asked me to cut the grass." Not one for outdoor activities, Abe cringes. "And when I went to the shed to get the lawn mower, I found all of my supplies. Shoved in a corner. In black garbage bags. Under a tarp."

Gabby gasps. "Did you ask why they were in there?"

He nods. "Dad said he and Mom were allergic to the fumes. Even though they've been around my supplies tons of times, and I've never even heard them sneeze."

"And if that were true," I say, "why didn't they just tell you? Why hide your stuff? Why the secret?"

Before he can answer, Gabby chimes in. "Something really weird's going on here, too. But it's making everyone miserable—not just me—so I don't know if it's like what's going on at your houses."

"Let's hear it," I say.

She clears her throat. Opens her mouth. And sings the first few bars of "The Star-Spangled Banner."

"You're singing a Fourth of July song in June," Abe says when she's done. "That is weird."

"The song doesn't matter," Gabby says. "It's what my family does whenever I sing. And you guys didn't do it right now, so I know it's just them."

"What do they do?" I ask.

She's sitting on a towel on the beach. A blue-gray ocean's behind her. After she raises one pointer finger, asking us to give her a second, she puts down her K-Pak and jumps up. As she runs across the sand, I notice a large white house in the distance. She reaches the house quickly, sprints across a deck, and peeks in the windows. The coast must be clear, because she charges toward us and plops back down onto the towel.

"Sorry," she says. "Sound travels really easily at the beach. Anyway, you all know how much I love to sing? Yodels, Christmas carols, pop songs, the alphabet, whatever? And how good I am at it?"

Abe snorts. Lemon strings together multicolored snowflakes.

"We do," I say.

"Well, three days ago . . . something . . . happened. It was the night before my dad's birthday. Over dinner we talked about how we should celebrate. No birthday's complete without its famous song, the one your friends and family sing before you blow out the candles on your cake, so I started practicing. At the table. In the middle of dinner."

"Why?" Abe asks.

"Why not?" Gabby asks simply.

"Um, because people were talking," Abe says.

"Restaurants play music while people talk all the time," Gabby points out. "I thought my song would make the meal even more enjoyable."

"So what happened?" I ask. "What'd your family do?"

Gabby pouts. "They put on headphones. All of them. I hadn't even finished the first note when Mom, Dad, and Flora each grabbed a pair from under the table and put them on. I asked what they were doing, and they didn't answer. Because they couldn't hear me."

"I'm not sure I'm following," I say.

"They blocked me out!" Gabby exclaims. "With special headphones that silence all noise when you wear them. Since then, anytime I break into song—which is, like, once every five minutes—they put them on. Then they take them off as soon as I stop."

"Have you asked why they're doing that?" Abe asks.

She nods. "Mom says my voice is so beautiful they don't deserve to hear it every day. I believed her at first, because my voice really is magical, you know?"

Abe swallows a groan.

"But," Gabby continues, "I've always sung the same, and they've never worn headphones before. So I don't know."

"It definitely sounds suspicious," I say. "How about you, Lemon? Notice anything weird since you've been home?"

He stares at something offscreen.

"Nope," he finally says.

"Are you sure?" I ask. "No one's saying or doing things they usually don't?"

"Nope."

"We should call Elinor," Gabby says, tapping her K-Pak screen.

"I don't know if that's such a good idea," I say quickly. Although Elinor's not an official member of Capital T (Abe nixed the idea when we talked about asking her to join our alliance last semester), I still considered inviting her to this meeting for her input. I didn't, because I thought it might be hard for her to get away from her mom. Also because I wrote her back three days ago and still haven't heard from her. "You saw where she lives."

"The hole in the desert?" Gabby asks.

"IncrimiNation's a school," Abe says. "Her mom works there. They must live somewhere else."

"Remember those abandoned houses?" I ask.

"The ones without windows or doors?" Gabby asks.

"And with dirt yards covered in garbage?" Abe asks.

"Where we found Elinor standing on an inner tube in a swimming pool filled with snakes instead of water?" I nod. "Home sweet home."

Gabby shudders. "Poor thing. We should organize another rescue mission."

"No thanks," Abe says. "I swallowed enough sand during that trip to throw up a second Sahara."

"Ew," Gabby says.

"You were awesome." I don't compliment Abe often (he does that enough himself), but last semester, when Elinor didn't return to school and we (nicely) hijacked a Kilter helicopter and flew to Arizona to free her from IncrimiNation, the trouble-making camp her mom runs, he *was* awesome. They all were. We had to be to escape Shepherd Bull and his gang of wild, dirty misfits.

"I guess we don't want anyone there overhearing anything they shouldn't," Gabby says.

"Right. And Elinor promised that her mom's much mellower when school's not in session. She didn't seem worried about going home." I wouldn't have let her go otherwise.

"Getting back to *our* parents," Abe says, "I think we need to go big."

"How?" Gabby asks.

"Not how. Who." He looks at me. "Annika."

I frown but don't disagree. Kilter's director and I have a complicated relationship, one I'm not sure I trust, but she tends to know things no one else does. If anyone can help figure out what's going on with our moms and dads, she can.

"Who's going to tell her?" Gabby asks.

She looks at me. So does Abe. Lemon continues stringing snowflakes like he's not even listening.

"Okay," I say. "I'll do it."

Chapter 5

DEMERITS: 410
GOLD STARS: 150

I haven't talked to Annika that much since last semester. One reason is because she can be super nice one second and super mean the next, so I'm not sure how to feel about her. But the bigger reason is because she accepted me into Kilter for what I did—or what she *thought* I did—to Miss Parsippany. She doesn't know the truth, which is that my substitute teacher is still alive. My apple hit her, but it didn't kill her. And thank goodness for that.

I should tell Annika this, since she and my Kilter teachers still think I'm a supremely skilled, one-and-done kind of marksman, but I've been stalling. Because the second she knows, she'll kick me out, and I'll probably never see my friends again.

But sometimes, talking to Annika pays off. I'm reminded of this while rereading the e-mail she sent last night.

> Greetings, beloved Kilter Academy parents!
>
> Heat dragging you down? Humidity frizzing your hair? Sweat staining the armpits of your favorite T-shirts?
>
> Then escape to Kamp Kilter! At this inaugural annual retreat, you and your family will forget all of your summer struggles during TWO WHOLE WEEKS of spectacular lakeside living. Nestled among the glorious Adirondack mountains, Kamp Kilter offers luxurious accommodations and waterfront fun in a cool, technologically enhanced climate.
>
> As we give your children a surprise session they'll never forget, you'll enjoy swimming! Sunning! Jet-Skiing! Canoeing! Hiking! Biking! Tennis! Rock climbing! Or if indoor activities are more your

thing, enjoy TV! Movies! Shopping! Fine dining! Napping! All in the comfort of our state-of-the-art air-conditioning system!

And put away that wallet! Kamp Kilter is FREE to all Kilter families! PLUS, parents will receive generous financial compensation for playing hooky from their jobs. The only thing you need to worry about is packing a swimsuit and getting here ASAP!

The Fine Print: Offer redeemable by families of current Kilter students ONLY. Trespassers will be punished accordingly. E-mail invite required for entry. Everything that happens at Kilter stays at Kilter, so attendees will be required to sign nondisclosure agreements. Violation of these agreements will result in immediate, permanent expulsion of the associated Kilter students.

Hope to see you soon!

Sincerely,

Annika Kilter

Founder and Director,

Kilter Academy for Troubled Youth

"How're you doing back there, sport?" Dad asks.

I look up from my K-Pak. We've been on the road six hours, but I'm still surprised to see him in the driver's seat and Mom in the passenger seat. In all my thirteen years, he's never taken the wheel if she's been in the car.

"Fine," I say.

"Hungry?" Mom asks.

"Nope."

"Thirsty?"

"Nope."

"Need a bathroom break?"

"Nope."

She smiles at me between the front seats, then faces forward again. I'd wonder why she was being so nice if I didn't already know that she's trying to make up for her past bad behavior. Plus, we're going to Kilter, which is like her favorite place on earth.

Returning to my K-Pak, I scroll through the short slideshow that came with Annika's e-mail. The photos include a turquoise lake, a white sandy beach, and flower-covered mountains. They show a place so beautiful you'd be crazy to spend your summer anywhere else.

I have to give Annika credit. After talking to Capital T, I e-mailed her our concerns. Two minutes later, she wrote back and said she was on it. Three minutes after that, I got the Kamp Kilter invitation. I showed my parents right away and can't remember ever seeing Dad so excited. Of course, that might be because we've never received a paid vacation before. Mom seemed less excited, which was weird considering she couldn't send me to Kilter fast enough a few months ago, but she was probably just caught off guard. It didn't take her long to agree that it'd be nice for us to get away as a family.

That was fifteen hours ago. And now here we are. In the car, on our way to two weeks of spectacular lakeside living. I don't know what else Annika has up her sleeve, but I'm impressed she got us so far so fast.

"Remember the last time we made this drive together?" Dad asks.

"Sure do." It's impossible to forget. Especially since I spent most of it fighting back tears while imagining the horrible but deserved punishment I'd receive at what was supposed to be the best reform school in the country.

How times have changed.

My K-Pak beeps.

"Exit here," I say, following the GPS directions.

Whistling, Dad signals and guides the car right. My K-Pak beeps again. I instruct him to turn left and stay on the twisty two-lane road for twenty-seven miles.

My K-Pak beeps again. This time, it's for a new e-mail.

TO: shinkle@kilteracademy.org
FROM: loliver@kilteracademy.org
SUBJECT: Kamp Kilter

S—

Almost there. But not sure it's a good idea. You?

—L

I hit reply, start typing.

TO: loliver@kilteracademy.org
FROM: shinkle@kilteracademy.org
SUBJECT: RE: Kamp Kilter

Hi, Lemon!

I think it's too soon to know what kind of idea it is . . . but I do know that I'd rather find out what's up with my parents with you guys at Kilter than by myself at home. And I also wouldn't mind swimming in the turquoise lake and watching movies on the school's enormous TVs!

So don't worry. We'll figure everything out!

—Seamus

I hit send. Then I start another note.

TO: parsippany@cloudviewschools.net
FROM: shinkle@kilteracademy.org
SUBJECT: RE: Happy Summer!

Dear Miss Parsippany,

Hi! It's great to hear from you. I hope you're having a lot of fun traveling. Were you visiting friends and family? Or just exploring new places?

Thanks for the coconut recommendation! I'll see if the Kilter chefs have some fresh ones I can try.

By the way, I'm on my way back to school right now. I thought I'd be spending the summer at home, but our director decided to throw a fun retreat for all our families!

As for Bartholomew John, I'm not sure where he is or what he's doing. I haven't seen him since Christmas, when he delivered flowers to my house. So the last I heard, he was a star employee at Cloudview Cards and Carnations. Which doesn't sound like something a troublemaker would be . . . but he's Bartholomew John, so who knows?

And I hope you don't mind, but can I ask why you asked?

Hope you're having a great time wherever you are!

Sincerely,

Seamus

As I reread the note, I think about how stunned I was when the doorbell rang Christmas morning—and Bartholomew John,

Enemy No. 1, sauntered in like he owned the joint. He didn't even wait for us to open the door. The only thing more shocking than that was that my parents seemed to find his visit completely normal.

Of course, that was before I found Mom up in the attic, surrounded by Kilter supplies. Then I figured she was probably so grateful to him for making me throw the apple in the school cafeteria and get shipped off to Kilter, she considered him an honorary son.

Miss Parsippany doesn't know any of this, though. Or what Kilter really trains kids to do. Telling myself she's better off in the dark, I hit send.

My K-Pak beeps with another new message.

TO: shinkle@kilteracademy.org
FROM: enorris@kilteracademy.org
SUBJECT: Where are you?

Hi Seamus,

I got to Kamp Kilter a little while ago. I just checked your place but it's empty. Does that mean you're still on your way? I hope so. . . .

—Elinor

My heart pounds as I write her back.

TO: enorris@kilteracademy.org
FROM: shinkle@kilteracademy.org
SUBJECT: RE: Where are you?

On my way, be there in no time!
☺

I hit send and lean between the two front seats. "Any chance we can go faster?"

"There sure is!"

Dad punches the gas. Mom yelps. I fly back into my seat. We're still several miles away, but thanks to skills I had no idea Dad or his ancient sedan possessed, the Kamp Kilter sign appears nine and a half minutes later.

The car skids to a stop by a small house. It looks like a log cabin, but made of steel instead of wood.

I slide down the seat for a better view. Dad rolls down his window and sticks out his head. We stay like this for a long moment. Because nothing happens. No one comes out of the house to greet us. No other cars pull up behind ours. We're parked at the edge of a deep, dark forest, but leaves don't rustle, birds don't sing, the air doesn't stir. It reminds me of the very first time we came to Kilter, when Mom rushed toward the windowless gray building and Dad and I stood outside the chain-link fence topped in barbed wire, trying to convince each other it was anything but terrifying.

Now I'm scared again. But this time of being kept out—not let in.

Before fear turns to panic, the steel cabin's door screams open. A figure steps out. It's wearing green cargo pants, a green cargo shirt, and tall black combat boots. The clothes are stretched thin across big, sharp muscles, like they're straining to hang on. Aviator sunglasses with mirrored lenses hide the figure's eyes.

"Hi, Annika," I say.

She approaches us silently. Dad pulls his head back into the car slowly. Like he's afraid one wrong move will make her yank the gun from the holster attached to her hip. Because he has no idea the weapon is a toy filled with water. Or that it's only for show.

Annika stops by Dad's open window. Her head turns toward mine. As I stare at my reflection in her mirrored sunglasses, my pulse quickens. My lungs pump faster. Despite our differences, I know she considers me a star pupil . . . but she can still shrink me down to pint-size with a single look if I'm not sure why she's giving it.

She holds my gaze. Then she looks at Dad, throws open her arms, and smiles. "Welcome to Kamp Kilter, Mr. and Mrs. Hinkle!"

Dad's head hits the back of his seat as he exhales and laughs. Mom laughs too.

"How was the ride?" Annika rests her palms on her thighs and stoops down so that she's eye-level with my parents. "Find us okay?"

"It was a breeze!" Dad says.

"Wonderful. We're thrilled you're here! Now let me get your bags." Annika disappears into the steel cabin. Two seconds later she pops out holding sparkly gray tote bags. "Here are a few things to get you started. Beach towels, water bottles, sunblock, sunglasses, straw hats, lip balm, flip-flops—you know, the basics!"

Dad takes the bags. Not braced for their weight, his arms drop. His triceps slam against the bottom of the open window.

"Oops! Careful." Annika lends Dad a hand. Together they lift the totes into the driver's seat. "Your K-Pads are also in there."

"K-what?" Dad asks.

"Your very own Kamp Kilter personal computers," Annika explains. "Jam-packed with information, including your cabin assignment, an interactive map of the grounds, and an e-mail and phone directory for all facilities and services."

"Like K-Paks," I say.

Annika ignores me. "They'll also tell you everything you need to know about itineraries, class schedules, movie showings, workshops, lectures, special activities, and more. They shouldn't leave many questions, but should you have any, our camp counselors are always available and ready to help."

"It sounds like you've thought of everything!" Mom declares.

It does. And considering Kamp Kilter has existed for less than twenty-four hours, I have to give Annika credit for this too.

"Just one more thing, and then you're off to having fun in the sun—or being made in the shade!" Annika disappears into the steel cabin again. When she reappears, she's carrying a large basket. "I need your cell phones."

Dad reels back as she thrusts the basket forward.

"We want you to be fully immersed in rest and relaxation, without any distractions. And uninterrupted family time is guaranteed to bring you closer than you've ever been. Is anything more important than that?"

My parents exchange looks.

"You'll get them back at the end of camp," Annika adds.

They force smiles and fork over their phones.

"Great!" Annika cradles the basket between her waist and arm. "Now just scoot over and make room for Horatio here."

A tall man wearing gray shorts and a gray T-shirt emerges from the cabin. He looks familiar, but I can't place him—until I notice the silver fanny pack around his waist. Then I realize he's one of the Good Samaritans, Kilter's version of security. Apparently he's been given a new look for his new position with Kamp Kilter.

Horatio opens the driver's-side door, nudges Dad over, and

sits down. Then he produces two silver ribbons, winds them around my parents' heads and across their eyes, and double-knots them. As Mom and Dad gasp and giggle, Annika opens my door, pulls me out of the car, and clamps one cold hand over my mouth.

"Have fun!" she calls out as Horatio buckles up and hits the gas. "And if you need anything at all, just ask!"

My pulse pounds in my ears as I watch them drive down a long dirt road. Annika brings her head toward mine and lowers her voice.

"A true Troublemaker can't be cured so fast . . . can he?"

Which I guess is her way of saying that bad kids don't deserve the kind of fun my parents are about to have.

A few seconds later, Dad's ancient sedan rounds a corner and is swallowed by trees. Annika releases my mouth. Nervous for my parents now that I can no longer see them, I resist sprinting after them.

I turn around instead and see a golf cart that wasn't there five seconds ago. An older man wearing black wool pants, a black turtleneck, and a black baseball hat sits as still as stone behind the wheel.

"Get . . . *in*," he hisses.

I jump in the cart. Because when Mr. Tempest, a.k.a. Mystery, a.k.a. Kilter's history teacher, tells you to do something, you do it.

You could die if you don't.

Chapter 6

DEMERITS: 430
GOLD STARS: 150

Oh my gosh, this is the most amazing thing I've ever seen! Isn't it the most amazing thing *you've* ever seen? I can't believe we get to live here!"

Gabby squeals and sprints away. Abe looks at me.

"Can we take out her batteries?" he asks.

I grin. He half smiles too, so I know he doesn't totally mind Gabby's hyperactivity.

"Oh my goodness! *Guys.* You have to see this!"

We're in the kitchen and follow Gabby's shriek to the next

room, where she's standing between the biggest flat-screen TV and fleece beanbag chair known to mankind.

"Wow," I say.

"Agreed," Abe says. "When Mystery dropped me off, I thought I'd be sleeping on the ground—not living in luxury underneath it."

I thought the same thing. Because after a silent ride that seemed to last days but only took minutes, Mystery dropped me off in front of a tent. Actually, that's too fancy a term for what it really was. Because tents have zippers. Some even have multiple rooms and windows. What I ducked under was a ripped black tarp draped over two sticks stuck in the ground. Like Abe, I expected to find a big patch of dirt. Maybe a cot. Definitely the promise of long, sleepless nights watching for bears and flicking away bugs.

But I found a gleaming silver trapdoor instead. And a computer screen attached to a pedestal. Once the section of tarp I'd lifted floated back to the ground, the screen flashed on and instructed me to place my palm to its surface. I did, the computer registered my print, and the trapdoor whooshed open. A clear glass tube rose up. Its door slid open, then closed after I stepped inside. I have no idea how far below ground it traveled. In fact, once it stopped I wasn't even sure I was still below ground, because the room it landed in was bright and sunny. The windows throughout the room looked real. They offered beautiful views of blue sky, a turquoise lake, a white sandy beach, and flower-covered mountains. Those looked real too.

I asked Abe how that was possible. He guessed live video feed. Which means the outdoor images we see are projections captured by digital camcorders scattered throughout the campground.

"What are those?" Gabby asks now, pointing to several small gray spheres spread across the ceiling.

Abe and I step farther into the room to investigate. I'm standing on my tiptoes for a closer look when the room blows up.

Against the deafening roar, my palms hit my ears. My knees hit the floor. My eyes squeeze shut. My entire body shakes.

And then, just like that, the noise stops. The room, and my body, still.

I move my hands an inch away from my ears. Open my eyes one at a time.

"Lemon?" I ask, not sure I'm still alive or that he's really standing in the living room doorway.

"Lemon!" Gabby leaps out of the beanbag, where she fell during the explosion, sprints across the room, and almost knocks him over when she hugs him.

"Are we dead?" Abe reaches one hand out from his hiding place under the coffee table. "Is this warm fuzzy thing a rug . . . or my insides smeared across the floor?"

"Ew." Gabby grimaces. Then she skips to the coffee table, takes Abe's hand, and helps him slide out. "Music can't kill you, silly."

"That was music?" he asks doubtfully.

Lemon holds up a short silver wand, then aims it at one of the gray ceiling spheres.

"That's okay!" Abe jumps to his feet. "I don't need another demo."

Lemon tosses the remote onto the couch and drops his duffel bag to the floor. I'm so happy to see him I want to hug him too—but he doesn't say hi. He doesn't even look at me. All he does is cross his arms over his stomach and slowly tilt to one side until his left shoulder stops at the doorway wall.

"How was your ride?" I ask.

"Long," he says.

"Were your parents so excited about Kamp Kilter?" Gabby asks.

He shrugs. "They're here. So . . ."

"What about your little brother?" Abe asks.

"Oh my goodness, little kids *love* camp," Gabby says. "A long time ago? When I was five? My parents sent me to Camp Songbird, this amazing camp for super talented musicians. And at first? I totally didn't want to go. I was, like, crazy homesick. I cried myself to sleep and—"

A doorbell rings.

Gabby gasps. "Company!" She claps her hands and races out of the room.

Abe looks at me. "*Now* can we take out her batteries?"

I smile at him, then look at Lemon. Or at the empty space he occupied half a second ago. Lemon's idea of hurrying is walking instead of shuffling, but his legs are about twice as long as mine are and can move fast when he wants them to. Before I can decide whether to go find him or give him space, Gabby bounds back into the room.

"Look who's *here*!" she declares.

"Your old Camp Songbird counselor?" Abe asks. "To say there's been a terrible mistake and that you should be there instead?"

I start to laugh—and then stop. Because I no longer

remember what Abe just said. Or where we are. Or why. Or even what my name is.

Fortunately, Elinor does.

"Hi, Seamus."

My mouth opens. Closes. Opens again.

"Hey, Elinor," Abe says.

"Hi." Her eyes—her warm, pretty eyes, which are the color of worn pennies—hold mine. When the cat refuses to return my tongue, they shift to my alliance mate. "Annika said I could stay with you guys. Is that okay?"

"Stay with us?" Gabby asks. "You mean live with us?"

Elinor nods.

"Yes!" Gabby grabs Elinor's hand and drags her from the room. "Oh my goodness, we're going to be roommates and best friends and stay up all night talking about trouble and boys and boys and trouble and . . ."

Her voice fades as they head down the hallway.

"She's not in the alliance," Abe says. "We have to be really careful not to—"

He's cut off by a loud buzzing. The noise comes from our K-Paks. I take mine from my pocket and accept the video chat request. Abe does the same with his. Annika's face appears on our computer screens.

"Hello, Troublemakers!" she says with a smile. "Welcome back to Kilter Academy. I know you didn't expect to return so soon, but I hope you're happy you did. I know I am! You must have many questions, and I promise to answer them all. We just have to take care of one item of business first. You might find it confusing, but please play along. Consider it your first troublemaking assignment of the summer!"

I feel a familiar wave of nervousness. It's been almost a year, and I still feel bad about trying to get into trouble instead of trying to stay out of it.

"Please report aboveground immediately," Annika says.

The screens go blank. Abe books it to the elevator. I follow him, trying not to worry about the pending mission, Lemon's weird behavior, my parents . . . Elinor living in our house.

Abe gets there first, but the elevator doesn't arrive right away. By the time it does, Lemon, Gabby, Elinor, and I are standing behind him. While we wait, I sneak peeks at Elinor's reflection in the shiny glass. Her skin's still the same color as creamy vanilla ice cream. Freckles are still scattered across her nose and cheeks like pink sprinkles. Her long dark-red hair is still pulled back in a braid, which is still tied in a green satin ribbon.

She's still the prettiest girl I've ever seen.

The elevator arrives. The door swishes open.

"Let's do this," Abe says, and lunges inside.

Gabby and Lemon join him. I step aside to let Elinor in first, and she does the same for me. We pause. Our eyes meet. She gives me a shy smile and steps inside. When I follow, Abe gives me a look. Then he pushes the up button, the door swishes shut, and we take off like a rocket.

"I have a question," Gabby announces after liftoff. "Annika invited our families to Kamp Kilter after Seamus told her about what was happening with our parents."

"What was happening with your parents?" Elinor asks.

"I'll fill you in on everything later," Gabby says. "But back to my question—do you think Annika had already planned to invite our families to Kamp Kilter, just later in the summer?"

"No," Abe says.

"Did any of you ever hear her or our teachers say anything about the camp while we were at school?" Gabby asks.

"No," Abe, Elinor, and I say.

"So do you think Annika created Kamp Kilter overnight?"

I look at Elinor. "Did your mom know anything about this?" Annika and Nadia Kilter, Elinor's mom, are sisters. They're not close, probably because Nadia runs IncrimiNation, a rival troublemaking school (if you can call it that), but maybe she'd talked about Kilter's programs in the past.

"No," Elinor says. "And I could tell it was the first she'd heard of it. When I showed her the invitation, her eyes got big and her face turned red, and then she stormed out of the house. She slammed the door so hard it fell off its hinges. That was the last time I saw her before the helicopter came."

"What helicopter?" Abe asks.

"Annika's. She knew Mom wouldn't bring me, so sent a Good Samaritan to pick me up."

Abe huffs. I try to read Elinor's expression to see if talking about her mom, who's even harder to figure out than my mom is, makes her sad, mad, or something else. I'm still trying to decide when Gabby continues.

"So then does that mean Annika built all of this . . ."—she motions around the elevator, points down then up—"in less than twenty-four hours?"

"Guess so," Abe says.

"But how?" Gabby asks.

He shrugs. "She's Annika."

The elevator stops. The door swishes open. We file out of the chute and through the raggedy tarp tent.

"Troublemakers!" a low voice booms. "Are you ready . . . to meet . . . your DOOM?"

Chapter 7

DEMERITS: 430
GOLD STARS: 150

It's just for show. . . . It's just for show. . . .
It's just for show. . . .

This reminder skips through my head like a scratched part on one of Dad's old Frank Sinatra records. But it doesn't make the scene outside any less intimidating.

"What are you waiting for?" a low voice roars into a megaphone. "Start digging!"

Dozens of my classmates are on the beach. At Annika's command, they scatter and sprint to rusty metal shovels standing upright in the sand.

"Did you *really* think you'd get three months off?" she demands. "Did you *really* believe that you deserved to do whatever you wanted after doing countless things *nobody* wanted you to?"

"Hurry up, Hinkle!" Abe hisses. He's already claimed a shovel a few feet away from our tarp tent. I head for one a few yards away.

"*Good* kids go to camp!" Annika continues. "They get to swim! Hike! Build bonfires! Toast marshmallows! Do arts and crafts!"

I lift the heavy shovel, aim it at the sand.

"*You* are not good kids! *You* have not earned these privileges!"

I scoop up sand, toss it to the side.

"You want to swim? Then find your own water!"

"Um, there's water right there?" points out Carter Montgomery. After me, he's the shortest kid in our class. "Like, a lot of it? Right behind you?"

He's right. Annika, wearing the same uniform she was when we arrived, stands with several other people dressed the same way in front of the huge, glittering lake featured in her photo slideshow.

Of course, Annika knows this. That's why she charges at

Carter, presses the megaphone to his ear, and says, "*Dig*, little man. *Dig!*"

He digs. So do Abe and Gabby. Elinor does too, which is surprising because she's famous for being Kilter's worst Troublemaker, a position that's made her repeat first-year classes multiple times.

Of the dozens of students scattered across the beach, only one doesn't follow our director's instructions.

Lemon. Normally, he'd do as he was asked at his own leisurely pace. This wouldn't make Annika happy, but it wouldn't get him kicked out, either. But now he does nothing. He simply stands by a shovel, rests one elbow on its handle, and stares across the lake.

When I follow his gaze, one of the guys standing with Annika catches my eye. He smiles, and I realize he's Houdini, our teenage math teacher. I give him a quick wave, then check out the other people he's standing with. They're all wearing green cargo shirts, button-down shirts, black boots, and aviator sunglasses, but I still recognize Fern, our gym teacher; Wyatt, our art teacher; Samara, our biology teacher; Devin, our music teacher; and Lizzie, our language arts teacher. Mystery, our history teacher, wears all black and stands apart from the group, reading a book.

"See a pretty bird, Hinkle?" Annika barks.

I pick up the pace.

"Hey." Alison Parker, another Troublemaker in my class, stands up straight. She shields her eyes from the sun with one hand and looks out across the lake. "Is that my dad? Jumping on a trampoline?"

Every Troublemaker stops digging and looks toward the beach on the other side of the water.

"Nice cabins," Gabby says.

"More like lodges," says Chris Fisher, another soon-to-be second-year Troublemaker.

He's right. Instead of the small rustic houses I've seen in movies about kids at sleepaway camp, Kamp Kilter cabins are enormous. Even from here, at least half a mile away, I can see that most are two-stories tall with wraparound porches and multiple chimneys. Some even have balconies and decks off the upper floors.

"Is that where our families are staying?" Abe asks.

Striding around holes, Annika groans into the megaphone. "If you must know, yes. While you're fighting for protection from the elements, blood-sucking insects, and carnivorous wild-life in these makeshift tents, your families will be enjoying air-conditioning by day, the warmth of cozy fireplaces at night, gourmet dining, and countless other amenities in their luxurious ten-star accommodations."

"But . . . why?" Chris asks.

Annika freezes. Then she spins around, brings the megaphone to her mouth, and yells, "Because that's what they deserve for putting up with you!"

Shoveling sand in eighty-five degree weather is no joke, so I'm already sweating. But at Annika's declaration, goose bumps spread across my arms and legs.

"Um, is my dad waving at me?" Alison asks, raising one hand to return the gesture. "Can he hear me?" She pauses. "Now he's nodding."

"Your families deserve a carefree summer vacation," Annika bellows. "We're going to give them that. We're also going to give them the comfort of knowing that your Kilter training will not stop until your transformation from terrible to model children is complete! So yes, microphones have been installed on this side of the lake and speakers on that side. Whatever you say inside and outside your tents will be broadcast live for them to hear inside and outside their new summer homes."

"What if they don't want to listen to us," Carter asks, "because they want peace and quiet instead?"

"Their grounds have speaker-free sections," Annika says. "They can also mute you when they're indoors. But I'm sure most of them will enjoy knowing exactly what you're up to most of the time!"

"I guess so," Alison says. "Dad just gave me a thumbs-up."

"Here is what your days will consist of!" Annika barks. "You'll rise before dawn and have ten minutes to forage for breakfast. Your options will include whatever Mother Nature provides on any given day—berries, twigs, bugs, fish, anything you can find or catch. After that, you'll travel across the lake and perform a variety of chores for our visiting families. After you've completed your chores to the satisfaction of your instructors, you will return to the regular Kilter campus for five hours of class time! If you're still standing after that, you'll forage for dinner as you hike back through the deep, dark woods."

"How far is campus from here?" Gabby asks.

"So far you may be eating dinner when everyone else is eating breakfast the next day!"

I picture the freezer full of fish sticks back home. When I was hungry all I had to do was go downstairs, dump my snack on a plate, and toss it into the microwave. Was alerting Annika and coming here a mistake?

It can't be. Because the fish sticks were thrown out. Something was wrong. It *is* wrong. We wouldn't have been called here so suddenly otherwise.

Plus, this itinerary is all part of Annika's show for our listening parents . . . isn't it?

"Upon your return you'll do a final cleanup of Kamp Kilter grounds!" Annika continues. "Then you will have five minutes of free time before lights out. At which point you'll retire to your makeshift tents and do your best to sleep on the cold hard ground!"

Several yards away, Carter Montgomery raises his hand.

"What?" Annika squawks.

"Um, where do we . . . ? That is, how do we . . . ? What I mean is—"

"Where are your restroom facilities?" Annika finishes.

Carter nods. Annika lunges at him, making him stumble backward. Then she stops abruptly and thrusts her pointer finger toward the ground.

"You want us to go . . . in a hole?" Alison asks.

Annika doesn't say anything. She doesn't move either.

"Nope," Alison says. "No way. Not going to happen. I'd rather hold it in until—"

"Ali," Gabby says, *"chill.* Didn't you see the amazing bathrooms with marble Jacuzzis and velvet towels down in our—"

She stops. Or *is* stopped—by a piece of silver duct tape gluing her lips together. Gabby drops her shovel and claps both hands to her covered mouth.

"Gabby," Abe groans. "Annika just said we need to play along so that—"

He's stopped too. This time I glimpse the silencer as it flies toward him. It starts out in a small roll, then unwinds as it shoots through the air. When it lands squarely over Abe's mouth, it's an even six-inch-long piece of tape.

The other Troublemakers look around the beach for the tape's source. Most check out our teachers, who stand motionless by the lake.

I don't. Maybe it's because of my marksman training, or maybe it's because we've spent so much time together. Whatever the reason, I know that Ike, my troublemaking tutor, fired the shots. This hunch is confirmed when I spot him hanging from the branches of a tall pine tree at the edge of the beach. He's holding a silver tape dispenser, like the kind Dad has in his office back home, only Ike's version has a handle and a trigger. When he sees that I see him, he smiles and waves. I do the same, then go back to digging before Annika catches me slacking.

"To answer your question," she says, aiming the megaphone at Carter, "yes, you will use holes in the ground to take care of your various biological needs. I'm not completely cruel, however, so the holes you use needn't be these. If you have enough strength to dig others in the privacy of the woods, by all means do so. As for bathing, you're very fortunate to have the beautiful Lake Kilter for your personal tub. Be advised that many sharp-toothed fish call this side of the water home—and they defend it fiercely. Also, bathing is considered a privilege and will be done only during your five free minutes at the end of the day."

Annika relays this information so convincingly, my stomach turns. Judging by the way my fellow Troublemakers squirm and frown, theirs do too.

"All that said, your families and their happiness are my top priority. I'll be very busy making sure their every need is tended to—starting now. Are there any other questions before I go?"

Annika's severe tone implies that there better not be. So I'm surprised—and nervous—when Alison raises her hand again.

"Sorry," she says, looking out across the lake. "But my dad's jumping around and waving his hands like crazy . . . so I think he has one?"

Annika turns to our teachers. "Samara? Would you please ask Mr. Parker what we can do for him?"

I now notice that all of the teachers are wearing small earpieces. Our biology instructor speaks quietly, then listens and addresses Annika.

"Mr. Parker would like to know if the families will get to spend time with Kilter students, ma'am."

"If that's what Mr. Parker would like, then yes. We can arrange brief get-togethers with Kilter students and their families to improve parent-child relations. However, Mr. Parker and our other valuable visitors should remember that like bathing, time with loved ones is a privilege for Kilter students. We must be careful not to reward them too much for things they haven't earned."

Samara brings two fingers to her earpiece, listens, and nods once. "Mr. Parker understands."

"Good." Annika turns to us. "Since this is the first day of Kamp Kilter, the lawns and accommodations are pristine and do not yet require your attention. Your regular chores will begin tomorrow. However, preparing for your families' arrivals kept our custodial and grounds crews from their normal duties on the Kilter campus. Because they've been helping you, you will now help them by doing their regular jobs. At my whistle, drop your shovels, form a single line, and march down the path behind tent number one. The path will lead you to campus, where you'll receive your assignments."

I glance at my friends. Abe and Gabby are trying, unsuccessfully, to tear the tape from their mouths. Elinor's still digging. Lemon's sitting down, building a sandcastle.

Annika whistles. We drop our shovels and form a line by the first tarp tent. Abe and Gabby are ahead of me. Lemon and Elinor must be behind me.

"Forward *march*!" Annika shouts.

We do—and fast. Soon the woods thicken. The path narrows. The trees grow taller, thicker. Their branches block the sun. The air cools. Light fades. Troublemakers stumble as it gets harder to see. I want to check on Elinor but know that if I take my eyes off the ground, I'll trip on an upraised root and make Troublemakers fall like dominoes.

"Oh my goodness," a girl whimpers up ahead. "Where are we *going*?"

"How long do have to play along?" another whines.

"There's no way our parents can hear us now," a male Troublemaker complains.

"Is anyone else afraid of the dark?" another asks.

Then, as suddenly as duct tape appeared on Abe's and Gabby's mouths, a golf cart shoots out of the blackness and skids to a stop at the front of the line. Just like the extended cart we took on a field trip to Annika's Apex—the dilapidated amusement park—my first semester, this one has enough seats for my entire class.

The door opens. Houdini peers down at us from the driver's seat. I notice that while we've been marching, he's been changing. Instead of the cargo uniform, he's now wearing his favorite teaching outfit: jeans, an orange T-shirt, a hooded sweatshirt, and black Converse. His curly hair had been slicked back on the beach, and now it's combed out and frizzy.

"He looks mad," whispers the Troublemaker behind me.

"He's never mad," another points out nervously.

It's true. Some of our teachers are more serious than others, but our math teacher is usually the most laid-back of the bunch. Yet now his eyes narrow as he watches us, like he's trying to decide whether we deserve a ride.

I'm beginning to think the answer is no when his face breaks into a wide grin.

"What d'ya want?" he asks. "A written invitation? Hop on!"

Chapter 8

DEMERITS: 430
GOLD STARS: 150

Once the door closes behind the last Trouble-maker, Houdini hits a switch. Red and blue strobe lights bounce off the walls. Disco balls lower from the ceiling and start spinning. Electronic music composed of beeps, beats, and sirens blasts. Troublemakers spin, twist, and wriggle on seats and in the aisle. It's an instant dance party that, after digging holes and trekking through the cold woods, my classmates are thrilled to attend.

But the party doesn't last long. Abe's doing the worm down the center aisle when the golf cart stops short. Everyone onboard lurches forward. Abe loses momentum and slides along the floor until his forehead slams into my ankle.

"Seriously, Hinkle?" he says, rubbing his head.

"Learn how to drive that thing," I say with a grin.

The door opens. Abe jumps to his feet. The music's still pumping, so kids wiggle and shimmy all the way down the steps and outside.

"Oh my *goodness*!" Gabby squeals.

"Is that really for us?" another Troublemaker asks.

"Kamp Kilter rocks!" a third exclaims.

When I reach the top step, I understand the fuss. Houdini's taken us to an enormous swimming pool. A dozen diving boards and waterslides are positioned around the pool's perimeter at different heights. Nearby, a big bin holds inner tubes and rafts. Thousands of white Christmas lights are strung high above the pool. Tiki torches burn around a picnic area filled with large tables and benches. Next to the picnic area is a patio, where Kanteen chefs wait to cook us our favorite meals.

"Get set to get wet," Houdini says near my ear.

"I didn't bring my trunks," I say.

"I don't think that'll be a problem." He points to a tall glass structure. It looks like the Kommissary but smaller—and filled with only one thing.

Swimsuits.

I stifle a groan and start down the steps.

"Gather round, my darling Troublemakers!" Fern, our gym teacher, declares. She's standing on a small island in the center of the pool. Minus Houdini—and Mystery, I see as I get closer—the rest of our teachers are there with her. "First, I just want to say how excited we are to have you back at Kilter so soon. And who's excited to be here?"

The group cheers. I look for Elinor and spot her on the other side of the pool. Our eyes meet. She smiles. So do I.

"As always, we have a lot of fun in store for you! And we're going to kick things off with a little game I like to call . . . Fishing for Trouble!"

She raises one palm, asking for silence. When the cheering dies down, she snaps her fingers. A narrow stream of water shoots up from the pool before her. It looks like an upside-down waterfall. Something small and silver bounces on top of the stream.

"Who here has had goldfish for pets?" Fern asks.

Several Troublemakers raise their hands.

"How fast did they swim?"

"They didn't!" Gabby calls out. "Mine just floated in a tiny bowl. I tried giving it more space in my parents' Jacuzzi, and I bought, like, a hundred fake ocean plants from the pet store, and also one of those cute little treasure chests that open and close, but—"

"Thanks, Gabby," Fern says, then addresses the rest of us. "Goldfish barely move. When they do, they don't go far—or fast. Which pretty much makes them the opposite of silverfish."

"Silverfish?" Chris Fisher asks. "There's no such thing."

"Smart Troublemakers don't make silly assumptions." Fern wags one finger at him, then turns to our art teacher. "Wyatt, I'd love seafood for dinner. Would you be a dear and catch me some?"

Wyatt rolls up his sleeves. He eyes the silverfish on top of the liquid column for several seconds, then lunges.

Fern snaps her fingers. The fish vanishes. Wyatt face-plants into the pool.

"Oops!" Fern exclaims. "Samara, want to give it a try?"

Widening her stance, our biology teacher looks up, down, and around.

"There!" Alison Parker shouts and points.

The silverfish hovers at one end of their concrete island—above the water, in midair. It doesn't have wings so must be another high-tech Kilter toy.

Samara sprints toward the end of the island. Inches away from its edge, she lifts both arms and leaps.

The silverfish waits. Then, as Samara's fingers are curling toward it, Fern snaps again. The fish zips away.

"Ouch!" Fern says as Samara belly flops into the deep end. "That had to hurt."

Our soaking-wet teachers climb out of the water. Their slippery target returns to Fern's open palm. It stays there as she explains the game.

"In Fishing for Trouble, the goal is simple: Make the catch. Reaching this goal, however, is nearly impossible. Because the Kilter silverfish is unlike any other fish you'll find in any other body of water in the world. For one thing, it's computerized. For another, it can't be baited or distracted from its purpose. Which is: to evade capture. I controlled its motion for the demonstration but will set it on autopilot for the game. Left to its own devices it will zig and zag at speeds of up to one hundred miles per hour. The only thing you have going for you is numbers. With so many bodies in the pool, there will be only so much unoccupied water. The silverfish's escape options will be limited. That said, it'll still give you a tough run for your money."

"Money?" Abe asks. "Does that mean the winner gets a prize?"

"Indeed. The Fishing for Trouble victor will receive . . ." She pauses. An electronic drumroll blares through the stereo speakers, then stops. "One *thousand* demerits! For one *thousand* credits!"

The group cheers again—a thousand times louder than before.

"The game will begin in five minutes!" Fern exclaims over the din. "Please visit the Kilter Swim Hut for your game gear!"

The Troublemakers resemble a school of multicolored fish as they all turn and run toward the glass store at the same time. I lag behind. Not because I don't want to play, but because swimming is about my least favorite physical activity. And that's not because I don't like to swim.

"Seamus!" Gabby squeals inside the store. "You *have* to wear these!"

It's because I don't like being practically naked in public.

"Aren't they perfect?" Gabby demands once I find her by a long rack of swimsuits. She holds up a pair of apple-printed trunks. "And they're the only ones here! It's like they were made just for you! Try them on!"

She thrusts the trunks at me, then joins Elinor at another rack.

"Four minutes!" Fern's voice bursts from overhead speakers.

"Excuse me?" I flag down a salesperson. "Where are the T-shirts?"

"Um, at the mall?" He gives me a look that says I should know better. Then he resumes polishing a mannequin's blank face.

I try not to look at the mannequin. Because it's male. It has huge biceps and a twelve-pack. It might be made of plastic, but it's still way more of a man than I am.

"Three minutes!" Fern warns.

I dart to the nearest dressing room, yank its curtain closed, pull off my shirt.

"Minute and a half!"

The dressing room has a full-length mirror. I want to avoid my reflection but can't miss my pale, scrawny chest. Its whiteness is blinding.

Anxious to get out of there, I finish changing, throw my T-shirt back on, and join the rest of the Troublemakers outside.

We line up around the pool. Our teachers are still on the

concrete island. There's not a gap along the edge big enough for my friends and I to stand together, so we split up. Abe bolts left. Gabby bolts right. Lemon shuffles to a spot near a tall waterslide. Probably because he plans to hide beneath it while the rest of us compete.

"Seamus," a soft voice says. "Over here."

My heart skips. Elinor's standing by the shallow-end steps and motions to the empty space between her and Austin Baker. The space is narrow, but thanks to my barely there chest, I fit with room to spare.

"Can you swim?" she asks.

I nod. "You?"

She pauses. "I'm really good in a pool of reptiles."

I look at her. "But this— Do you mean— Are you saying you don't know how—"

"Time's *up*!"

A horn blows. Lights flash. Fern tosses the silverfish overhead like it's a quarter, and we're waiting to see who goes first.

But then the silverfish glows white, spins, and nosedives down. The instant it hits water, every Troublemaker but me leaps in after it. Including Elinor, who comes up gasping for air.

"Over there!" Alison points to the deep end. She must not be thinking clearly in all the excitement, since sharing the target's location can only invite competition.

And fast. All Troublemakers kick and flail and paddle in that direction. So does Elinor. Whose feet seem to be made of lead as she stumbles across the shallow end, still gasping for air and wiping water from her eyes.

"Interesting technique."

I look up. Houdini's standing next to me, studying his K-Pak screen. I sneak a peek and see Troublemakers spinning and tumbling underwater. Every half second a tiny white light zips between them, making them spin and tumble some more as they try to change directions. When I see Elinor doing the same, her cheeks puffed out as she holds her breath, her eyes squinty but open, I'm relieved.

"What is?" I ask.

"This. Staying put. Knowing that the silverfish will go where no one else is. Trusting that it'll come back to the shallow end eventually, and when it does, all you'll have to do is jump. When everyone else is scrambling to catch up. It's smart." He nudges me with his elbow. "Of course, I'd expect nothing less from our star student."

He's right about the technique. But he's wrong about me. I can't be a star student, at least not at this very moment, because I have no technique. I'm just too embarrassed to take off my shirt.

"Uh-oh." Houdini's face turns serious. He takes a walkie-talkie from his shorts pocket. "We've got a possible K-2 in Q-1. Lifeguard on standby."

"Copy that," answers an unfamiliar voice. "LG in route."

"Lifeguard?" I scan the pool. "Does that—? Did someone—?"

I stop when I spot Elinor. Her head's above water one second, below it the next. Her arms slam the surface as she tries to keep herself afloat. Oblivious Troublemakers create a dangerous whirlpool around her as they swim after the darting silverfish.

"Send in the lifeguard," I say, my voice thin. "Elinor's in trouble."

"Sit tight, Hinkle," Houdini says, his voice calm. "Everything's under control."

"But she's not a strong swimmer."

"This is the best way for her to get better."

I can't see it, but I know my snow-white skin now burns red. Anger and worry shove blood through my veins as an image of

Elinor lying on the ground in the middle of a blizzard, her arm hurt and face twisted in pain, comes to mind.

"Good idea," Houdini says as I take off my shirt. "The silverfish should be—"

I jump into the pool. The water's choppy from so many people bounding around, and that makes it hard to swim. The other Troublemakers don't help either. As they continue to chase the silverfish, they push and knock into one another—and into me.

"Seamus!"

Eric Taylor slams into my side. My feet hit the floor. I stand for a better view and spot Elinor ten feet away. She's drifting into deeper water.

"Seamus—" Her head dunks below the surface, pops back up. "I can't—" Down it goes again.

I dive underwater. Hoping it'll be easier to swim below the waves, I hold my breath and open my eyes. Without goggles I can only make out colors and figures. Elinor's swimsuit is emerald green. Locating that shade, I kick hard and head for it.

I'm halfway there when Elinor disappears. The other Troublemakers vanish. I can still feel my arms and legs, but I can't see them. I can't see anything. The whiteness is too bright, the water too rough.

"There it is!" a muffled voice shouts.

"Out of my way!"

"It's MINE!"

The muffled voices get louder. I close my eyes. Open them again. Press my lips together to keep from gasping in a gallon of water.

The silverfish. It's right before me, floating in front of my face. It's glowing softer now, so I can make out its shiny fins and tiny metal scales. Its black, lifeless eyes seem to stare right at me, daring me to reach for it.

Dozens of hands emerge from the surrounding whiteness. The silverfish lingers a second more, then zips out of their reach—but stays within mine. If it doesn't move again I can reach it in two kicks.

But then I glimpse a flash of red.

Elinor's hair.

My heart lunges. I kick twice. Away from the silverfish.

And toward Elinor.

Her braid drifts behind her in the rough water, so I reach it first. Still kicking, I stretch one arm as far forward as it'll go. I don't want to hurt her neck, but if I tug the end of her braid just enough to close the gap between us, then—

"What the—"

The words escape my lips before I can stop them. Water gushes into my mouth, down my throat. Something has me from behind. It takes all of my strength to blow out the water and clamp my lips shut. Trying not to choke, I kick and paddle as hard as I can.

It's no use. I move backward, not forward. The green ribbon at the end of Elinor's braid grows smaller.

Paddling even faster, I glance behind me. I expect to see Austin Lewis or one of my bigger classmates pulling me away from the silverfish. Instead, I see a propeller. Like the kind motorboats have.

Only this one's ten times bigger.

I kick harder. The propeller blades spin faster. My heart hammers. My lungs burn. I try not to picture my legs being sliced and diced like paper through Dad's favorite shredder—but I do anyway.

The liquid vortex drags me from the deep end and across the shallow end.

"Elinor!" I cry out.

Water clogs my throat, fills my lungs. I'm pretty sure I'm drowning as I'm sucked out of the pool . . . and into complete darkness.

Chapter 9

DEMERITS: 430
GOLD STARS: 650

What was that about?"

My eyelids snap open. I realize that I can see. But I'm not looking at the clear blue sky and fluffy white clouds of heaven. Or the flickering red flames of that other place—since, let's face it, my recent behavior doesn't deserve a warm welcome anywhere else.

I see a silver lamp. A white velvet couch. A glass desk. A chair made of diamonds. A white leather lounge chair, which I'm lying across.

Annika. Wearing a long white dress and standing by a wall of water.

"What happened?" My voice is scratchy, but it works.

She nods behind me. "George? Do you mind?"

A clear bucket appears out of nowhere. According to the markings on its side, it's filled with three gallons of water. Plus one soggy Band-Aid.

I sit up. "George? Is that really you?" The man holding the bucket certainly looks like the Good Samaritan I got to know well when Capital T (nicely) hijacked his helicopter with him behind the wheel.

George winks.

I grin. "How's Ms. Marla? And Rodolfo? And your vegetable garden? Did your prize-winning tomatoes earn another blue ribbon at the country fair?"

Ms. Marla is Kilter's Hoodlum Hotline operator—and GS George's new girlfriend, thanks to a little matchmaking on my part. Rodolfo's her three-legged Chihuahua. Gardening is GS George's favorite summer hobby.

His face lights up. "Thank you for asking! Everyone's great, and the garden's really coming along. We planted some new zucchini seeds that—"

"Ahem."

GS George and I look at Annika. She raises her eyebrows.

"My apologies, ma'am." GS George places the bucket on the floor by my feet and retreats to the opposite wall, where he stands still and stares straight ahead.

"What's that?" I point to the bucket.

"That," Annika says, slowly strolling toward me, "is what was extracted from your stomach the instant you popped out of the Inner Tube—a fast-moving underground chute. It transported you here from the pool, clearing all ingested fluid along the way."

Now that she mentions it—and that my head's clearer—I vaguely recall feeling topsy-turvy motion after I was sucked into the darkness. Like I was riding down a super-fast enclosed water-slide.

"Where's here?" I ask. "What is this place?"

"My subterranean viewing station."

"What do you view?" I ask.

"Anyone and anything I need to."

My eyes return to the bucket. "What's with the Band-Aid?"

"Accidental intake. One of your classmates had a boo-boo. The Band-Aid covering it came off during the game. You swallowed it along with all that water."

I wince, bring one hand to my stomach. "Gross."

"There's something worse." Reaching one end of the wall of water, Annika presses a button on the adjacent wall. The water stills. As it does, I see my classmates—including Elinor, thank goodness. They're still swimming and dunking and bobbing.

"This is the pool right now," Annika says.

"Everyone's moving slower. They must be getting tired."

"Of course they're getting tired. They've been chasing an uncatchable Kilter silverfish for twenty minutes."

"Uncatchable? Fern said it'd be hard, but that it was still possible to—"

Annika holds up one hand. "I'll ask again. What . . . was that . . . about?"

I open my mouth to answer. It's hard to tell her what she wants to hear, though, since I don't know what she's asking.

"The silverfish was right in front of you," she says with a huff. "I gave you an eternity to catch it. A thousand credits—they could buy the troublemaking supplies of your choice—were there for the taking. And you let them swim away. You lost out on all those credits—*and* earned five hundred gold stars."

I think fast. "It was too easy."

Annika smirks.

"You want us to challenge ourselves, right?" I ask. "So we're always becoming better Troublemakers? The silverfish was right there—but I wanted to work for it. I wanted to catch it using the skills I've learned at Kilter. I wanted to *earn* the win."

"And risk losing to your classmates in the process?"

Now I smirk. This is to say: Right. Like that would happen. Not because I think my victory was a sure thing, but because I know she'd want me to think it was.

This must be a good move because Annika lifts her chin, turns on one heel, and strolls alongside the wall of water. Once her back is to me I check out the pool again. Abe and Gabby have teamed up—or else Gabby has latched onto him. That's likelier. Either way, she's right behind him, doing everything he does a second after he does it.

I spot Lemon, too. Or his feet. I know they're his because they're scarred from the time he walked across a bed of burning coals just for fun. Now they're dangling in the deep end. The rest of him must be outside of the pool, sitting on a low diving board.

I'm still looking for Elinor when Annika stops and spins around on her other heel.

"I'm sorry for the sudden suction," she says, "but I wanted

to meet with you. And I know you don't enjoy being singled out, no matter how much you often deserve to be, so I thought it best to do so while your classmates were consumed by the silverfish hunt."

"But if you wanted to keep them distracted, why'd you give me the chance to catch the silverfish? Since that would've ended the game?"

"They would've been spinning in circles long after you grabbed it and left. Had we needed more time, Fern would've tossed in a backup silverfish. One that would've disappeared once you were in the pool again." She pauses. "I want you to have as many resources as possible, but I can't simply send you on a Kommissary shopping spree. That would attract attention and suspicion."

"Right," I say. "Thanks."

"You're welcome. Now," she says, her voice firmer, "we have much to do and no time to waste. I need your help with another top secret project."

I sit up straighter. "Is it Mr. Tempest?"

"That old bag of bones?" She waves one hand. "He's the least of my problems."

This is really saying something. Last semester Annika asked me to help keep an eye on Kilter's history teacher because she was very busy and he was very mysterious. She said he'd often run off, disappear, and ignore her e-mails and phone calls. She asked me to help keep an eye on him. I did, and found out a lot more about Mystery than I ever wanted to. Like his love of sharp axes, which I saw him steal from the Kommissary. And his secret cottage deep in the Kilter woods, which was decorated in pink and filled with stuffed animals and dolls that I saw him sneak out of Annika's childhood bedroom.

"It's your parents," Annika says.

"They're worse than Mystery?" I know Mom and Dad have been acting weird, and that that's why we're here—but I'm still surprised.

Annika presses a button on her K-Pak. A screen lowers in front of the wall of water. She presses another button and ten squares fill the large screen. A different live scene fills each square.

"Is that Kamp Kilter?" I recognize the luxury cabins, trampoline, and white sandy beach covered in sunbathers.

"Indeed." She faces me. "You were right to contact me. Your parents were exhibiting very abnormal behavior."

"Tell me about it."

"When Troublemakers return home for the summer after their first year at Kilter, there's always an adjustment period. Students must balance behaving and misbehaving. They want to behave to keep their parents happy, but they want to misbehave in order to keep sharp their newly learned skills. Parents walk a tricky tightrope too. They're usually thrilled to have their kids home, but they don't want to go overboard with love and affection and risk undoing all the work we did on their formerly uncontrollable offspring. On the flip side, they trust that we were tough enough during the school year that continuing a bad-cop charade over the summer would either be overkill or pointless, since they could never duplicate our immensely effective approach."

I think of my parents, trying to decide which side of the tightrope they walked.

Annika continues. "Initially the balancing act makes for a lot of formal yet polite exchanges between parents and children. Eventually home life returns to a more pleasant version of what it was pre-Kilter. For example, just like before, parents give kids chores. Unlike before, kids do them with just enough protest to suggest that progress has been made but more is needed."

"Because they don't want their parents to think they're cured and not send them back for a second year."

"Correct." Annika studies the screen for a long moment. "I've been doing this almost nineteen years . . . and not once have I heard of parents making trouble for their returning children. Doing so only asks for it in return. Their kids would inevitably resort to former bad behavior." She looks at me. "Why would any parent want that?"

I think of Mom. "No idea."

"That's why I brought you all here as soon as you wrote. Their behavior was unprecedented. I couldn't let it continue." She pauses. "Seamus, do you remember your first real-world combat mission?"

"When Houdini and I taught eleven-year-old Molly Lubbard's mother a lesson?"

"Yes. Do you remember *why* you taught her a lesson?"

"Because she wasn't very nice. She made Molly clean the entire house while she hung out at the spa every day. And if she didn't like something Molly did or didn't do, she'd lock her in the basement—knowing Molly was scared of the dark."

I frown at the memory. For three days Houdini and I spied

on Mrs. Lubbard and studied live video feed of the happenings inside the family's home. When we finally acted, I used my marksman skills to knock the knob off the basement door and free Molly, and then left Mrs. Lubbard a note instructing her to change her ways or else.

"Do you know what happened after you left the Lubbards?" Annika asks.

I shake my head. She reaches inside the pocket of her dress, takes out a long, skinny silver wand, and aims it at a flat-screen TV. The TV turns on. Molly Lubbard and her parents appear. They're riding bicycles through a meadow filled with flowers.

I watch for a second. "They look different."

"That's because they're happy. And they're happy because of what you did." Annika pauses. "Seamus, do you know why I created a school for professional Troublemakers?"

"Because you don't like adults very much?"

"I like some adults just fine." She walks toward me. "Let's try this: Why do your classmates think they're here?"

"To have fun." That's what Lemon told me my first semester, when I couldn't stop wondering why we were being taught how to make more trouble.

"Right. And they do. But Kilter's true purpose is much bigger than that. I won't go into all the details, but suffice it to say for now that what you did for the Lubbards is what I want all Kilter graduates to do. Your mission was in Kentucky, but my hope is that eventually, we can help children all over the world."

"Why don't you tell students that? Why the big secret?"

"Those who need to know, do—when the time is right. Telling students too soon can distract them from their studies. Not to mention there are those whose loyalty—or lack thereof—can't be trusted with such valuable information in the real world."

This makes sense . . . I think.

"Allow me to cut to the chase," Annika says.

"Shoot."

"Nadia's up to no good."

"Your sister?" And Elinor's mom?

"You saw her school. Her students, if you can call them that, are animals. That's how she likes them. The dirtier and stranger, the better. And I *know* she's behind your parents' odd behavior."

This sounds like a huge stretch to me—mostly because Nadia, and IncrimiNation, are in Arizona. That's thousands of miles away from our house in New York. She doesn't have their phone numbers or e-mail addresses, so how would she contact my parents? Even more puzzling, *why* would she contact them?

"Like I said before," Annika says. "When parents act worse, kids act worse. I think my sister's trying to get my students to act more like hers in hopes of poaching them from Kilter and bringing them to her poor excuse for a school."

"So you brought our parents here so she couldn't get to them?"

She leans forward. "And to ask you to help me find out exactly what she has up her dirty sleeve. So we can keep Kilter's true purpose on track. And help hundreds . . . thousands . . . *millions* of kids around the globe."

My limbs tingle. She wasn't kidding. Monitoring Mr. Tempest seems like small potatoes compared to this mission. And although she's also right that I don't enjoy being singled out . . . I have to admit, right now, I kind of do.

"Okay," I say, since she seems to be waiting for an answer. "I'll do it."

She beams. "Wonderful!"

"On one condition."

She freezes.

"Or more like . . . four conditions."

She sighs, stands up, and strides to the opposite wall. Halfway there, she aims her K-Pak at the large screen. The screen rises, revealing the outdoor pool. When she reaches the wall, she smacks the button with her palm. There's a loud whoosh. I watch Abe, Gabby, and Lemon get sucked away from the other Troublemakers and across the pool.

There's another whoosh. I look behind me and see a small door slide up the wall.

Abe plops out first. Then Gabby. Then Lemon. They're soaking wet and clearly confused. GS George gives them towels and aims an enormous hair dryer at their heads.

I turn back to Annika. "Forgot one."

She swallows a groan. Smacks the button again.

There's a third whoosh.

And out comes Elinor.

"What's going on?" Gabby asks, patting her face with the towel.

"Whatever it is better be worth more than a thousand credits," Abe says, squeezing out his trunks.

"Don't worry." I grin at my friends. "It is."

Chapter 10

DEMERITS: 1430
GOLD STARS: 650

The rest of my first day at Kamp Kilter is a blur. Without telling Lemon, Abe, Gabby, and Elinor everything she told me, Annika explains that she needs our eyes and ears to help figure out what's going on with our parents. Abe and Gabby are thrilled to be part of the mission. Lemon doesn't say anything, so I'm not even sure he's listening. And Elinor asks if she's really supposed to be included. To which Annika replies, through gritted teeth, "But of course."

After that we're sent back through the Inner Tube chute.

When we fly out into the pool, the silverfish game is still going on. My feet haven't even hit the floor when the target appears before me. Its light dims. Its empty black eyes find mine. This time, I reach out and grab it. When my head pops above water, a siren sounds. Lights flash. Our teachers cheer and congratulate me on winning one thousand credits. One by one, tired Troublemakers crawl out of the water and collapse onto the grass. Kanteen chefs hurry over with refreshments. Before long everyone's revived and dancing along to the Funky Faculty, our teachers' rock band.

I don't dance. I barely hear the music. Because I can't stop thinking about everything Annika told me. I think about it during the rest of the party, our ride back to Kilter Kamp, and while getting ready for bed.

I'm still thinking about it the next morning, when my K-Pak buzzes with a new e-mail.

TO: shinkle@kilteracademy.org
FROM: parsippany@cloudviewschools.net
SUBJECT: RE: RE: Happy Summer!

> Dear Seamus,
>
> Thank you for writing! It sounds like you have a great summer ahead of you. And how wonderful that your school director is throwing a retreat for students and their families! She must care a lot about you.

I stop reading. *Does* Annika care? She's given me reason to doubt it in the past—like when she ignored Elinor's burn on top of the mountain—but after telling me about Kilter's true purpose, now I'm not so sure.

I keep reading.

> As for all my traveling, I'd like to say it's part of an extra-long vacation. But most of it's for work. You must know it was extremely difficult for me to leave my position as a substitute teacher after what happened in the Cloudview Middle School cafeteria. I love kids and helping them learn. For a time, I planned to resume teaching once I was fully recovered. But then an amazing job opportunity

presented itself. One that included the chance to visit all the places I talked about in my last note, and countless more.

So I took the new job. Besides visiting amazing places, I get to meet amazing people. It's not teaching, but in some ways, it's better.

Thank you for the Bartholomew John update. I was just wondering how he was, as I often do about students I've had the privilege to know. In the short time we spent together, he struck me as a . . . special . . . individual. One with lots of raw potential.

Bartholomew John? A special individual with raw potential? I guess that's one way to describe him.

In any case, whenever you're home again, I'd really appreciate another Bartholomew John update. I'd contact him myself, but after what happened in the cafeteria I'm afraid he'd try to be much nicer than he actually is in hopes of demonstrating how acting like a bad kid helped him become a good one.

And I'm a firm believer that honesty is ALWAYS the best policy. Except when it's not. You are too, right?

Well, we've begun our initial descent into Dubai so I should wrap this up! Have a great time with your family. If you have a spare moment in between fun activities, please feel free to write. It's always a delight to hear from one of my favorite recr—

The message ends here. I scroll down to see if the rest of it is at the bottom of the message box. I'm still scrolling when my K-Pak buzzes with a new message.

TO: shinkle@kilteracademy.org
FROM: parsippany@cloudviewschools.net
SUBJECT: Oops!

Sorry—I hit send before I was finished. Darn turbulence!

What I meant to say was that it's always a delight to hear from one of my favorite students ever. Which you are!

Have fun! Write soon!

With Warm Regards,

Miss Parsippany

Puzzled, I reread both notes. When I'm done, I still have a few questions.

#1: What's Miss Parsippany's new job? She told me a lot about it without saying what she actually does.

#2: Why didn't Miss Parsippany say what she actually does?

#3: Has too much time at Kilter made me super paranoid and suspicious of all adults?

The last question is the only one I can answer.

Yes. Too much time at Kilter must be messing with my head.

"Rise and shine, campers!"

I jump and drop my K-Pak. Annika's face fills the flat-screen

TV on the wall opposite my bed. Standing before the lake, she shouts into a silver megaphone.

"You have exactly three minutes to drag your lazy bones out here! One second late and you'll join Kamp Kilter's brand-new sewage sorting committee!"

The screen goes black. I fling off the covers and throw on clothes. Then I swing by the bathroom, taking a few extra seconds to comb my hair and tame my eyebrows so that Elinor doesn't confuse me with a wild forest animal. After that I book it to the kitchen and grab a blueberry muffin. I scarf down breakfast as I sprint to the elevator, where Abe's already waiting.

"About time," he says.

"I'm the second one here," I say.

"I've been here twenty minutes."

I remind myself that we're on the same team. Then my K-Pak buzzes, stopping me from reminding him, too.

TO: shinkle@kilteracademy.org, ahansen@kilteracademy.org, loliver@kilteracademy.org, enorris@kilteracademy.org, gryan@kilteracademy.org

FROM: annika@kilteracademy.org
SUBJECT: Good Morning!

Hello, my talented Troublemakers!

I hope you enjoyed the rest of the party! I also hope you got a great night's sleep. You'll need it today.

This note is to confirm that your top secret mission begins NOW. You are to be on the lookout for odd behavior, strange signals, weird conversations, unfamiliar hand gestures, sneaked glances, and any other sign that something's amiss with Kilter parents. Additional indications of my sister's involvement include random piles of dirt, a nauseating stench, and the unshakeable feeling that evil eyes are watching your every move. (Think a mobile IncrimiNation.)

I expect detailed reports in my in-box by six p.m. this evening. Of course, should anything particularly alarming arise throughout the day, please let me know right away.

Hugs!

Annika

"Sixty seconds!" a male voice booms from the speakers scattered throughout our underground house. It sounds like Houdini.

I pocket my K-Pak as Gabby races down the hall. Elinor follows behind her, somehow looking even prettier in the morning than I've seen her any other time of the day.

"Forty-five seconds!"

"Hinkle," Abe says. "You need to go squeeze the sleep from your friend. Fast."

Lemon. I peer down the hall. His door's still closed.

"Annika might not be serious about the sewage sorting," Gabby says, "but she'll still be mad if we're late."

She's right. I dash down the hall.

Having shared a room with Lemon my first few months at Kilter, I know he's not exactly a morning person. When his alarm goes off, he hits the snooze button. Then, when it goes off again, he grabs the clock and yanks the plug from the electrical outlet. A few minutes after that, the alarm on his K-Pak clock—which he sets because he knows he'll need backup—goes off. That alarm eventually works, but because it sounds like a wind chime in a gentle breeze, he's able to ignore it for as long as half an hour.

And today, we don't have that kind of time.

I knock on his bedroom door. "Lemon?"

Nothing.

I knock again, then crack open the door. "You awake?"

The middle of the long lump lying in bed rises and falls. He's breathing, but that's about all he's doing.

"Twenty-five seconds!"

I dash across the room, dodging paper airplanes and arrows covering the floor, and nudge his shoulder. He throws off the pillow and shoots up. I jump back.

"Finn?" His eyes are wide, unfocused. "What happened? Are you okay? Did I—"

"Lemon." I step toward him. "It's me. Seamus."

His eyes find mine, return to normal size.

"I'm really sorry to barge in, but—"

"Twenty seconds!"

"We need to go. Like now. Annika's waiting. Our mission's starting. We have—"

"Eighteen seconds!"

"—to get in the elevator and up to the beach. Just put on some clothes while I find your shoes and . . . Lemon?" I stop sifting through paper stars for his worn moccasins. "What are you doing? Why are you lying down?"

"Not going." Lemon pulls the pillow over his head.

"You have to go. We all do. You heard Annika. She needs us to help—"

"Thirteen seconds!" Houdini shouts.

"Hinkle!" Abe shouts.

I stare at Lemon's motionless body, torn. He's my best friend. Whatever he needs—sleep, space, no questions asked—I want him to have. But this mission is important. And Capital T can't do it without him.

Then it hits me.

"What about Finn?" I ask. "He's here, isn't he? Don't you want to see him?"

Jackpot. Lemon flings away the pillow, grabs his moccasins from under the bed, and sprints from the room.

"Ten seconds!"

I'm the last one inside the elevator. Abe hits the up button. The glass door slides shut. During our ride I sneak glances at Lemon, who's now wide-awake and staring at the glowing red arrow above the door.

The elevator stops. The door slides open. Abe and Lemon elbow and nudge each other to be the first one out.

We reach the beach just as Annika, who's standing before the lake with our teachers, holds an air horn overhead and lets it rip. The noise sends birds flying from the trees. Once every living thing within a ten-mile radius is awake, she swaps the air horn for a megaphone.

"Reed Jenkins! Natalie Warner! Liam Jones!"

There's a scuffle behind us. I look over my shoulder and see three Troublemakers pop out from under three different tarp tents.

"You're *late*!" Annika says. "Tardiness suggests that you feel your time is somehow more valuable than mine! And this suggests that at home, you feel your time is somehow more valuable than your parents'! Neither is *ever* the case!"

"Sorry," Reed says, his face turning red. "I couldn't find my K—"

"Wyatt," Annika barks into the megaphone. Our art teacher steps out from the line. "Please take these troubling truants to the sewage sorting lair."

Reed's face goes white. Natalie and Liam exchange worried looks. I want to assure them that this show is for our parents' benefit, since they must be listening on speakers across the lake, but don't. Partly because doing so might really annoy Annika, and also because Wyatt takes them by the ears and whisks them away before I can.

"As mentioned yesterday," Annika continues, "you'll have ten minutes to forage for breakfast in the woods. After that you'll transport yourselves across the lake. On shore, Kamp Kilter staff members will give you your assignments. Any goofing off and you risk permanent ejection from Kamp Kilter. In the event of such punishment, your families will be forced to end their vacations early. And you don't want that, do you?"

There's a low murmuring throughout the group.

"I can't hear you!" Annika yells.

"No!" we shout.

"Good. Now, I assume you have your K-Paks. Keep them on you at all times! You'll soon receive e-mails about Role Reverse, a fun new activity."

"Fun?" Alison Parker asks. "But I thought—"

"That may have been an exaggeration!" Annika yells into the megaphone. "I should've been clearer and said a *not-entirely-miserable* activity. But if all goes well, it's one that should help you and your families have fun together upon your return home."

"Role Reverse?" Abe asks. "Is that like role playing?"

"Precisely," Annika says. "Additional information is forthcoming. For now, go! Eat! Try to be the children your parents wish you were!"

The group bolts for the trees. Some Troublemakers actually search for edible twigs and berries. Others down granola bars, bagels, and other breakfast items they must've taken from their kitchens. Then they all moan and groan when they realize they should've saved their appetites.

"Oh. My. *Goodness!*" Gabby squeals. "That's the most food I've ever *seen*!"

When I see what she means, I'm impressed too. A long table has been set up in a large clearing. It looks like it should be in a fancy restaurant, not in the middle of the woods. It's covered by a white tablecloth and holds real plates and silverware, candles, and vases of flowers. It also holds towers of food. There are pancakes. Waffles. Eggs. Bacon. Sausage. Toast. Fresh fruit. Glass pitchers of orange juice, hot chocolate, and steaming maple syrup. Crystal bowls filled with cream cheese, jam, and peanut butter. Behind the table, three Kanteen chefs man three silver stoves on wheels, occasionally dashing to an oversize refrigerator for more ingredients.

"We have eight minutes!" Abe announces.

"Then we better get eating!" Eric Carle says.

"Are those fish sticks?" Elinor asks from across the table. "Covered in maple syrup?"

I smile, not sure what makes me happier: that my favorite Kilter breakfast is on the table . . . or that Elinor remembered what my favorite Kilter breakfast is.

"Looks like," I say. "Thanks."

Mouth watering, I aim a fork at the fish stick at the top of the tower.

But it disappears before I can stab it. So does the one underneath it. And the two underneath that. And the four underneath that. In case I missed something, I look down at my plate. But it's empty. So is the fish-stick platter when I look at it again.

"Does someone else—"

Love fish sticks? That's what I try to ask. But the question's cut short.

Because I'm grabbed by shirt collar. Yanked off the ground.

And sucked into the sky.

Chapter 11

DEMERITS: 1430
GOLD STARS: 650

Maple-syrup-soaked fish sticks? No offense, but that has to be the grossest thing I've ever heard of. And smelled."

"They're not soaked," I correct Ike. "They're dipped. Soaking would make them soggy—and that *would* be gross. Since the crunchy coating is what makes them so delicious!"

My tutor and I are sitting in a tree above the long breakfast buffet table. This is where I landed after he snagged the back of my shirt with a super-strong fishing hook and reeled me in. We're so high up I can barely hear my classmates talking below.

Holding his nose now, Ike frowns and examines a fish stick.

"How do you know you won't like it?" I ask.

"If I feel sick just thinking about it, I'm pretty sure it's not for me."

I grin. "One bite. For me."

Ike releases his nose. "Fine. *If* you do something for me."

"Deal."

He reaches behind him and holds up a long stick. "Ever seen one of these?"

"A fishing pole?"

He turns over the stick so I can see the writing on the other side.

"The Kilter Katcher 5000," I read aloud.

"Guaranteed to elevate your camping experience by ensnaring any target—hook, line, and sinker. Allow me to demonstrate." He jumps to his feet and crouches down like the branch is a surfboard. "See that donut Abe's holding?"

"Nope." Abe, and the rest of the Troublemakers, are not only far away, they're hidden by the tree's thousands of leaves.

"Look." Ike points to the Kilter Katcher.

I lean closer. "Is that a radar screen?"

The small square is attached to the top of the pole. As I watch, Ike adjusts the silver reel on the underside of the pole. The image on the screen grows larger. My Capital T alliance mate brings a huge, sugary ball toward his mouth.

"That's Abe," I say. "And that's definitely a jelly donut."

Ike spins the reel. On the screen, the red bull's-eye moves. When it's centered on the donut, Ike squeezes the reel. The bull's-eye freezes. The Kilter Katcher releases silver fishing line.

"Now *this* is breakfast." Ike bites into the jelly donut, which has gone from Abe's hand to his in about a second.

My chin drops. "That's how you stole my fish sticks so fast? And got me up here?"

"Yup." He shoves the rest of the donut into his mouth, chews, and licks the powdered sugar from his fingers. "Your turn."

I sit up straighter on the tree branch. Ike hands me the Kilter Katcher. For such an impressive weapon, it's surprisingly light.

"What should I catch?" I ask.

"We'll start easy. I'll give you ten demerits for that caterpillar two branches down."

I frown. "Won't I hurt him?"

"Were you hurt when I caught you?"

No, but Ike's obviously had practice. So I'm still nervous as I spin the reel and move the bull's-eye over my furry target.

"Good," Ike says when the radar's locked in place. "See the handle on the side of the reel? That's your firing lever. Pull it down to let 'er rip."

"Sorry, little guy," I whisper. Then I pull down the lever and cringe.

"Missed."

I look down. "How? The bull's-eye was locked right over it."

"The line's tangled in leaves." Ike leans against the tree trunk and clasps his hands over his stomach. "Sorry. I should've mentioned that the Kilter Katcher can't do your job entirely. Once it's released, you have to guide the line toward its target. The instant you pull down the lever, the screen will change. It'll show you the line's route as well as obstacles in its path. Using the reel like a video-game controller, you have to watch the screen and move the line around those obstacles."

"But it's so fast," I say.

"That just means you have to be too."

I consider this, then give the Kilter Katcher a strong tug. The line rips free of the leaves and flies back up into the pole. I find the caterpillar on the screen and refocus the bull's-eye. I lock it in place, take a deep breath, and pull down the lever.

The screen changes instantly. I pretend I'm playing video games in my bedroom back home as I stare and adjust the reel. The tiny digital hook moves around tiny digital limbs and leaves.

"It made it." I look at the screen, down at the target, and back at the screen. "I think it—"

"Voila." Ike nods to the end of the pole, where the fuzzy caterpillar is now cradled in the hook like a baby in a swing. "You just earned ten demerits. Congrats."

"Thanks." I lower the pole, remove the caterpillar, and gently place it on the branch. "And congrats to you—you just earned a bite of maple-syrup-dipped fish stick!"

"Not so fast. That was just a warm-up. Your real challenge is next."

"Bring it on."

"Annika."

"You want me to catch *her*?"

"No—although that's tempting."

For a second, I forget about the Kilter Katcher. Because Ike's probably the happiest guy I know. He smiles a lot. I've seen him serious and focused—but never in a bad mood. But now? When he talks about catching Annika? He sounds different. He *looks* different. As if he thinks trapping our director is a good idea . . . but for bad reasons.

But then he shakes his head and smiles, and he's happy Ike again.

"I want you to catch her sunglasses. Snatch them right off her face. For a hundred demerits."

I smile too. "No problem."

"Don't be so sure. The caterpillar was close. Annika's a quarter of a mile away—and she's a moving target. Even if the hook reaches her, it has to find her face. And there's always a chance she'll see the hook and dodge it."

"Hinkle!" a male voice shouts far below us. *"Where are you?"*

Abe. Our top secret mission.

I look at Ike. "Annika gave us ten minutes for breakfast. Can I take a rain check? And catch her sunglasses later?"

"If you do it right it won't take long."

"Hinkle!" Abe hollers. "We *will* leave you!"

My pulse quickens. Not wanting to disappoint Ike, I adjust the reel and study the screen. After a few tries, I zoom in on the beach and see Annika talking on her K-Pak. She walks as she talks, which makes it hard to lock the bull's-eye on her sunglasses.

Annika pauses. The bull's-eye hovers over the right lens of her sunglasses. My breath catches. I lock the bull's-eye, yank the lever, and release the line.

Two seconds later, I'm smiling at my reflection in Annika's mirrored sunglasses. Which Ike's wearing as he chows down on a maple-syrup-dipped fish stick.

"Pretty good, right?" I ask.

He swallows. "Don't know if I'd order it in a restaurant . . . but it's staying down. So that's good."

I hand him the Kilter Katcher. "Thanks! This was fun. But I kind of have to go."

"Understood."

I wait. He licks his fingers.

"Sorry," I say, "but do you think you could . . . ?"

"Oh! Sure."

I turn slightly so he has a better shot at my back. He lifts the Kilter Katcher and casts the line in one quick motion. The hook latches onto my shirt. The line lifts me from the branch and begins lowering me down.

"Thanks again!" I smile and wave.

The line stops. My body jerks.

"Seamus?"

I look up at Ike. He's looking down at me. His mood seems to have changed again. But he's not mad. Maybe sad? Definitely serious.

"Annika has you working on a special project . . . doesn't she?"

My mouth opens. Nothing comes out. Because I'm not sure what to say. Ike's my honorary big brother so I don't want to lie to him. But Annika's Kamp Kilter mission is top secret and I don't want to disobey her.

Fortunately or unfortunately, my silence must answer for me. Because Ike leans down and whispers three words.

"Be very careful."

Chapter 12

DEMERITS: 1560
GOLD STARS: 650

"We're not going to make it," Gabby says.

"Yes, we are," Abe says.

"But water's in the boat. The boat's sinking. That means *we're* sinking."

"You can swim, right?" Elinor asks.

"Yes," Gabby says, "but so can the flesh-eating fish that live in the lake. I bet they're faster than I am. And hungry, too!"

"If you'd all stop talking and start filling your cups, we'd go a lot faster."

I look at Lemon. So do Abe, Gabby, and Elinor.

"Shouldn't you be napping?" Abe asks.

It sounds like a sarcastic question, but Abe's serious. Because normally at this point in any challenge, Lemon would be relaxing while everyone else was hurrying to get the job done. Out on the lake and under the warm sun, he'd be asleep in seconds.

But today Lemon's at the head of our hole-riddled canoe. He's using two of the plastic cups Annika gave us to scoop out the rising water and dump it back into the lake. And he's moving so fast, his gray T-shirt's already black with sweat.

"Lemon's right," I say. "The other boats are almost there."

"There" is the other side of the lake, home to our parents' luxury cabins. According to Annika's latest e-mail to me and my friends, we'll start our day with the rest of the Troublemakers and split up after the assignments have been given. Our classmates are either really strong, excited, or afraid of the flesh-eating fish in the lake, because we all left shore at the same time, and they're way ahead of us.

I can't say I'm helping. I mean, I *am* helping—I'm scooping out water and dumping it back into the lake—but I'm also distracted.

I can't stop thinking of what Ike said before he released me all the way to the ground.

Be very careful? Of what?

"You okay?"

I glance up. Elinor's looking at me as she crouches in the ankle-deep water, trying to plug two holes with her feet. Remembering that as our weakest swimmer she has much more reason to fear sinking than Gabby does, I fill and dump my cup faster.

"Yup." I smile. "Just thinking."

"I'm a good listener," she says.

"I know. Thanks. Maybe we can talk—"

Later? That's how I'd finish the sentence—if Lemon didn't leap out of the canoe. The boat's still rocking when he grabs the front with one hand and starts paddling with the other.

"Who released the Olympian?" Abe asks.

Which is another good question. Because thanks to Lemon's superhuman swimming, I fill and dump only three more cups of water before we reach the shore.

We hop out and drag the canoe a few feet up the beach so it doesn't drift away. Then we hurry toward the other Troublemakers, who are gathering around Samara, our biology teacher.

As we run, I look around for my parents. But besides us and a few Good Samaritans, the beach is empty.

Halfway to the group of Troublemakers, Lemon stumbles over a rock. I grab his arm to help steady him—and to slow him down.

"Hey," I say. "Have a sec?"

"Not really. Everyone's here. Samara's about to give out assignments."

"We have our assignments. Annika gave them to us yesterday." When he glances at the group, clearly worried that I'm holding him back, I add, "They're all drying off. And they're soaking wet. That'll take at least a minute."

He takes a deep breath and releases it in a loud rush. "What's up?"

"Um, well . . . I was just wondering . . . is everything okay?"

"Why wouldn't it be?"

"I don't know. It's just . . . you kind of seem . . . a little off?"

"Off?"

"Well, like . . . the origami?"

"What about it?"

"You're really into it."

"So?"

"So you never were before."

"It's a new hobby. I'm off because I've developed an interest in the ancient Japanese arts?"

"No. Of course not. And 'off' is probably the wrong word. It just seems like an odd choice. Considering your other hobby, I mean."

"Which is?"

My eyebrows lift. "Playing with fire?"

"I can have more than one hobby."

"Definitely. But those two together seem kind of dangerous. What if you're throwing flames one day—and they catch on a strand of paper snowflakes?"

He shrugs. "I'll put out the fire. Like I always do."

"Okay," I say, "well, then how come you didn't dig a hole with the rest of us yesterday? Or play the silverfish game?"

"I've never been an overachiever when it comes to Kilter assignments."

"Yes, but you still do them. Even if it's later or slower than everyone else."

He sighs. "I don't know. I didn't plan to spend the summer

here, so maybe my brain's still in vacation mode." He pauses. "Is there anything else?"

I think about it. "I guess not."

"Great."

"Sorry. I didn't mean to—"

He puts one hand on my shoulder. "Don't be. It's okay. You were concerned. Because you're my best friend. I'm lucky to—"

"Care to join us, boys?"

We look down the beach. Our classmates have formed a circle around Samara.

"Shall we?" Lemon asks.

"Let's," I say.

He sprints toward them. My legs are about half as long as his, so it takes me a few seconds to catch up to the group. When I do, Samara's calling out names and chores.

"Chris, laundry! Alison, window washing! Jake, toilet scrubbing!"

At this, a few Troublemakers snort. Others giggle.

"Abe, mopping! Gabby, ironing! Lemon, dusting! Elinor, silverware polishing! Seamus, indoor-plant maintenance!"

Samara gives out the rest of the chores. When every

Troublemaker has one, she lowers her clipboard and addresses the group.

"Rules for the day! You'll do your chores in your parents' cabins. When you're done, you'll e-mail me or another faculty member, and we'll come evaluate your work. We have extremely high standards, so I wouldn't e-mail unless you're absolutely certain you can't do anything more! If the job isn't done to our satisfaction, we'll make you start all over—*and* punish you with demerits!" Samara pauses and gives us an exaggerated wink. Then she continues. "Also! Your families are on vacation. *You* are not. Some of our softer-hearted parents might be inclined to hug you and kiss you and include you in their camp activities. We've advised them not to, but accidents happen. In any case, you are under no circumstances to have any fun with your families. Is that clear?"

Nicole Fields, a tall Troublemaker in the Athletes group, raises her hand.

"What?" Samara asks.

"What about the hugs and kisses?" Nicole asks.

"What about them?"

"Can we accept them—and give them back?"

Samara turns, quietly confers with our other teachers, and faces us again.

"Yes. However, the affectionate exchange must last no longer than two seconds."

"How will you know if a hug lasts longer than that?" Gabby asks.

Samara leans forward. Her eyes narrow. "Do you really want to risk finding out?"

Gabby gulps, shakes her head.

"Good!" Samara straightens. "Moving on with the rules. You'll be assigned a different chore each day. Every inch of your parents' cabin will be pristine by week's end. Got it?"

We all nod.

"Great! One last rule. After an initial daily greeting you will not initiate or engage in conversation with your families. You're here to work, not chitchat. We've told your parents this and explained the benefits of leaving you alone. After a silent summer, perhaps you'll appreciate the privilege of having people close to you who truly care about how you're feeling and what you're thinking every single day." Samara gives this a moment to sink in. Then, "Any questions?"

"Yeah," a male Troublemaker calls out. "When's lunch?"

My classmates chuckle. Samara smiles.

"Austin Lewis, you just earned ten gold—" She catches herself. "Ten demerits!"

"What?" Austin huffs. "Why?"

"Because good children never ask for rewards." She motions behind her. "Your supplies are back here. Load up and head out!"

Every Troublemaker dashes toward a line of folding tables. The tables are piled high with sponges, buckets, bottles of bleach, and about a million other cleaning items. One teacher stands behind each table and tells us what to take. Lizzie says I'll need a watering can and trimming shears, which I learn is a fancy term for scissors. She also tells me which cabin my parents are in (#1), and where it is (on a hill to the left of the tennis courts).

Once I'm ready to go, I look around for my friends. We can't talk about what we're really going to do inside our families' cabins in front of everyone else, but I wouldn't mind a few nods or waves so I know we're all still on the same page.

I'll just have to hope they remember the day's real goal. Because Gabby and Abe are already off and running. Lemon must've been the first one to get supplies—and the first to head for his family's cabin—because I don't see him anywhere. Elinor's still here, but I can't catch her eye because she's talking to Samara with her back to me.

"Don't you have somewhere to be . . . *Seamusss*?"

I freeze, but my skin crawls, as if my name was hissed by a real snake that's now slithering up my arms.

"You know Annika doesn't like dawdling," the snake adds near my ear.

Mystery. At least I think it's him. It definitely sounds like him. And I feel as uncomfortable as I usually do whenever I'm around him. But he looks different. Probably because I've only ever seen him in head-to-toe black, and now he's wearing white shorts and a white T-shirt.

"Since when do you care about what Annika wants?" I ask.

"Since I've realized just how wonderful a service she provides families," he says.

"Took you a while."

"Quick opinions are often wrong opinions."

"Okay," I say, and head for the tennis courts.

I'm glad the walk to my parents' cabin is long. I have a lot to think about. Like this weird Mystery encounter. Ike's warning.

Lemon's insistence that everything's fine. Miss Parsippany's last e-mail. What the heck I'm supposed to do with trimming shears.

Halfway to the tennis courts, my K-Pak buzzes. Checking my K-mail, I read and walk at the same time.

TO: year2troublemakers@kilteracademy.org
FROM: samara@kilteracademy.org
SUBJECT: That's Not All!

Hi, Troublemakers! Miss me yet? ☺

This note is to say what I couldn't during our morning meeting for fear of your families over-hearing. And that is: You have homework! To be completed today, in addition to and while you're doing your chores. (You didn't think we'd keep you here all summer without giving you a chance to practice your troublemaking skills, did you?)

So remember that great biology lesson last semester? The one on faking sickness? That taught you several ways to fool your parents into believing you should stay in bed instead of going to school? Of course you do. That much fun is impossible to forget!

After hocking a whole lot of loogies and holding your breath until your faces turned red and feverish, you guys were masters. Now it's time to up the ante! Rather than playing sick yourselves, your assignment today is to convince one family member that he or she is under the weather. (You may break the no-talking rule for this purpose ONLY.) We'll know you've succeeded when said family member checks into the Kamp Kilter infirmary. Send more than one family member to the infirmary, and you'll earn extra demerits and Kommissary credits. Send NO family members to the infirmary, and you'll earn a boatload of gold stars—and lose a boatload of Kommissary credits.

Good luck, Troublemakers! Do me proud.

—Samara

P.S. Like good children would, you'll receive gold stars for completing your daily chores—which you MUST do. So you'll definitely want to get into as much trouble as possible to make up for the mandatory loss of credits!

"Seamus!"

My heart skips. I'm climbing a tall staircase up a steep hill to my parents' cabin, and now I stop and look down. Fifteen feet below, Elinor looks up at me.

"Can I come with you?" she asks. "My mom's not here so I don't have a family cabin to clean. Samara said I could pair up with a friend."

"And you want to pair up . . . with me?"

She smiles. "Is that okay?"

I nod. She jogs up the stairs. When she reaches the step below mine, I take her towel and silver polish to carry the rest of the way.

Newly energized, I climb the remaining steps like they're flat on the ground and not stacked at an eighty-five-degree angle. Every few seconds I glance behind me to make sure Elinor's okay. And every few seconds, she smiles and makes my heart beat even faster.

My chest stays warm and mushy all the way to the top of

the hill, across the large front yard, and onto Cabin #1's wide front porch. With Elinor by my side, I don't think it can feel any other way.

But then I lift the heavy silver KA knocker. Tap it against the door. And feel my heart harden the instant Dad answers, sees me standing there—and slams the door in my face.

Chapter 13

DEMERITS: 1560
GOLD STARS: 750

Do we have the wrong cabin?" Elinor asks.

"Nope," I say. "That was my dad."

"He looked like he thought you were a ghost. Or a burglar."

"He did."

"Why?"

"That's what we have to find out."

I step to the left and peer inside a large window. Curtains are pulled across the glass inside, but there's a sliver of open space between them. It's just wide enough for me to see Dad drop to his knees by the living room table and quickly gather whatever's on it. Then, arms full, he jumps up and flees the room.

"Should we knock again?" Elinor asks.

The door flies open. "Seamus!" Dad exclaims. "Elinor! What a pleasant surprise! Please come in!"

Elinor and I exchange glances. She steps through the doorway first. I follow.

"You have a lovely cabin," Elinor says once we're all inside.

She's right. We're standing in the huge living room, which has hardwood floors, a cathedral ceiling, and a two-story fireplace. Each wall is different. The one facing the lake is made entirely of glass, so even standing on the other side of the room it feels like you're floating on a cloud. Another is made of multicolored rocks. Another features water streaming from the ceiling to a long, narrow pool on the floor. The last is made of twisting, tangling tree branches. The room looks like a hip indoor forest.

"Would you like to sit?" Dad asks. "Can I get you something to drink?"

After that hike up the hill, I'd love a glass of water. But we have a job to do. And the sooner we get to it, the sooner we can figure out why Dad's acting like I'm a houseguest instead of his son.

"Actually," I say, "do *you* need something to drink? You look a little warm."

Dad's face freezes. "I do?"

"Your face is red. And kind of sweaty." Spotting a thermostat on the rock wall, I walk over and check the temperature. "Sixty-five degrees. That's pretty cold. The air-conditioning must be working. And you're wearing shorts and a short-sleeved shirt." I turn around. "What do you think, Elinor?"

She stands before Dad and holds up one palm. "May I?"

"Um, well, what—"

He gives up on trying to form a sentence when Elinor presses her palm to his forehead. She turns to me, eyes wide.

"He's burning up," she says.

"He is?" I ask.

"I am?" Dad asks.

"Wildernitess," I say, thinking fast. "It's a sickness. A serious one. That you get in the woods."

"Like poison ivy?" Elinor asks.

"Worse. It sucks your energy. Zaps your appetite. Turns your muscles to mush. It's really common in people who are used to being in houses and malls and cars—and then are suddenly dropped in the middle of a forest. It's like their bodies' way of rejecting fresh air." I raise my eyebrows at Dad. "And it starts . . . with a fever."

"You're right," he says.

I pause. "I am?"

"He is?" Elinor asks.

"Yes!" Dad bustles around the room, grabbing his wallet from the coffee table, his penny loafers from the mat by the door. "I've been feeling a bit off but thought it was just the excitement of being on vacation. I didn't consider that I might be coming down with something—but it makes sense! I'd better get checked out before it gets any worse."

He snatches the lanyard holding his Kamp Kilter ID and key card from a hook on the tree-wall and starts to open the front door.

"Wait," I say.

Dad stops, one foot in the living room, the other on the porch.

What are you doing? Why are you lying? What are you hiding?

Who are you and what did you do with my real dad?

I swallow down these questions and go with another. "What about Mom? Wildernitess is highly contagious. Maybe she should get checked out too?"

He shrugs. "Your mother's already out. I'll be sure to talk to her about it later!"

"That was easy," Elinor says when he's gone. "He didn't even ask why we were here."

"And he left us alone in the house."

She pauses. "Isn't he usually the normal one?"

"Compared to my mom?" I nod. That's what I'd told Elinor once last semester. Because back then, it was true.

"Do you think she's rubbing off on him?"

This is an interesting question—and one I haven't considered. I already know that Mom loves Kilter and wants me to be as bad as I can be. I still don't know *why*, but I do know that. Is it possible that she told Dad about Kilter's real purpose? And somehow convinced him that I should be a professional Troublemaker?

I'd like to share these thoughts with Elinor but don't. She doesn't know that Mom knows about Kilter. I've been tempted to tell her and my other friends, but I don't want wondering about her to make them wonder about me. After almost losing them all when Mom revealed I was a murderer (before I knew I wasn't), I can't risk that again.

"I have no idea," I say instead.

"Do you think we should've kept him around a little longer?" she asks. "To see if he said or did anything strange?"

"He said and did a lot in the few minutes he was here." I tell her what I saw before entering the house, and how I want to find what Dad was trying to hide.

"Should we do our chores first?" she asks when I'm done.

"Good idea. We'll finish as fast as possible and then get to our real mission."

We retrieve our supplies from the living room and head for the kitchen. Elinor opens drawers and looks for silverware. I go to the sink and fill the watering can. When the can's full, I turn off the faucet and heave out the heavy container.

I'm about to go to the living room when a thought occurs to me.

"Can I ask you something?"

Elinor looks up from a gleaming spoon. "Anything."

We've come a long way—because I know she means it. And this is an especially big deal since Elinor's troublemaking talent is lying.

"Is this weird for you?" I ask. "Looking for evidence against your mom?"

She shrugs. "Maybe a little. But we wouldn't be looking if she'd just plant flowers and bake cookies and be a normal mother."

"Okay. Well if it does get really weird, or if you're uncomfortable at all and want to stop . . . you'll let me know?"

She gives me a small smile. "I will. Thank you."

I smile too. Then I go to the living room and get to work. There are six plants. I water them all until their brown soil turns black. Then I take the trimming shears and survey the plants' leaves. Most are smooth and green, but a few are wrinkled and gray. Using the shears, I focus on clipping the dead leaves from their stems.

I pause only once, when I hear Elinor singing softly in the kitchen. Then I'm distracted by images of future Elinor and future me doing chores around our future home. In this scenario, Elinor's just as pretty as she is now. I'm taller. And we're doing chores because they're a good excuse to spend time together, not because someone told us to.

"Focus," I tell myself.

"Did you say something?" Elinor calls from the kitchen.

"Ficus!" I call back. I think that's the real name of a real plant Mom has at home. "This one's out of control!"

When I'm done in the living room, I take the watering can

and head for the next room. I stop at the first door I come to—and it's locked. Looking down the rest of the hall, I see that every other door is wide open.

I'm instantly suspicious. I'd check the top of the doorframe for a key, but I can't reach. I'm tempted to drag over a chair—but decide I should finish plant duty first. Annika's top secret mission is most important, but I don't want to invite attention if Samara makes a big deal about who didn't finish their chores later.

I dart into the next room. Judging by the rumpled blankets and open suitcases, it's the one Mom and Dad are using as their bedroom. I quickly find and trim four plants, then take a K-Mail break.

TO: loliver@kilteracademy.org, ahansen@kilteracademy.org, gryan@kilteracademy.org
CC: enorris@kilteracademy.org
FROM: shinkle@kilteracademy.org
SUBJECT: So?

Hi! Just wanted to see how everything's going. Any weird observations yet?

Elinor and I had some right away. (She's helping

me since her mom's not here and she doesn't have a cabin to clean.) Will tell all later!

—S

I hit send. Before I can pick up the watering can, my K-Pak buzzes.

TO: shinkle@kilteracademy.org, loliver@kilteracademy.org, gryan@kilteracademy.org
CC: enorris@kilteracademy.org
FROM: ahansen@kilteracademy.org
SUBJECT: RE: So?

My parents aren't here. Correction: their BODIES are here. But their brains have clearly been sucked out and replaced with unidentifiable matter. Details later.

Side note: Your girlfriend's working with you? That sounds like mixing business with pleasure. And THAT sounds like a bad idea. One that could seriously compromise our group's goals.

—Abe

Heart thumping and cheeks blazing, I press reply. It's bad enough that Abe's singling out Elinor and me again . . . but to call her my girlfriend? *And* copy her on the note? That's totally unnecessary.

I'm about to start typing when my K-Pak buzzes again.

TO: ahansen@kilteracademy.org, shinkle@kilteracademy.org, loliver@kilteracademy.org
CC: enorris@kilteracademy.org
FROM: gryan@kilteracademy.org
SUBJECT: RE: RE: So?

Abe, did the aliens that stole your parents' brains also take your heart? So what if Seamus and Elinor want to hang out together all the time? I think it's GREAT! ☺

XO!

Gabby

I've just finished reading Gabby's e-mail when another new one comes in.

TO: ahansen@kilteracademy.org, shinkle@kilteracademy.org, loliver@kilteracademy.org
CC: enorris@kilteracademy.org
FROM: gryan@kilteracademy.org
SUBJECT: Oops!

Sorry—forgot to mention my parents! Nothing to report yet. I actually haven't seen them. Maybe they're still sleeping?

XOXO!

Gabby

Still reeling from Abe's first note, my heart hammers like I'm sprinting around the room. Before anyone can send another mortifying message, I start typing.

TO: ahansen@kilteracademy.org, gryan@kilteracademy.org
FROM: shinkle@kilteracademy.org
SUBJECT: HEY!

> Elinor and I are just FRIENDS. And we're just trying to WORK. So since there's nothing else to say, can you not talk about us anymore? Please??
>
> —S

I send the note and wait. My in-box stays quiet. I'm happy Abe and Gabby listen to my request, but I wouldn't mind hearing from Lemon about his parents.

A minute later, when there's still no word from my best friend, I put away my K-Pak and go to the glass doors on the other side of the bedroom. They lead to a balcony. Since the house sits on a huge hill, maybe I can see all of the other houses—including Lemon's family's—from there. At the very least I can make sure he didn't fall asleep in a lounge chair or set up an origami station on the beach.

I have one hand on the knob when something catches my attention.

Mom's coupon folder. The one that looks like a mini filing cabinet stuffed between red plastic covers. It's on the nightstand next to the bed. Mom never goes anywhere without it, so normally I wouldn't give it a second glance.

But I do now for two reasons.

#1: It's here, at Kamp Kilter. Where everything is free.

#2: The folder's flat. At home it's always stuffed with small paper squares offering ten cents off paper towels, fifty cents off tofu, and other shopping deals. Here it looks empty.

But it's not. I realize this when I go to the nightstand and pick it up. It doesn't hold coupons, though. It holds a book—a real one, with paper pages.

I check behind me to make sure I'm alone, then slide out the book. I wonder if it's the same one Mom was reading in the kitchen back home, that she tried to cover up when I came into the room.

When I see the title on the front cover, I know it is.

MY LIFE WITH SEAMUS
by Judith Hinkle

"This is private property," I tell myself. "And none of your business."

Only my name's on the front cover. So how is it anything *but* my business?

Heart thudding, I open the book to the first page. It was written thirteen years ago, on my birthday. My mom's handwriting was the same then as it is now. Neat. Even. With no cross-outs or any other sign that she started to say something she didn't mean.

Which makes her first entry especially interesting.

He's perfect.

After all this time, all these months—no, years—of hoping and waiting and hoping some more, he's here. And he's even more breathtaking than I could've ever imagined.

I'm reluctant to spend even a few minutes apart from him, so I'll keep brief these first thoughts in what will eventually be a lengthy dedication to the light of my life. But suffice it to say that this is the happiest I've ever been. The joy is truly overwhelming, and will only grow. Of this I'm certain. And that's for one reason, and one reason only.

My son.

Seamus.

I look up. Blink. Could I possibly have read that right?

The morning sun faces away from this room. The light's dim. Deciding I need a better, brighter view, I take the book outside.

At the balcony's railing, I look down and start rereading.

Once again I'm instantly struck. But not just by my mother's words.

By white balls. Dozens of them, maybe more. Flying over the balcony railing, they hit my chest. Bounce off my head. Stunned, I stumble toward the glass door, which my back hits. And I drop to the floor.

I try to get up. But the aliens that sucked out Abe's parents' brains must've come for mine, too. Because the world starts to grow fuzzy.

And then it disappears.

Chapter 14

DEMERITS: 1610
GOLD STARS: 750

Name?"

"Ssshhaymmmm . . ."

"Age?"

"Thirrnnn . . ."

"Do you know where you are?"

"Killt . . . er . . ."

"Killed her? He said 'killed her!' Why's he talking about the teacher he—? Um, OW? What—"

"Would you please pipe down? Not everyone knows what

Seamus did to get in here. If he wants to spill the beans, that's his business. Not ours."

"But he said—"

"He doesn't know what he said. He's a vegetable right now."

"Would you *both* please pipe down? It's hard enough hearing him in all this ruckus without you two bickering like Rodolfo bickers with Esmeralda."

"Who's Esmeralda?"

"The spoiled Pomeranian next door. My poor baby can't bury a bone without that one squeezing through the fence and digging it right back up. Why, the other day—"

"Wait! Did his eyelids just twitch? I swear I just saw them twitch."

"Maybe I should sing? Injured people really respond to beautiful music. It, like, heals them from the inside out. If I just—"

"Gabby."

"Seamus? It's Elinor. Can you hear me?"

The world lightens. Soon I can see actual colors. Gabby's pink T-shirt. Abe's blue baseball hat. Ms. Marla's red lips.

Elinor's copper eyes.

"What happened?" I whisper.

Gabby squeals. Abe exhales. Ms. Marla winks.

"You had a little accident," Elinor says. "You're in the infirmary."

"Are you kidding? That was no—"

Elinor shoots Abe a look. Then she turns back to me. "I found you lying on the balcony. Totally out of it. Surrounded by ping-pong balls."

"Whoever was playing has some arm," Gabby says. "To send so many balls that high? And hard enough to put Seamus in a coma?"

"Seamus wasn't in a coma." Sitting on a stool next to me, Ms. Marla leans closer and shines a light into each of my eyes. "He doesn't have a bruise or bump to speak of. It's hot out there. My guess is he was surprised on top of overheated, and his body just took a little break. How do you feel now, sugar?"

I'm not sure. It's hard to separate potential physical pains from mental ones.

Because Elinor found me lying on the balcony? Was I drooling? Did my T-shirt ride up when I fell? Did she see my chest and learn just how white white can really be?

"I think I'm okay," I finally offer. Then, "Ms. Marla, what are you doing here?"

"Making sure everyone makes it home alive at the end of the summer."

I take in her white coat and the stethoscope. "You're the camp nurse?"

"Indeedy."

"What about the Hoodlum Hot—"

Her hand clamps over my mouth. "Whoa, take it easy there! You just came to. Don't want to overexert yourself!"

Unable to move my lips, I move my eyes and look around. The infirmary is a large white room. There are cots. Posters of smiling kids and adults wearing Kamp Kilter T-shirts. Shelves filled with jars of tongue depressors, cotton balls, and Band-Aids. It looks like a fairly normal infirmary. With one exception.

It's packed.

"Whsocrwd?" I ask against Ms. Marla's palm. She gives me a look, warning me not to say the wrong thing, then removes her hand. I try again. "Why's it so crowded?"

"Must be something in the air this morning." Ms. Marla smacks a Band-Aid onto my forehead. "But good news! You're healthy as a horse, and free to go."

With that, she pushes away from me and rides her

stool-on-wheels over to the next patient: a grown woman who appears to be totally fine except for her worried frown.

"Samara must be an excellent teacher." Abe stands next to Elinor and lowers his voice. "Tons of parents are getting checked out for fake symptoms."

My head starts spinning. Slowly at first, then faster.

"I remember what happened." I look at Abe. "You're right. It wasn't an accident." Then, "What's wrong with your hands?"

He holds them up. They're completely blue, from wrist to fingertip. "I washed them at my parents' house. Only what I thought was soap was some kind of weird ink. It came out clear but turned blue on my skin." He lowers his hands. "Ms. Marla gave me some special ointment. I should be back to normal by tomorrow."

"Me too," Gabby says.

Her hands look fine. But, "Why are you wearing sunglasses?" I ask. "Inside?"

She leans closer. "Cleaning's hard work. I got hungry so decided to look for a snack. I opened the refrigerator in my parents' kitchen, and—BAM!"

"Gabby," Abe hisses. "Keep it down! Geez."

"Bam," she whispers. "Stars."

"Like the kind in the sky?" I ask, confused.

"Shaped like that, but these were battery operated and taped all over the inside of the fridge. When I opened the door, they started flashing like crazy. I was so surprised it took me a second to close the door—and then I still saw them. They were that bright."

"You saw them shining through the refrigerator door?" Abe asks.

"No, silly," Gabby says. "You know how when someone takes your picture, the flash goes off—and then you keep seeing light? Until your eyes adjust again? It was like that. Only times a hundred, because there were at least that many stars. Then it was hard to see anything else. I can see fine now, but Ms. Marla gave me these super-cute sunglasses to protect my eyes, just in case."

I look at Elinor next. "Are you okay?"

She nods.

"Nothing strange happened while you were polishing silverware?"

"Not until I heard a lot of noise and found you on the balcony."

"Great," Abe says, clearly wanting to move on. "We're all fine. Now can we talk about what's happening?"

"Yes," I say. "But not here. Too many ears."

"How about the dining hall?" Gabby asks. "It's too late for breakfast and too early for lunch, so maybe it's empty?"

"Sounds good." I sit up, give my head a second to adjust to the sudden movement, and start to stand. "Let's go."

As we make our way to the door, I look around the crowded infirmary. It's crawling with parents, but I don't see mine. It's also crawling with kids, but I don't see Lemon.

I'm not sure how I feel about my best friend's absence. My friends and I aren't the only Troublemakers here so it doesn't seem like we were the only targets of mysterious pranks. Why was Lemon excluded? Or, what if he wasn't excluded—and is in such bad shape he couldn't make it to the infirmary?

When we're sitting in the empty cafeteria, I ask these questions aloud.

"Did you see the size of our parents' beds?" Gabby asks. "Lemon probably plopped onto one and fell asleep."

"Maybe," I say. "But he seemed pretty awake this morning."

"Did he write you back?" Elinor asks. "When you e-mailed to check in with everyone before?"

"No," I say. "And I'm kind of worried."

Gabby gasps. "Elinor, the sundae bar's open. Want to check it out?"

The girls leave.

"I'm worried too," Abe says when they're out of earshot.

"You are?" I ask. "Good. I was beginning to think I was the only one who—"

"Not about Lemon. The dude's weird. If he's acting differently, I'm sure it's just a new kind of Lemon-weird. And not because anything's wrong."

"So then what are you worried about?"

"Not what." His eyes dart toward the sundae bar. *"Who."*

"Go on," I say.

"You're not going to like it."

"Try me."

He pauses. "Elinor."

My heart skips. "She said nothing happened to her."

"That's the problem."

I glance at Elinor, who's now laughing with Gabby as she pours hot fudge over her ice cream.

"Think about it," Abe says. "We're trying to bust her mom. Her mom's not here, so she asks if she can help out in your parents' cabin. You guys split up. Then one second you're on the balcony alone, and in the next, you're knocked out. And who finds you first?"

I don't say anything.

"Kind of convenient, don't you think?" he asks. "That Elinor wasn't with you when balls started flying . . . and then when they stopped, she was?"

"She was the first person to find me because she was the only other person in the house. And she helped me."

"After she hurt you."

"No."

"Maybe."

"*No.* She was inside. The balls came from outside."

"And there's no way she could've gone outside after you split up, and come back inside once she'd stopped firing?"

Of course she *could* have. We were apart long enough that that'd be physically possible.

But she wouldn't have.

"What about you guys?" I ask. "You and Gabby? If Elinor was so busy targeting me, how'd Gabby end up half-blind and you with blue hands?"

"Elinor filled the soap dispensers and rigged the fridge beforehand. Obviously."

"And the other Troublemakers? Was she behind whatever happened to them, too?"

"Well—"

"Forget it. That question doesn't even deserve an answer. But Abe, what exactly are you saying? That Elinor isn't working with us? That she's actually secretly working for her mother—who, let me remind you, trapped her in a swimming pool of snakes? And who she couldn't get away from fast enough when we went to rescue her last semester?"

He thinks about it. "Yes."

I laugh. "No offense, but that has to be the craziest thing you've ever said. I know Elinor. And she knows me. There's no way she'd—"

"Hinkle."

"No, you need to—"

"Hinkle."

I freeze. So does my mouth, which is still open from being interrupted. Because Abe's face is white. And when I follow his wide-eyed stare to a window near the cafeteria coffee station, I know why.

"Do you see what I see?" he whispers.

I see a dirty brown bandana. Tied around an oily, pimpled forehead. Holding back hair so greasy, it shines like the light in Gabby's rigged refrigerator. Whoever's wearing the bandana is outside, ducking under a cafeteria window.

Still staring, Abe and I answer his question at the same time.

"Shepherd Bull."

Chapter 15

DEMERITS: 1610
GOLD STARS: 750

No way!" Gabby exclaims.

"Yes way," Abe says.

"I can't believe it," Elinor says.

"I'm sure you can't," Abe says.

"Why didn't you say anything?" Gabby asks.

"We didn't want to talk about it until we knew it was safe," Abe says.

"But—where?" Gabby asks. "How? When?"

"Who?" Annika adds.

We all look at our director. She's sitting at the head of a gleaming silver yacht. This is where Houdini brought us after we got back to our campsite, I e-mailed Annika and said we had big news, and she sent the golf cart. Houdini drove us to another lake, this one bigger and bluer than the one our parents are enjoying, and then took us by motorboat to the yacht floating half a mile off shore.

"*Who* is Shepherd Bull?" Annika repeats.

"Only the dirtiest, smelliest, meanest boy-giant that ever lived!" Gabby says.

"How do you know him?" Annika asks.

"We don't," I say. "Not really. But we've seen him before. At IncrimiNation."

Annika sits up straight. "So I was right. My sister *is* up to something."

"Looks like," Abe says.

"What else do you know about this boy?" Annika asks.

"He has a lot of dirty friends," Abe says. "When we were at their school, they blindfolded us in gross gym socks, tied us up, and locked us in a closet."

"And he seems to be some kind of leader," I add.

"Where did you see him today?" Annika asks.

"Outside the camp cafeteria," I say. "Spying on us through a window."

"Was anyone with him?" Annika asks.

"We don't know," I say. "He was gone by the time we ran outside."

"And you don't know where he went?" Annika asks.

"Nope," Abe says. "We checked the woods and other buildings, but there was no sign of him."

Annika looks at Elinor. "What do you know about this?"

"Yeah," Abe says. "What *do* you know?"

Like the rest of us, Elinor's sitting on one of the yacht's comfy lounge chairs. Now she sinks deeper into the cushion and says, "Nothing."

"You've spent time at your mother's school," Annika says. "Occasionally against your will, often against your mother's. At the very least, you were there several weeks last semester before your friends came and got you. You're saying you don't know anything more about this dirty boy-giant than what's just been shared?"

Elinor looks down at her hands, which she's clasping and unclasping. "They're right," she says, her voice soft. "He's a leader. My mother usually gives him orders, and then he tells the other kids what to do."

Annika waits. "That's it? You don't know where he's from? How old he is? What his special troublemaking talents are? Why your mother favors him?"

Elinor's head snaps up. When she talks now, her voice is low but sharp. "He's mean. So mean, whenever I see him coming I turn around and go the other way."

At this I want to run over to Elinor and give her a huge hug. But Annika smirks and speaks before I can.

"No wonder."

"No wonder what?" I ask.

"That my sister takes any chance she can get to dump her—" Annika stops herself. "Never mind! Now, tell me. What should we do about this situation?"

I look at Elinor again. She's dabbing her eyes with her T-shirt sleeve.

"That's what we wanted to talk to you about," I say evenly. "We thought you might want the Good Samaritans to take care of it. By finding Shepherd Bull and any other trespassers, and kicking them out."

"Definitely not," Annika says. "At least one Incriminator is on the premises. There may be more. This is an unexpected development, but it's also an opportunity. Here, on our turf, we have an invaluable chance to learn more about the enemy in ways we didn't anticipate."

"How?" Abe asks.

"Engage them," Annika says. "Let them do whatever they've come to do, and while they're doing it, watch. Listen. And, of course, defend yourselves as necessary."

"Hang on," Gabby says. "You want us to spy on our parents, spy on the Incriminators, *and* do all of our regular homework and assignments?"

"Is that a problem?" Annika asks.

"Nope!" Gabby gives two thumbs-ups to show she really means it.

"That's what I thought. And remember: You're well trained and up to the challenge. Just think of the Incriminators as new items you've picked up from the Kommissary and play with them like the toys that they are."

Gabby laughs. Abe grins. I look at Elinor, who looks down at her lap.

"Moving on," Annika says. "Abe's and Gabby's families will be here shortly."

"They will?" Abe asks.

"Why?" Gabby asks.

"Role Reverse," Annika says. "I told you about it the other day."

"You also said we'd get e-mails with more information." Abe whips out his K-Pak, taps the screen. "And I didn't get any."

"You're all much busier than your classmates are," Annika says, "so when this meeting came up, I thought it was a great chance to knock out two birds with one stone. I notified your parents, and they agreed to meet here." She pauses. "You sound nervous. Why?"

"I'm not nervous," Abe and Gabby say at the same time. But Abe's voice cracks and Gabby starts biting her nails, so I think they are.

"You shouldn't be," Annika says. "This is just a way for me to see you and your parents interact firsthand. I hope it provides more clues as to why they've been behaving so strangely. But before they arrive, who'd like to fill me on what you observed in your families' cabins today?"

Abe recovers enough from his surprise to tell Annika everything that happened before the Shepherd Bull spotting, including my ping-pong attack. His ink-stained hands. Gabby's light display. The other Troublemakers we saw in the infirmary. He doesn't tell her about my dad's weird behavior, because I didn't get a chance to share that with him or anyone else. I could do it now, and I probably should, considering this is what we're at Kamp Kilter to do . . . but I don't. Maybe because I know this is information Annika would like to have, and after she almost made Elinor cry, I don't feel like giving it to her. Or maybe I don't want to rat out Dad until I'm 100 percent sure he's doing something worth ratting him out for. Either way, I keep this to myself.

Annika listens carefully and takes notes on her K-Pak. When Abe's done, she thanks him and asks us to do the same good work tomorrow.

Then a door opens behind us. I turn and see two older couples and a teenager hurry onto the deck. I recognize Abe's dad and Gabby's older sister from their appearances during our alliance V-Chat back home. I assume the other adults are Abe's mom and Gabby's parents. The men are wearing damp shorts and T-shirts, the women sundresses over bathing suits. They all look like they just came from the beach.

"Welcome!" Annika jumps up and hugs the new arrivals. "Wonderful to see you!"

As they greet one another and chitchat, I sneak peeks at my alliance-mates. Elinor's looking at her lap. Abe's pacing across the deck. Gabby's gazing longingly out at the water, like she'd rather fall overboard than stay here.

A moment later, Annika asks everyone to take a seat. Then she says, "Mr. Hansen, Mrs. Hansen, Mr. Ryan, Mrs. Ryan, and Flora, thank you so much for taking a few minutes out of your busy vacation schedules to join us for this special meeting."

"Is this going to take a while?" Flora asks.

"Don't be rude!" Mrs. Ryan hisses to her daughter.

Flora ignores her mother and looks at Annika. "I was tanning. I'll look like a half-eaten Oreo if I don't get another twenty-three minutes of prime sun time on my stomach. You understand."

Annika forces her lips into a smile. "Of course. Let's get started." A waiter appears with a clipboard and pen. Annika takes both and continues. "We all know why we're here: to help your bad kids become good ones. By sending them to Kilter you've entrusted me with this huge responsibility, and I hope you're pleased with the progress made so far."

"Oh, yes," Mr. Ryan says.

"There's more work to be done," Mr. Hansen says.

"You're right," Annika agrees. "And I think Role Reverse will be an excellent tool for getting at the real root of your children's behavior."

"Role Reverse?" Mr. Hansen asks skeptically.

Annika explains. "Either you or your wife will play Abe. Abe will play one of you. Gabby and her parents will do the same."

"Play him how?" Mrs. Hansen asks.

"During a brief skit of sorts, you'll act and speak as you believe he would. He'll act and speak as he believes you would. Through this interaction, we'll gain insight into how you view him and vice versa. The results may be surprising, and they'll definitely be helpful."

"What do you mean by a 'skit of sorts'?" Mrs. Ryan asks.

"A scenario," Annika says. "From real life." The adults still look confused, so she adds, "Let's keep it simple. There must've been a specific incident that prompted you to send your kids to Kilter. Reenact that moment." She looks around. "Who'd like to go first?"

"*I* will." Flora jumps up. "Let's do this, Geek Girl."

Head low, Gabby stands.

"That's very kind, Flora," Annika says. "But I'd rather one of your parents—"

"Look at me!" Flora declares, covering her heart with both hands. "I'm Gabby! And I'm doing homework! Again! Because I *love* homework! Math! Science! English! History! The more boring the subject, the better!" Flora pauses, cups one hand to her ear. "What's that? A phone call for me? That can't be! Because I don't have friends! I don't have time for them! I'm far too busy reading and studying and getting straight As!"

Flora stops, then flings her arms to the side and folds over at the waist in a dramatic bow. I wonder who she's really talking about, because the person she's playing sounds nothing like the bubbly, friendly, super-social Gabby I know.

"Moving on," Annika says. "Mrs. Ryan, you'll play Gabby. Gabby, you'll play your mom. Mrs. Ryan will start."

Flora drops into her chair. Gabby's mom stands up slowly, like she'd much rather stay seated. Preferably back on the beach than here on Annika's yacht.

"Action!" Annika exclaims.

Mrs. Ryan jumps. Gabby's head snaps up. They look at each other uncertainly. After a few awkward, silent seconds, Mrs. Ryan begins.

"It's the middle of the night," she says, her voice soft. "My family's sleeping all snug in their beds. Now's the perfect chance to scare them!"

"That's not exactly how it went," Gabby says.

"That's not for you to say right now." Annika wags her pointer finger. "Please continue, Mrs. Ryan."

Gabby's mom does. "I don't know why I've been so unhappy lately, or why everyone's making me mad . . . but they are. So I must keep trying to make *them* unhappy. And this is the perfect chance." She reaches into her skirt pocket, pulls out nothing, and raises her hand like the nothing is something. "Blindfolds! For Flora. Mom. And Dad." Mrs. Ryan pretends to tie invisible blindfolds three times. "I'll triple-knot them so they're impossible to take off. Then I'll go to the front door . . ."—Mrs. Ryan tiptoes across the deck—"open it . . ."—pretends to open a door—"and set off the security alarm!" She claps her hands over her ears. When she speaks again, she practically shouts. "The beeping is so loud! They're freaking out! And they can't take off the blindfolds so they can't see where they're going or what's happening! For all they know a bunch of burglars are stealing everything we own!" She laughs. "Mom and Dad just ran into each other! And fell to the floor! Flora just tripped over her sneakers! Perfect!"

Mrs. Ryan continues to describe the chaotic incident. I glance at Annika and see her studying Gabby's mom and jotting down notes. I glance at Gabby, whose face is bright red.

Finally, Mrs. Ryan stops. Her face is bright red too. She's breathing heavily. Behind her, Mr. Ryan shifts uncomfortably in his chair. Flora smirks.

"Your turn, Gabby," Annika says.

Words burst from my alliance-mate's mouth. "I'm having the best dream ever! Flora and I are at the spa! We're getting manicures and pedicures! After this we'll go shopping! And out to dinner! And maybe catch a movie! Just the two of us! Oh, wait—so is this a dream? Or am I awake? Because that's what we do every weekend!"

"Not every—"

"Shh!" Annika cuts off Mrs. Ryan.

"What's that?" Gabby continues. "The security alarm? Is someone in the house? Is Flora in danger? I must find her! I must make sure she's okay! I don't know what I'd do if anything happened to my favorite daughter!"

Gabby stops. Her chest rises and instantly falls. Over and over and over again.

"Gabby," Mrs. Ryan says, her eyebrows low. "Is that what you think? That I care about your sister more than I care about you?"

Gabby doesn't answer. She takes her seat instead.

"Mr. Hansen?" Annika asks. "Abe? You're up."

Abe and his dad stand and face each other like this is the Wild West and they're about to duel. Mr. Hansen starts.

"It's my birthday. I've just opened my present from my parents . . . and it's a football. Another one. This one's not even new. The leather's faded. It's soft and mushy, probably because it was blown up a hundred years ago. It's the worst gift I've ever gotten." Mr. Hansen tosses up an invisible ball, catches it. "Dad says we should go to the park and throw it around. He keeps talking about quality time, and father-son bonding, and all sorts of other mumbo jumbo."

"Quality time?" Abe asks. "Bonding? You never said anything about—"

Annika shushes him. His dad continues.

"But hanging out with my *dad*? Please. I'd rather eat this football than throw it around with him. If he doesn't get that by now, I'll just have to make him." Mr. Hansen takes the invisible ball and seems to squeeze it. "I'll pop this and turn it into a lamp shade. Maybe then Dad will finally understand how I feel about him."

Mr. Hansen stops. Abe starts.

"It's my son's birthday! A perfect reason to give him his eighth football—and millionth reminder that I wish he were bigger! Stronger! Into sports! If I had a daughter, the art thing would be cool. But Abe shouldn't be painting or drawing or sketching! He should be throwing and catching and grunting! If he did any of those things, maybe I could be proud of him!"

Abe stops. His dad's frowning.

"Your father loves you very much," Mrs. Hansen says, voice wavering. "So do I. That old football was his as a boy. He just wanted you to—"

Mrs. Hansen is interrupted by a shrill beeping. The noise comes from Annika's K-Pak. She picks it up, turns it on, and taps the screen.

"I'm very sorry," she says a moment later, "but I have to leave for another meeting. We'll end here."

No one moves. Not even Flora. Abe, Gabby, and their families exchange curious looks, almost like they're really seeing one another for the first time.

But then two waiters appear on the deck. They motion for the families to stand and leave, and escort them to the door. When they're gone, Annika thanks us for our cooperation.

"You got it," Abe says, and gives her a small salute. "Is there anything else?"

Annika starts to shake her head, then stops and looks around. "Actually, yes. Where's Lemon?"

Chapter 16

DEMERITS: 1630
GOLD STARS: 750

Where *is* Lemon?

By the middle of the night, I have a long list of where he's not. Like our underground house. The barbecue dinner hosted by Lizzie, our language arts teacher. The karaoke party after that. The golf-cart ride back to camp. His bedroom. The bathroom, living room, or kitchen.

I e-mail him every few hours. At three in the morning, when I still haven't heard back, I reread my notes to make sure I didn't say something upsetting.

TO: loliver@kilteracademy.org
FROM: shinkle@kilteracademy.org
SUBJECT: Hi!

Hey, Lemon!

Just wanted to let you know that Abe, Gabby, Elinor, and I just met with Annika. We looked for you before we left our parents' side of the lake, and we also e-mailed and tried v-chatting, but we didn't find or hear from you. You had dusting duty, right? I hope you didn't get lost in a big gray cloud! LOL.

Anyway, the meeting was interesting. I'm sorry we didn't wait longer for you but it was kind of an emergency. I'll fill you in on everything later.

Speaking of later, Lizzie's having a BBQ at her place! Should be tons of fun. Can't wait to see you there.

—Seamus

TO: loliver@kilteracademy.org
FROM: shinkle@kilteracademy.org
SUBJECT: Me again!

Hi, Lemon!

Man, I'm stuffed! Whoever decided gooey melted cheese and hot meat was a good match was RIGHT.

I'm sorry you missed out. See you at the karaoke contest? I hope so! Gabby's sure to get a little out of control, so we'll need all the help we can get dragging her offstage every now and then. ☺

—Seamus

TO: loliver@kilteracademy.org
FROM: shinkle@kilteracademy.org
SUBJECT: See you at home?

Hi there!

Missed you at karaoke! It was great. I'm not sure who was the bigger star: Gabby or Abe. She sang until her voice gave out and she started croaking like a frog, and he eventually carried her offstage so someone else could have a turn. I felt kind of bad about that, but Gabby got over it pretty fast when she realized who'd picked her up. Then she didn't want to be put back down!

Anyway, we're headed home now. Hopefully we'll see you there?

—Seamus

TO: loliver@kilteracademy.org
FROM: shinkle@kilteracademy.org
SUBJECT: Are you okay?

Hey, Lemon,

Sorry to keep bothering you, but when you get a chance, could you please let me know you're okay? Because it's getting late and I haven't seen you since this morning. I'm sure you're totally fine, but if you wouldn't mind telling me I'm being silly, that'd be great.

Thanks!

—Seamus

TO: loliver@kilteracademy.org
FROM: shinkle@kilteracademy.org
SUBJECT: Is this . . .

. . . about our talk earlier? When I asked about the origami? You didn't seem mad then, but maybe you are now after thinking about it all day. Either way, I'm sorry! Really. Let's talk more ASAP, okay? Like right when you get home? Which will be . . . ?

TO: loliver@kilteracademy.org
FROM: shinkle@kilteracademy.org
SUBJECT: It's midnight

Where ARE you???

I stop reading and rest my K-Pak on my stomach. It's been three hours since my last e-mail. I'm tempted to write again, but what good would it do? Especially if he really is mad at me? Or if he's been captured by Incriminators, which is my newest—and scariest—theory. Maybe I should wake up Abe and see what he thinks. When we talked about Lemon's absence earlier, all he said was that it's not his problem if Lemon doesn't feel like participating. But that was hours ago. Surely he'd be worried now if he knew our alliance's fourth member was still missing?

Deciding he would be (and that I can make him be if he's not), I hop out of bed and look for my slippers. They're shaped like calculators and have thick soles covered in multiplication, division, addition, and subtraction symbols, so you leave a mathematical trail anytime you walk across carpet. Dad gave them to me for my birthday, and I wear them all the time.

I'm still looking for them when I hear a thud. I freeze and listen.

There it is again. The second thud is followed by another. And another. The noises are fast. And getting louder.

I stumble across the room and fumble for a light switch. When the lamp turns on, I look for a weapon. People in movies always use hockey sticks and baseball bats to fight off burglars and intruders, but I don't have any of those. My few marksman weapons are in the front hall, where I left them after practicing between activities today. I grab the best of my options—a pillow—and lunge toward the door.

"Seamus! Hey! How's it going?"

I stand in the open doorway. My mouth opens. The pillow drops. I stare at Lemon—or the stranger who could be his twin. This person has shaggy hair. And furry eyebrows. And he's wearing my best friend's worn moccasins. But he's also smiling. Instead of shuffling along at a snail's pace, he's practically skipping down the hall.

"Where is everyone?" he asks, hurrying past me. "It's as quiet as detention in here!"

He disappears into his room. I pick up my chin and pillow from the floor and follow after him. I stop again when I reach his bedroom doorway and watch him kick off his shoes and flop onto his bed.

"Lemon," I say. "It's three in the morning."

"Is it? Huh. Time really does fly when you're having fun. Who knew?" Then, "Why aren't you sleeping?"

"Because—" My voice is loud. Not wanting to wake up anyone else, I lower it before continuing. "Because I was *worried*."

"Is something wrong?"

"You tell me," I say.

"What do you mean?"

"I mean you've been gone all day. I wrote you, like, twelve times. I didn't hear one word back. I thought something happened."

Lemon clasps his hands behind his head and shrugs. "Well, here I am! So you can stop worrying and get some sleep."

"Where were you?"

"Where I was supposed to be. At my family's cabin."

"All day and night? When all of the other Troublemakers left their families' cabins before dinner?"

"Yes."

"What were you doing there?"

He fluffs his pillow and gives me a small, apologetic smile. "Seamus, I'm sorry I didn't write you back, and that you were worried. But I promise everything's fine. Now I'm kind of tired. Can we talk more in the morning?"

It *is* the morning. The sun will be rising in no time. But I don't say this. There's no point.

Lemon's already snoring.

Returning to my room, I close the door and crawl back into bed. I'd really like to sleep, but I can't. My head's spinning too fast.

So I pick up my K-Pak and start typing.

TO: parsippany@cloudviewschools.net
FROM: shinkle@kilteracademy.org
SUBJECT: Honesty

Dear Miss Parsippany,

Hi! Thanks for writing me back. I hope you're having fun wherever you are!

So in your last note, you asked if I believe that honesty's the best policy. And honestly? I don't know.

Take today. A lot happened. My dad slammed a door in my face. I made him think he was sick, which made him go to the camp infirmary. I found my mom's diary and read a few of her private thoughts. I was attacked by ping-pong balls. I learned that at least one scary kid broke into camp and is following my friends and me around. I ate an enormous cheeseburger and will probably have a stomachache for days. And I got upset with my best friend for acting like someone I don't even know. The only really good thing that happened is that I got to spend time with Elinor, but even that got messed up because a) I was attacked by ping-pong balls, and b) Abe told me he thinks she's some kind of traitor working for the wrong team.

It was totally exhausting.

So here's where your question—and my confusion—comes in. Because up until now, I haven't been completely honest. If I were, the school director would know I'm not really supposed to be here. Because I didn't really do what she thought I did to get accepted to Kilter Academy. If she knew the truth, she'd definitely kick me out. And since I've wanted to hang around because I thought there have been things I needed to hang around for, I've let the lie live on.

But sometimes, I don't know if this is such a good idea. Because if I were totally honest and told Annika I'm not who she thinks I am, and if she kicked me out, then I could go home. I'd leave all of this behind. And life would go back to normal. I don't know if that'd be better or worse, but it'd definitely be less complicated.

Have you ever lied because you thought it was better than telling the truth? If so, why?

Anyway, thanks again for writing! I hope you're having fun and that your latest plane rides have been turbulence free. ☺

Sincerely,

Seamus

P.S. Speaking of plane rides, you never said what your new job actually is. Would love to know!

I reread the note, check for typos, and hit send. Feeling a little better after getting some of that off my chest, I put my K-Pak on my nightstand, lie back, and close my eyes.

I've just dozed off when something jolts me awake.

It's my K-Pak, buzzing with a new message. From Miss Parsippany.

Or not.

TO: shinkle@kilteracademy.org
FROM: server@cloudviewschools.net
SUBJECT: ERROR

Dear Recipient:

Your message, SUBJECT: Honesty, failed to reach its intended recipient. That mailbox, PARSIPPANY@CLOUDVIEWSCHOOLS.NET is INVALID.

Do not reply to this message.

Sincerely,

Information Technology Department

Cloudview Schools

"That has to be it," I say. "So she doesn't have to worry about him on top of everything else."

We watch Mr. Tempest kick off his sneakers, hitch up his shorts, and bound into the lake to help pull in an approaching boat. When the Troublemakers are close enough to start hopping out, he offers his hand to assist.

"Have a magnificent day!" he says before bounding over to another boat.

We head toward our teachers. They're gathered by the supply table down the beach. Now that we know the day's routine, there's no big meeting. Samara simply gives us our house-keeping assignments and the other teachers give us supplies. I'm on window-washing duty, so Devin, our music teacher, hands me a bucket, a bottle of Smudge-Be-Gone, and a huge roll of paper towels.

Elinor's on fireplace detail. She gets a bucket, a short broom, and something to pick up ash that looks like the pooper-scooper Ms. Marla keeps handy for Rodolfo.

As we head for my parents' house, we don't speak for several minutes. Unlike other silent stretches we sometimes fall into, this one isn't because I'm so nervous to be around Elinor that I don't

Chapter 17

DEMERITS: 1630
GOLD STARS: 850

Good morning! How are you? Nice to see you! Isn't it a glorious day?"

It's the next morning. Abe, Gabby, Elinor, and I are standing on our parents' side of the beach, watching Mystery greet Troublemakers coming ashore.

"What's he *doing*?" Gabby asks.

"What's *wrong* with him?" Elinor says.

"He must be popping some brand-new, super-serious senior-citizen vitamins," Abe says. "Or else Annika finally told him to shape up or ship out."

know what to say. Also unlike other silent stretches, I'm so lost in thought I barely notice.

"You're pretty quiet this morning," Elinor finally says.

I look up. "Am I?"

She nods. "Everything okay?"

"Yeah. I guess I'm just worried about Lemon." And Miss Parsippany. And my parents. And a few other things that don't make for pleasant morning chitchat.

"He must've gotten in really late last night."

"He did."

"And he was still the first one up. And in the boat on our side of the lake, and out of the boat on this side. And in line to get his chore and supplies."

It's true. After leaping out of the canoe and pulling it as he swam, just like he did yesterday, Lemon got us to shore in record time—and then hit the beach running. While he was talking to Samara, we were still climbing out.

"Does he really love cleaning?" Elinor asks.

"Not that I know of. When we shared a room, I was always walking around his mountain of laundry and emptying his overflowing wastebaskets and washing toothpaste off his side of the bathroom mirror. So if he does, it's definitely a new interest."

"Like origami?"

"Just like it."

We keep walking.

"So I was wondering," Elinor says a moment later. "Do you think . . . I mean, is it possible . . . that is, what if . . . ?"

I give her a reassuring smile. "It's okay. You can ask me anything."

She takes a quick breath. The question rushes out. "Do you think Lemon's working with the Incriminators?"

I trip, drop my bucket.

"Sorry!" Elinor squats down to help gather the fallen supplies. "That came out of nowhere. It's just—he's been acting *so* different. So un-Lemon. I mean, when was the last time you saw him light a match?"

"Last semester."

"That's a long time ago. So I've been thinking about what might make him do a one-eighty like that." Elinor shakes sand from the fireplace pooper-scooper, places it in the bucket, and stands. "And then it came to me: Shepherd Bull."

"What about him?" I ask, climbing to my feet.

"He's here. And I know him. Not well—because like I told Annika, I try to avoid him as much as I can. But enough to know that when he wants something, he gets it. And usually does a lot of damage in the process. For example, one time another Incriminator found a new cowboy hat in the storage room of the old General Store."

She pauses, apparently to make sure I remember the General Store. IncrimiNation's campus is an abandoned desert town. Many classrooms are vacant buildings of former businesses. The General Store, still filled with postcards and lizard-printed coffee mugs and cactus-shaped salt-and-pepper shakers, is one of these buildings.

I nod. Elinor continues.

"Shepherd Bull saw the kid wearing it and decided he wanted it. The other kid wouldn't give it up. So Shepherd Bull picked him up, turned him upside down, and held him by the ankles until the kid gave him the hat."

"Lemon's too smart for that. He'd see Shepherd Bull coming from a mile away and beat him at his own game."

"He is smart—and it sounds crazy. Impossible even. I'm sorry for suggesting it. You're best friends and I don't want you to think that I think he'd betray Capital T like that. But can you think of another reason why he'd be acting like a totally different person?"

I want to. I really, *really* want to.

"No," I admit, and start walking again.

Elinor doesn't say anything else. Not as we pass the tennis courts, or head up the steep staircase, or cross the yard leading to my parents' cabin. I feel her look at me every now and then, and as we step onto the front porch it occurs that to me that she's probably worried that she upset me, or made me mad—and that I should probably promise her I'm fine. Because I'm not upset. Or mad. I'm just incredibly confused.

But before I can, the front door swings open. Dad reaches forward and pulls me into a huge bear hug.

"Seamus! Elinor! It's *so* great to see you again. You did *such* an amazing job yesterday! My fork was so shiny at dinner last night I used it as a mirror while picking my teeth. And the *plants*!" He gasps and releases me. "Can we just say, botanica fantastica? I've never seen such perfect greenery! At least not indoors!"

"Thanks, Dad. We—"

"You have everything you need, yes? And know where

everything is? Great! Enjoy yourselves! I'm overdue for a little fun in the sun!"

He brushes past us and scampers down the porch steps. I'm so surprised by his abrupt greeting and departure that it takes me a second to call after him.

"What about Mom?"

"Out!" he shouts back. Then he reaches the steep staircase and disappears down the side of the hill.

"It's cloudy," Elinor says.

"Not a great day for fun in the sun," I say.

We go inside. As I'm closing the front door, my K-Pak buzzes. So does Elinor's. We check our e-mail and read at the same time.

TO: year2troublemakers@kilteracademy.org
FROM: wyatt@kilteracademy.org
SUBJECT: Today's Troublemaking Task!

Hey hey, T-makers!

Nice job convincing your parents they were sick yesterday! By late afternoon Nurse Marla was so overwhelmed with patients she couldn't tell a thermometer from a Q-tip. (No joke. I actually saw her stick a plastic ear-junk excavator in Mrs. Madison's mouth! I also saw Mrs. Madison chomp down on Nurse Marla's finger when she realized the mistake. Ouch!)

But today's a new day! Which means a new troublemaking assignment.

Remember that time in art class when I asked you to draw pictures that'd spook your parents whenever they opened and closed the fridge? Well, today you're going to do something similar—only without paint, pastels, or any other traditional art material. Besides those exceptions, the medium's totally up to you, as is the canvas. Whatever it takes to achieve the goal of shocking your parents!

As always, success will be rewarded with demerits and credits. Failure will result in a permanent visit to Nurse Marla's Hospital of Horrors. Just kidding! As always, failure will result in shiny gold stars.

Create away!

—Wyatt

"I bet Abe's happy," Elinor says.

"I can already hear his victory cheers," I say.

We look at each other. Smile. Whatever tension was between us during the second half of our walk here melts away.

"Should we clean first and investigate later?" I ask.

"Sure."

She takes her supplies and goes to the fireplace. I take my bucket, Smudge-Be-Gone, and paper towels, and start toward the living room's wall of windows. Then I think better of it and change direction.

En route to the hallway, I pass the wall of tree branches and have an idea. I turn around again and head for the kitchen. I open the freezer and pull out the big bag I'd hoped would be there. I dump the bag's contents into a bowl, pop the bowl into the microwave, and press start. Three minutes later, I remove the bowl and return to the living room.

Elinor looks up when I come back in but keeps sweeping the fireplace without asking questions.

Three more minutes later, I'm done.

"What do you think?" I ask, surveying my work.

"Wow." Elinor surveys too. "Impressive."

"Freaky impressive?"

"Definitely."

Good. That's what I was going for when I stuck the warm, soggy fish sticks onto sharp points all over the wall of branches.

"Is that a house?" Elinor asks.

"Yup. And the fish sticks will probably start to fall apart before my parents see them. Which means the house will start to fall apart. Kind of like our real one did back home."

Elinor looks at me. "I'm still a good listener."

"I know. Thanks." I nod toward the hall. "I'll start in the bedrooms. Yell if you need anything."

"You too."

I leave the room, check the locked closet, which is still locked, and head for my parents' bedroom. Once inside, I close the door slightly, leaving a wide enough gap that Elinor can still see me and won't worry or wonder what I'm up to. Then I put down my supplies and head for the nightstand.

It's still there. Mom's coupon folder. With her journal inside.

"You have to do it," I tell myself quietly. "Not just for your own good. For everyone's."

I do believe that knowing Mom's secret thoughts will

somehow help me fix our family. But I still feel guilty as I slide out the journal, flip forward a few pages, and start reading.

Today was a terrible day.

My chest tightens. According to the date at the top of the page, Mom had this terrible day ten years ago, when I was three.

My adorable boy was playing in the sandbox with another adorable boy named Bartholomew John.

I stop reading. Cringe. Keep going.

They were building castles and getting along swimmingly. They shared shovels and helped each other dig moats. For a time I thought I was watching the beginning of a beautiful friendship.

But then everything changed. Seamus' castle grew taller than Bartholomew John's castle—and Bartholomew John couldn't have that. As soon as he noticed the height difference, he grabbed a rock from the—

"Seamus?" Elinor calls out.

I snap the journal shut and drop it on the nightstand. Then I dart to the open bedroom door.

"Yeah?" I call back.

"Are you hungry?"

My stomach grumbles. "I could definitely eat!"

"Want me to see what I can find in the kitchen?"

"Sure! Thanks!"

I wait until I hear cabinets opening and closing, then spin around and hurry back across the room.

"Hey. What . . . ? Where . . . ?"

I stare at the nightstand. The coupon folder's gone.

I check the floor, under the bed, and behind the nightstand. When it's not in any of those places, I stop and think. I had my back turned for ten seconds. How could it just disappear? Was I so surprised by Elinor calling my name that I only *thought* I put it back where I found it? Did I accidentally drop it somewhere else instead?

That must be what happened. Because when I scan the room, I see it on the dresser, five feet away.

I hurry over, find where I left off, and keep reading.

Seamus' castle grew taller than Bartholomew John's castle—and Bartholomew John couldn't have that. As soon as he noticed the height difference, he grabbed a rock from the dirt outside the sandbox, pulled back his arm, and hurled it right at poor Seamus' head.

I don't remember any of this, but I can totally picture it. Hurling rocks at my head sounds like something Bartholomew John would love to do. Even as a toddler.

"Seamus?" Elinor calls out.

I place the journal on the dresser and dart to the open door. "Yeah?"

"Do you like pancakes?"

"Sure!"

I return to the dresser. The coupon folder's there.

But the journal's not.

I crouch down and peer under the dresser. When nothing's there, I stand up.

"*What* is going on?" I ask nobody.

Because the journal's back on top of the dresser.

I close and rub my eyes. When I open them again . . . the journal's gone again.

"Looking for trouble, *Troublemaker*?" a low voice asks.

My heart stops. My skin tingles. I spin to the right. The left. Right again. I don't see anyone, but I do see the journal. On the bed. The nightstand. The top of my parents' suitcase. It disappears and reappears, as if under the spell of a magician's wand.

My troublemaking training kicks in. I lunge for my supply bucket and yank out the squeegee. The journal's still on my parents' suitcase, so I throw myself in that direction, whirling the squeegee overhead.

By the time I reach the suitcase, the journal's gone. I stand still and scan the room.

Just wait. Listen. Give your instincts a chance, and they won't let you down.

Ike's voice fills my head. These are his instructions whenever

I'm so excited to learn something new—and to get it right—that I do it all wrong.

Every inch of my body aches to bolt around the room, but I force it to stay put. Then I close my eyes again. Wait. Listen.

"HA!"

This flies from my mouth as the squeegee flies from my hand. Opening my eyes, I see that my instincts worked. The window-washing weapon's handle is lodged in the wall next to the bed. Stuck in the hole with it is the ankle end of a dirty tube sock. A piece of chewed bubblegum is glued to the toe end of the dirty tube sock. On the floor three feet below the hole is Mom's journal.

I know that whoever was in the room with me is gone now, but I look around anyway. Then I tug the squeegee and sock from the wall and drop both into my bucket. I pick up the journal, find the part where Bartholomew John threw a rock at my head in the sandbox, and quickly finish reading the entry I started before being attacked.

My son cried like a baby.
And I cannot have that.

Ouch. This stings—and makes me want to keep reading. But I'm anxious to tell my friends what just happened, so I return the journal and coupon book to the nightstand, where I originally found them. Then I sprint from the room and head for the kitchen.

But the kitchen's empty. Smoke billows from a pan on the stove. I hurry over, turn off the heat, and keep running.

"Elinor! You'll never guess—"

I skid to a stop. Elinor, who's on her knees by the fireplace, stands up.

"Seamus? What—"

She doesn't finish her sentence either. Probably because when she sees what I see, she can't.

The fish sticks. On the wall of branches. When I left the room a few minutes ago, they were arranged in the shape of a broken house.

But instead of a picture, now they form three letters—and one terrifying message.

I

C

U

Chapter 18

DEMERITS: 1630
GOLD STARS: 850

Who sees you?" Annika asks.

"Shepherd Bull," I say.

"And his dirty friends," Gabby adds. "Because Shepherd Bull couldn't have been in the bedroom and the living room at the same time."

"Interesting." Annika walks across the yacht deck, hands clasped behind her back. "What about the rest of you? Were you attacked too?"

"Not today," Abe says. "But we weren't at our parents' cabins very long before Seamus called us on v-chat and told us what was going on. If Incriminators were around, they probably heard us talking about them and decided not to make a move."

Annika reaches one end of the deck, turns, and walks some more. She's been pacing since we got here twenty minutes ago. I e-mailed her right after I told my friends what had happened, and she sent a cart as soon as our chores were done and we got the clearance to leave from our teachers.

"We need supplies," Abe says. "From the Kommissary."

"As I said the other day," Annika says, "you may engage them—but not run them off."

"But if we don't have the right tools," Abe says, "they might run *us* off."

Annika stops, cocks an eyebrow in his direction.

"Believe me," he says. "I don't like admitting it. Because we're good. *Really* good. But those kids are crazy."

Annika keeps walking. I glance at Elinor. Our eyes meet. She shrugs as if to say she has no idea what her aunt is thinking. Eventually, Annika stops. Right in front of me.

"Do *you* feel you need additional supplies?" she asks.

"They can't hurt," I say.

"And you think you can give my sister's students a run for their money without stopping them from proceeding with anything else they may have planned?"

"Yes," I say.

She nods. "Very well. I'll program the cart to take you to the Kommissary."

"Great." Abe jumps up. "Thanks, Annika. We'll just—"

"Not so fast." Annika motions to a waiter. He goes to the door on the far side of the deck.

"Oh no," Abe says. "Please don't tell me my parents are here again."

"I think you and your families would benefit from another Role Reverse session," Annika says. "But no, your parents are sitting this one out."

I hold my breath. If the Hansens and the Ryans aren't participating . . . does that mean mine are?

"Welcome aboard, Mr. and Mrs. Oliver!" Annika declares as Lemon's parents step out onto the deck. "And Finn, great to see you!"

Exhaling, I smile and wave to Lemon's little brother, who hides behind his mother's legs.

"Thank you," Mr. Oliver says. "But is everything okay? A golf cart came for us and whisked us away so suddenly, we were worried something had happened to Lemon."

"He wasn't with you?" Annika asks. "In your cabin? I assumed you'd all come together."

"We weren't in our cabin," Mrs. Oliver says sheepishly. "We were . . . out."

"I see." Annika frowns, then looks at me. "Any idea where your best friend might be?"

Lemon's whereabouts are turning out to be a bigger mystery than Mystery himself. Before I can try to buy him time, the deck door flings open.

"Sorry!" Lemon dashes onto the deck. "I'm here! Hi, Mom! Hi, Dad! So great to see you, little brother!" He hugs his parents and pats Finn's head. "What'd I miss?"

"Nothing yet," Annika says. "But Lemon, I'm not pleased with your tardiness. Your friends have been here thirty minutes. It was bad enough not coming when they did, but then not coming with your parents either? And keeping them waiting?"

"Oh, we haven't been here long." Mrs. Oliver puts an arm around her eldest son. "It's okay."

"No, it's not." Annika strides to her deck chair, sits, and holds a clipboard in her lap. "But I'll deal with that later."

"May I ask what we're doing here?" Mr. Oliver asks. "The teacher who told us we were to meet you didn't mention why."

"Of course! And I do apologize for the lack of information. You're here for Role Reverse."

Mr. and Mrs. Oliver exchange looks.

"Surely you've heard about it from the other parents," Annika says. "No? That's odd. It's been such a hit." She shrugs, then proceeds to tell them what she told Abe's and Gabby's parents about the insightful activity, and suggests that they reenact the moment that made Lemon's parents decide to send him to Kilter.

"I don't think that's such a good idea," Lemon says.

"I don't think that's for you to say," Annika says.

"Can't we act out a different time?" Lemon asks. "Please?"

"That'd be fine with us," Mrs. Oliver says quickly.

Annika tilts her head, clearly wondering why the entire Oliver family doesn't want to do as she's asked. This, of course, only makes her want them to act out that specific moment even more.

"Lemon," she says, "you may play either your mother or your father. Who do you choose?"

Lemon's quiet for a long moment. Then he mumbles, "Dad."

Annika looks at his parents. "Mr. Oliver, you'll play your son. Okay?"

Mr. Oliver swallows and nods.

"And . . . action!" Annika declares.

If this were a movie, we'd be watching the slowest, least dramatic opening ever. Because nothing happens. Mr. Oliver and Lemon don't speak. The rest of us are silent. Even Finn is quiet as he sits in his mother's lap.

"Dude," Abe finally says, not unkindly. "The faster you do it, the faster it's over."

Which is enough of a pep talk to get Lemon to speak.

"How could he do this?"

"Louder!" Annika commands.

"How could he do this?" Lemon tries again, slightly raising his voice. "I've never understood this . . . hobby . . . of his. I know we used to build fires together a while ago, during our father-son camping trips, but then Finn was born. And we stopped going camping. We stopped doing a lot of things. Anyway, there wasn't a reason to build campfires anymore. Yet he kept playing with matches, lighters, and other flame-sparking things. I didn't approve, but we always kept fire extinguishers on hand. And he was always so safe. So careful. But then . . . this. *Finn*."

Lemon pauses. Mr. Oliver moves to pull him into a big hug.

Annika clucks her tongue. "Stay in character, please!"

Dropping his arms, Lemon's dad says softly, "It was an accident. I'm sorry." He looks at Annika. "That's all he was thinking in that moment. I know it."

"Fine." She makes a note on the paper on her clipboard. "You may be seated. Elinor, you're up."

Elinor gasps lightly. "My mom's here?"

"Don't be silly. But you've displayed your theatrical talents at Kilter more than once. Surely you can play both parts."

Elinor's sitting next to me. I lean toward her and whisper, "You don't have to do this." She might be in the Dramatists group at Kilter, but that doesn't mean she's comfortable taking center stage—especially by herself, with such personal material.

She gives me a small smile. "Thanks. But it's okay."

Our chairs are arranged in a half circle. She gets up and stands in the middle of the arc. Annika's chair faces ours, so she's sitting behind Elinor.

"I'll do my mom first." She closes her eyes and, for a moment, is perfectly still.

I glance at Annika. She's typing on her K-Pak, not even paying attention. Knowing her, she probably put Elinor up to this just to make her uncomfortable.

"Useless!"

I jump. So does everyone else on board. Now Elinor's eyes are wide open. Her nostrils flare.

"Poor excuse for a daughter!" she exclaims. "It's Mother's Day. *My* day. And what would make me happy? If my kid would just listen to me. Do what I tell her to the rest of the year, but without arguing. Is that too much to ask?" Elinor shakes her head. Fast. "But what does she do instead? She cleans the house, from roof to floor. She brings me breakfast in bed. She asks if we can take a walk together, just the two of us. I mean, really? A walk? Doesn't she know how busy I am? I don't have time for walks! And if she'd only do what I want her to, *she* wouldn't either!"

Elinor stops. Closes her eyes again.

"Mommy," Finn whispers. "What does her mommy want her to do?"

Make trouble. Mrs. Oliver doesn't know this, though. She probably thinks Elinor's a wonderful daughter for doing all those things for her mom on Mother's Day. I know I do. Unable to answer, she shakes her head and kisses the top of Finn's head.

"I made her French toast," Elinor begins again. Her voice is softer now. She looks like herself, only sadder. "That's her favorite. And I asked her to go for a walk, because I wanted to spend time together. I wanted a chance to talk. About the weather. Movies. Music. Whatever. I wanted to get to know her a little bit. And for her to get to know me a little bit. Because she's my mother . . . but in a lot of ways, we're strangers." Elinor looks down. "I'm sorry I disappointed her again."

She brushes at her eyes. Gabby jumps up and throws her arms around her. Mrs. Oliver pulls Finn tighter. Mr. Oliver puts one hand on Lemon's shoulder. Abe frowns and clenches his fists, clearly upset by what he just heard.

Glancing at Annika, I see her lips tremble. A single tear slides down her cheek. For perhaps the first time ever, she seems to feel something for her niece besides annoyance.

"Well done, Elinor," she says quietly. "Well done."

Chapter 19

DEMERITS: 1720
GOLD STARS: 850

Oh. My. *Goodness!* These. Are. So. *Cute!* Aren't they? Hello? Guys? Do you even see this?"

See this. See you. As in . . . *me.*

"You alright, Hinkle?" Abe asks, ignoring Gabby.

I nod. Even though I can't stop thinking about the rearranged fish sticks in my parents' cabin.

"Don't worry," he says. "If the Incriminators want to play, we'll give them a game they won't forget. That's why we're here."

"Here" is the Kommissary. As soon as the Olivers returned to camp, Annika had a golf cart take us to our shopping destination. The second Abe, Gabby, Elinor, Lemon, and I were seated and buckled, the cart took off like a rocket. Traveling at the speed of light, we shot through what seemed to be hundreds of acres of dark forest, and reached the school store in minutes flat.

"Watch me!" Gabby exclaims now.

We do. She's standing a few feet away, by the eye-enhancement products. I'm not sure what we're supposed to be looking at because at first nothing seems to happen. She blinks a lot, like she has something in her eye, but that's it.

Until she sneezes. And we get caught in a blinding glitter storm.

"Vision Vortex Lash Extensions!" Gabby exclaims. "How amazing are *they*?"

"Not as amazing"—Abe coughs—"as my"—chokes—"retaliation"—coughs again—"will be!"

I turn away, wipe my eyes with my sweatshirt sleeve. When I turn back, the silver cloud has started to dissipate. A billion tiny, shimmering shards float down, covering our shoes and the floor.

"How do they work?" Elinor asks, shaking the shine from her hair.

"First," Gabby says with a grin, "they trick you into believing they're just normal eyelashes. Even though they're really long and silver. I could just be wearing special mascara, you know? But every time you blink, pressure builds at the base of each lash. Sneezing is the trigger. When you're ready, you just . . . ah-*choo*!" She releases a smaller sparkly cloud. "And voila! A total tinsel tornado."

"The Incriminators will have no idea what they walked into," Elinor says.

"I think I'll get twenty pairs." Gabby slides the Kommissary's entire supply of Vision Vortex Lash Extensions off of the metal display bar and dumps them into her shopping basket. "Now let's find you something!"

Gabby hooks one arm through Elinor's, and they hurry down the aisle.

"I don't like the looks of this," Abe says.

"Why not?" I ask. "Shepherd Bull and his friends will never expect to get caught in a sparkle storm. That could come in handy."

"I'm not talking about Gabby's demo." Abe jerks his head toward the next aisle, where Gabby and Elinor talk and giggle. "They're getting close. *Too* close."

"They're friends," I say. "What's wrong with that?"

"Like it or not, Gabby's an alliance member. Elinor isn't."

"And remind me again why not?"

He counts off the reasons on his fingers. "Um, let's see. She zones out during class. She barely does the assignments. It took her years to graduate from a freshman Troublemaker to a sophomore one. Her mother's turning bad kids into dirty criminals."

"Not everyone wants to be the best Troublemaker ever," I say. "As for her mom, you know they don't get along. And did you forget that she helped us win the Ultimate Troublemaking Task? And that she's been helping us since?"

"Because she's your girlfriend. Which, no offense, is a temporary situation that will totally end. And when it does, there will be no loyalty or kept secrets."

"She helps because she's my *friend*. And your friend. And Gabby's. And Lemon's."

Abe pauses. "What about today?"

"What about it?"

"She wasn't with you. When you were in your parents' bedroom."

I roll my eyes. "Could you *please* give up the whole Elinor-spy theory? I told you, there's no way she'd—"

"Mess with your head? By moving things around your parents' room? And changing your gross fish mural?" Abe nods once. "You're right. She wouldn't . . . if she were one of us. A Capital T member. Who could be trusted."

I pick up my shopping basket from the floor and start walking.

"You were messed with twice!" Abe calls after me. "One Incriminator couldn't be in both places at . . ."

His voice fades as I reach the end of the aisle and round a display of waterproof toilet paper. A sign at the top guarantees WORRY-FREE TP-ING!

I drop a few rolls into my basket and keep browsing.

Aside from the reason for our visit—and Abe's accusations—it's been a pleasant shopping experience. When we arrived, Good Samaritan George greeted us and told us we had the store to ourselves. During the school year the Kommissary's always packed with Troublemakers checking out the latest arrivals and buying supplies needed for homework or tutor training sessions. That makes it hard to see everything—and to buy weapons you might not necessarily want anyone to see you buying, since you might want to secretly use them on classmates to complete assignments. Giving other Troublemakers a sneak peek into what's coming puts them on high alert, and gives them the chance to thwart your attack. So it's nice that my friends and I have the run of the place.

It's also nice that besides Gabby's and Elinor's giggles, the occasional rustle or explosion as my friends try out weapons, and the mellow music coming from overhead speakers, the store's quiet. So I can really think while I shop.

One subject keeps coming to mind: Mom's journal. Specifically what I read right before leaving the room to find Elinor.

My son cried like a baby.

And I cannot have that.

"Breaker-breaker one-nine."

I stop next to a display of Dump Ropes. They look like normal jump ropes, but according to the video playing on a small TV, they trip and tangle around the legs of unsuspecting users, knocking them down.

Next to the TV is a silver box with a skinny black antenna. It doesn't seem to be part of the Dump Rope display. And it broadcasts a familiar voice.

"We got a brown micro in white water. Do you copy?"

I pick up the box, hold it near my mouth. "Lemon? Is that you?"

"Seamus! Awesome. Don't move. I'll be right there."

I follow his instructions. Soon I hear a loud beep as the Kommissary door opens and closes.

"Hey!" Lemon jogs down the aisle, breathless. "Thanks for waiting." He stops before me and grins. If he's still upset after his family's role-playing session, he doesn't show it. "How'd I sound?" I must look puzzled because he adds, "On the Turbo Talkie?" He holds up a small silver box. It's identical to the one still in my hand.

"Oh! Great. I heard what you said, loud and clear. Although I have no idea what it meant."

"It's code for chocolate chip cookie with milk." He smiles. "Was there any static? Did my voice break up at all?"

"It was like you were standing right next to me."

"Awesome. The package promised a thousand-mile hearing range, but I didn't—"

He's stopped by a white ribbon. It sails over the top of the Dump Rope display, hits his nose, and winds around his head, covering his entire face. When it's done, only his eyes remain exposed. He tries to talk, but the ribbon hardens like a walnut shell, freezing all of his features.

"Not bad," Abe says, coming up behind us. Standing before Lemon, he holds up a plastic spray bottle and pulls the trigger. Clear liquid shoots out from the nozzle and hits Lemon's face. The ribbon softens. Droops. Slips down. Soon it looks like a scarf around Lemon's neck. "Papier-Mâché Mold. Guaranteed to conform to your target and lock them in a personal arts-and-crafts cave."

Old Lemon would be annoyed right now. But New Lemon laughs.

"Good one, Abraham! You really had me there." He nods to my hand. "Can I have that? I want to go pay."

I give him the Turbo Talkie. He jogs down the aisle, whistling.

"What do you think happened with his little brother?" Abe asks quietly. "That made his parents send him away?"

"No idea," I say. But I plan to find out—when the time's right.

"By the way," Lemon calls over his shoulder, "there's some crazy party going on over at the Performance Pavilion. Maybe we should check it out!"

Abe looks at me. "I didn't hear anything about a party tonight. Did you?"

"Nope. And if there *were* one, wouldn't it be closer to camp? Like the pool party was?"

Annika had told us that with the exception of the Kommissary, which would open only at her request, the regular Kilter campus was closed for the summer. The Performance Pavilion is located on the regular Kilter campus. Which means no one should be there now.

"Are you thinking what I'm thinking?" Abe asks, his voice grim.

I nod. "We'd better hurry up and pay for our supplies. We're going to need them."

"I'll get the girls. You make sure fun-loving Lemon doesn't leave without us."

He sprints toward one end of the aisle. I head for the other end. When I reach Lemon, he's talking with GS George at the register.

"Eight hundred credits?" Lemon asks. "Are you sure that's the right price?"

"Absolutely," GS George says.

"But I only have eight hundred and ten," Lemon says.

"Well, are these worth nearly wiping out your account?" GS George asks.

No. For one thing, we can use our K-Paks like walkie-talkies.

For another, unless there's more to them than Lemon let on, Turbo Talkies don't start, grow, or extinguish fires. So why does he want them? Especially when buying them means he can't buy anything else that'll help his troublemaking talent?

"Yes," Lemon says. "Wipe away."

He makes his purchase. Abe, Gabby, Elinor, and I make ours. Soon we're outside and hurrying across campus. The Performance Pavilion is about half a mile from the Kommissary. On foot it normally takes ten minutes to reach, but it takes much longer tonight. Because instead of following the paved walkways, we play it safe and travel in the dark cover of trees and shadows.

By the time we reach the Performance Pavilion, I think we're too late. The building is dark. Quiet.

"Lemon," Abe says, "are you sure this is where—"

Before he can finish his question, there's a loud *BOOM*. The ground shakes. The Performance Pavilion lights up, as if someone flipped a switch. The sudden, deep noise is followed by music. Shouting. Cheering.

Abe and Lemon head for the entrance.

"Hang on!" Gabby declares, stopping them. She reaches into her Kommissary bag, tears open a package of Vision Vortex Lash

Extensions, and puts them on. Then she blinks, releasing a small sparkle shower. "Okay. Let's go."

Hugging walls and hiding in shadows, we make our way inside and through the arena. Each time the music and voices die down, I think the party's ending—but then there's another *BOOM.* The floor shakes. The music, shouting, and cheering start up again, even louder than before.

By the time the main stage comes into view, the party's in full swing. And it's obvious our invitations weren't lost in the mail.

"Are those . . . ?" Gabby's voice trails off.

"Incriminators?" Abe finishes. "I don't know anyone else that dirty."

"But there are so many of them," Gabby says.

She's right. As we squat behind a low wall at the back of the auditorium, I scan the rows of seats—and guess that at least fifty of Nadia's students made the trip from IncrimiNation. Some are sitting, many are standing. They all face the large stage.

"How have we not seen them around before now?" Abe asks.

"They're really good at hiding," Elinor says.

"We better be too," I say.

Because the Incriminators want to find us. That's obvious

when there's another *BOOM* and a gigantic picture of Alison Parker, our classmate, appears on the screen hanging down from the ceiling to the stage. As we watch, the screen changes to show video footage of Alison making trouble with Kommissary supplies around the Kilter campus. With each new image, the gathered Incriminators cheer and shout louder. The last screen-shot lists Alison's likes and dislikes, her troublemaking strengths and weaknesses, and the location of her parents' camp cabin. That information lingers for several seconds, then the screen goes dark—and there's another *BOOM*.

Carter Montgomery appears next. Then Reed Jenkins. Natalie Warner. Liam Jones. And many more of our classmates.

Finally, the screen goes dark and stays that way. I think the show's over.

But then I hear more booming. Quieter than the explosive sound effect that announced each new Troublemaker, but just as frightening. The sounds get louder and seem to travel across the stage.

Then they stop. A spotlight flicks on.

And shines down on Shepherd Bull.

Standing center stage, he shouts over the whoops and

clapping. "So there they are! Some of Kilter Academy's best Troublemakers—and IncrimiNation's biggest pains!" He lets the crowd boo and hiss a minute, then holds up one hand. When the crowd quiets down, he yells, "They all deserve our attention! No Troublemaker will get off easy this summer! But *four* of them will feel our heat the most. Because there's bad . . . and then there's the worst. And that's what these Troublemakers are!"

Shepherd Bull throws up his hands. A series of booms, all louder than the ones we've heard before now, seem to rock the Performance Pavilion from its foundation. The Incriminators scream and stomp their feet as three more screens lower from the ceiling . . . and four familiar faces appear.

Abe's. Gabby's. Lemon's.

And mine.

Crouched down next to me, Elinor takes my hand.

"What do they *want*?" she asks.

The answer couldn't be clearer.

"Revenge."

Chapter 20

DEMERITS: 1720
GOLD STARS: 950

TO: shinkle@kilteracademy.org
FROM: parsippany@wahoo.com
SUBJECT: Zipped Lips

Dear Seamus,

Thanks so much for your last note! Hearing from you always makes my day.

First thing's first: I'm very sorry. You probably received a notification stating that your e-mail didn't reach me because my in-box no longer exists. If so, you must've been quite surprised! I was too. Fortunately, as you can see, my in-box does exist, although it's now attached to a different address. Since I never said I'd never again teach in the Cloudview School System, I assumed they'd keep my e-mail address active indefinitely. Apparently that wasn't the case, and they deactivated my account without warning. In any event, I apologize for the confusion! From now on you can reach me at my new e-mail address above.

Now on to apology #2. You asked what I meant when I said that honesty's always the best policy, except when it's not. You also asked if I'd ever lied. I should've been clearer in my last e-mail. When I said that honesty's always the best policy, except when it isn't, I simply meant that sometimes, it's better to edit the truth. Pare it down. Leave out details. Shape it into something the person you're telling will have an easier time processing.

I'll give you an example. Many years ago, my

mother bought a new dress. It was lime green. Too short. With too many ruffles. Please don't think I'm a terrible person . . . but the dress made her look like a stuffed party piñata.

See? I bet you winced just reading that. I winced while writing it, and this happened decades ago! Which is why, when my mother asked how she looked, I said "nice." I didn't say "fabulous," because that definitely would've been a lie. But I didn't say "bad" either, because the whole truth would've really hurt her feelings. So I went with an altered version of the truth. Sometimes that's just better for everyone. For whatever it's worth, I'd keep this in mind whenever you're tempted to come clean to Annika about what you did or didn't do, or who you really are or aren't.

I hope that answers your question! If you have any others, ask away!

With Kind Regards,

Miss Parsippany

P.S. Any new Bartholomew John news?

"Earth to Seamus."

I put down my K-Pak. "I'm listening."

"Really," Abe says drily. "What'd I just say?"

"Earth to Seamus."

Gabby giggles. Elinor smiles. Even Lemon, who's kicking and paddling in front of the canoe, flashes a grin.

"Way to bring down the house, funnyman," Abe says. "Now can we please be serious? And discuss the plan?"

"We *discussed* the plan." Gabby dips her plastic cup into the lake water pooled in the bottom of the boat. "For, like, hours last night. And this morning. We're going to engage the enemy. See what they've really got. And fire back."

"Without totally bringing them down," I add. "Since Annika wants us to watch them in action."

"And you're sure she wouldn't change her mind about that?" Abe asks. "Especially if she saw what we saw onstage yesterday?"

My K-Pak buzzes. I look down at my in-box and see Annika's name pop up on the screen. "I am, but she just e-mailed, so I'll write her back, tell her what we saw, and confirm that we should stick with the original plan. Good?"

"Great! Marvelous! Glorious! Stupendous! Exquisite! Scrumptious!"

For a second I think Mystery actually overheard our conversation—even though Lemon's just reached water shallow enough for his feet to touch sand—and is answering me. But then I realize he's addressing Troublemakers in the canoe ahead of ours as he helps them onshore.

"That's what today is!" he sings. "Great, marvelous, glorious, stupendous, exquisite, and scrumptious! Don't you agree?"

"I might have to borrow some of his super senior-citizen vitamins," Abe says. "The dude's got pep."

We all hop out of our boat before it reaches sand to avoid Mystery's bizarre greeting. Once onshore, we run to our teachers for our chore assignments and supplies. I get laundry detail—and a jug of detergent, another of bleach, and a box of fabric-softener sheets.

"How do I do it?" I ask Houdini after he's done loading me up.

"See this sweatshirt?" he asks. "I've bought the same one thirty-seven times. Whenever it really starts to reek, I just toss it and buy a new one."

This, apparently, is his way of saying he doesn't know. Because he doesn't do laundry.

I thank him for the supplies and turn around to look for Elinor. She's standing with Abe a few yards away. They seem to be having a serious conversation. When Abe sees that I see them, he waves me over.

"Elinor's working with me today," he announces when I reach them.

I look at Elinor. "Is that what you want?"

"She wants to help the group," Abe says. "Right?"

"Of course," Elinor says. "But—"

"She has mopping duty. My parents' floors are awful. If she gave them a good scrub today, that'd be really helpful."

I start to protest, but Abe catches my eye. *His* eyes say everything he doesn't want to say out loud. Which is the same thing he wrote in an e-mail to me late last night.

Which was: Elinor wasn't included in Shepherd Bull's presentation of Troublemakers to Incriminators at the Performance Pavilion. And if they're really here to get back at us for stealing Elinor from their school, then she should've been. Abe's convinced this is because she's secretly working for the other team.

I'm not. I still don't believe Elinor would ever do such a

thing. Abe's e-mail also said that he doesn't trust me to see who she really is. So if I'm smart, I'll let him keep tabs on her today. It could only help my case.

His eyes say that, too. They're very expressive.

"Fine," I tell him. Then to Elinor, "Call if you need anything."

They leave. Looking around, I see that Lemon and Gabby are already gone. So are most of our classmates. I pick up my supplies and start across the beach.

The jugs of detergent and bleach are heavy, but they feel like jugs of feathers compared to my head. There's just so much in it. Like, is Abe right? Could Elinor be some kind of spy? Maybe to earn points with her mom? How come I haven't seen *my* mom since we got here? Does she leave the house before dawn every morning to do top-secret work for Annika? How come Dad can't seem to get away from me fast enough? What will the Incriminators do with us if they have the chance? And why'd Miss Parsippany once again not say what her new job is?

I'm so busy sorting through all of these thoughts and questions, I don't notice the flyers covering the sand until one sticks to my sneaker. Then I stop, yank the flyer from my shoe, and read.

KILTER FAMILIES!

READY TO GET YOUR GROOVE ON?

JOIN DJ HOUDINI AND THE FUNKY FACULTY FOR

THE 1st ANNUAL KAMP KILTER BEACH BASH!

ENJOY A NIGHT OF MUSIC,

FOOD, FIREWORKS, AND FUN!

WHERE: KAMP KILTER BEACH

WHEN: SATURDAY, 8 P.M.

Note: Attendance is mandatory—because at Kamp Kilter,
FUN is mandatory!

A beach bash. Great. While I'm lugging around a hundred pounds of worry, my parents are living it up.

I shove the flyer into my shorts pocket. Then I keep walking.

When I reach the base of the long, steep staircase, I stop again. I drop the jugs to the sand, take my K-Pak from my other shorts pocket, and read Annika's latest e-mail.

TO: shinkle@kilteracademy.org
FROM: annika@kilteracademy.org
SUBJECT: So?

Dear Seamus,

I hope you enjoyed your shopping spree. Did anything happen after that?

—Annika

I glance around to make sure no one—like Shepherd Bull or one of his criminal companions—is lurking nearby, trying to see my computer screen while waiting to pounce. When the coast seems clear, I press reply and start typing.

TO: annika@kilteracademy.org
CC: ahansen@kilteracademy.org, loliver@kilteracademy.org, gryan@kilteracademy.org, enorris@kilteracademy.org
FROM: shinkle@kilteracademy.org
SUBJECT: RE: So?

Hi, Annika!

Something did happen after our shopping trip. But before I tell you about that, I wanted to tell you about Mr. Tempest. He's been acting kind of strange. Like, really happy. That's probably a good thing, but I thought you should know in case it isn't.

Back to business—and an Incriminator update. After our Kommissary trip last night we heard noise coming from the Performance Pavilion. We investigated and found dozens of Incriminators gathered for some kind of informational meeting—about Abe, Lemon, Gabby, me, and the rest of our troublemaking class.

We're on the case to find out exactly what they're up to. Do you still want us to engage them without taking them down?

Let us know! Thanks!

—Seamus

I send the message. I'm reaching down for the cleaning jugs when my K-Pak buzzes.

TO: shinkle@kilteracademy.org
CC: ahansen@kilteracademy.org, loliver@kilteracademy.org, gryan@kilteracademy.org, enorris@kilteracademy.org

FROM: annika@kilteracademy.org
SUBJECT: RE: RE: So?

Thanks for the update. Proceed with Incriminators as planned IF YOU HAVE TIME. Remember: Your parents are the priority!

—Annika

Huh. It's not like I expected her to be super concerned about us being targeted, but she didn't even comment on the Incriminators' meeting. I might be offended if I didn't have too many other things to worry about.

I pocket my K-Pak, pick up my supplies, and hurry up the stairs. I cross the yard and start up the porch steps. Before I reach the door, I hear Dad whistling inside. I crouch down by a window and peek through the gap in the curtains. He's sitting on the couch with his back to me. The coffee table's covered in books and papers, but I can't make out titles or words.

Remember: Your parents are the priority!

Annika's reminder helps me focus. I know exactly what I need to do.

I dash down the porch steps and around the back of the house, where I stash my cleaning supplies under a bush. I slink across the deck, climb onto a railing, and grab a low-hanging tree branch. Wishing I had Ike's Kilter Katcher, I lift myself up and scoot and shimmy across branches. After a few minutes—and several splinters—I reach a second-floor window. Unlike all of the other windows, this one's foggy. Also unlike the other windows, it's cracked open. Dad always opens the bathroom window while taking his hot morning shower. Thankfully, he hasn't changed his routine at Kamp Kilter.

Gripping the branch with one hand, I reach forward with the other and push up the window. When there's a wide enough opening, I lower my torso to the branch and aim my head at the opening. Moving an inch at a time, I slide through the space. As soon as more of me is inside the bathroom than outside, I grab the edge of the marble counter and pull. The force of my legs flying through the window shoves my entire body off of the counter. I land on the floor with a thud.

I hold my breath. Wait.

Dad's still whistling. He didn't hear me.

I scramble to my feet and peer around the door to check the

hallway. When my K-Pak buzzes, I see that the new message is our daily troublemaking assignment, and I exit my K-Mail without reading it. If our parents are the priority, then the troublemaking assignment can wait.

But two steps later, I find another distraction.

Mom's journal. It's sitting on the dresser in their bedroom. Inches away from where I'm standing in the hall.

Glancing toward the living room, I don't see Dad. I hear him, though. Now he's humming. But it doesn't sound like he's moved from the couch.

Deciding it's worth the risk, I leap across the hall and into my parents' bedroom. I take a second to appreciate my ballerina-soft landing, then grab the journal and flip ahead a few years. Thanks to the time crunch, I have to skip, not stroll, down memory lane.

This entry was written five years ago, when I was eight.

We had another incident today. Seamus and I were spending the afternoon at the park. Several kids decided to play hide-and-seek. Seamus seemed content to sit alone on a seesaw, but I encouraged him to join the game.

I stop, listening for Dad. He's still humming in the living room. I keep reading.

He started playing. And for a while, everything was fine.

Until Seamus was the seeker.

Is it my fault? Did I baby him too much? Did I wrap him too tightly in soft blankets all those years ago? These are the questions I've been asking myself ever since my son found Bartholomew John crouched under a picnic table and happily announced his discovery. And Bartholomew John insisted that he hadn't been found—and shoved Seamus to the ground. At which point, rather than insisting he'd won, Seamus ran over to me and cried.

Physically he was fine—but I wasn't. My heart broke. Because he was embarrassed. And I felt awful that he didn't feel strong enough to stand up for himself.

I have my work cut out for me. But whatever it takes, I WILL get the job done.

There's a noise down the hall. I put the book back where I found it and tiptoe to the bedroom door. Peeking out, I see Dad coming toward me—and I duck back inside. A second later, his footsteps stop. I lean forward.

In the hallway, the door that's always locked is now open. Dad's bottom sticks out past the door's edge as he bends down and rummages around. This lasts nearly a minute, then he stands up straight.

"Whoo-boy!" Dad exclaims, patting his belly. "This tank needs some fuel. Chow time!"

Good. He's going to the Kilter Kafeteria. Now I can read more of Mom's journal—and figure out how to get inside that closet.

"What'll it be this morning?" Dad asks, heading down the hall. "Bacon? Eggs? Cheeseburger and fries?"

My stomach turns as I hear him open and close the refrigerator, then clang around pots and pans. He's making himself breakfast. Which means he's not leaving.

This answers one question, anyway. Just like every other morning, Mom's not here. If she were, she'd be cooking—a low-fat, healthy meal.

Still in their bedroom, I wonder what I should do. Keep watching him from a safe distance inside the house? Or sneak back outside, knock on the door like I've just arrived for my daily cleaning detail, and see what he does?

I think about it, then go with option number three.

Play with fire. Not the way Lemon does (or used to).

The way Mom would want me to.

I peer down the hall. The coast is clear, so I tiptoe from the bedroom.

"Real maple syrup!" Dad declares, making me jump into the next open doorway. "Made from Kamp Kilter tree sap! What a treat!"

He continues whistling and banging pots. I continue creeping down the hall.

Five steps later, the wood floor creaks. I freeze. Listen.

Dad falls silent. Like he's listening too.

A few seconds later, he keeps whistling. I keep walking.

When I reach the door that's usually locked, I stop and smile.

Dad left it ajar. I don't even have to turn the knob and worry about it clicking—and inviting attention.

But then I open the door farther. And my smile vanishes.

What I thought was a closet isn't really a closet. It might have been once, but now there are no coats. Or bath towels. Or anything else Mom keeps in our hall closets at home.

Books are stacked on the floor. And they're not literary classics or accounting texts, which until now are the only kinds of books I've ever seen Dad read. Skimming the titles, I see *Keeping Your Kid in Line. How to Sabotage Your Son. 101 Rules for Pure Parental Power.*

There are pamphlets, too, like "Popular Smack and Slang." "The 10 Most Common Lies Kids Tell." "Childproof Your Life." Some are taped to the inside of the door, with certain phrases highlighted. Scanning quickly, I see one phrase repeated—and highlighted—more than any other.

WANT AN ANGEL? BE THE DEVIL!

This question-and-answer is emphasized by other items in the former closet. Like the wings made of white feathers that are also stuck to the door. There are big wings. Little wings. Wings with glitter. Wings that flutter when you touch the "Press Here" button that holds them together.

There are rings, too. Big rings. Little rings. Rings with glitter. Rings that glow when you touch the "Press Here" button at their bases. A few rings are stuck to the inside of the door. Some hang from the door knob. Others hold together clusters of pamphlets. I assume they're halos. Just like the kind angels wear.

Including me. Or the angel someone really wants me to be.

I know I'm the target of these self-help guides because of the former closet's biggest item.

A life-size cardboard cutout. Of me. Made from the photo Dad always carries in his wallet—the one he took last year, when we went mini-golfing and I got my first hole in one. The cardboard cutout's even waving the putter overhead, just like I did when the ball went in with a single stroke.

The only difference between the cutout and the original photo . . . is the gold 3-D halo perched on top of my cardboard head.

"Hello?"

Dad. I'm so stunned I almost forgot where I am.

"Okay. Got it. Yes, I'll be right there."

I hear footsteps. A faucet turning on. Water running. A loud sizzling.

Heart hammering, I step back, swing the closet door. It clicks shut and I sprint on my tiptoes down the hall, away from the kitchen. But then I remember that I found the door slightly ajar. And I spin around and sprint-tiptoe back.

When I reach the closet door, I hear another one open and quickly close. The sound seems to come from the living room—and the front door. Now, with the exception of my pulse pounding my eardrums, the house is silent.

This is a great chance to snoop freely. But I'm distracted by Dad's voice inside my head.

Hello?

Okay. Got it. Yes, I'll be right there.

He sounded serious. Urgent.

I race down the hall and glance in the kitchen. The counter's still cluttered with eggshells, packages of bacon, and bottles of maple syrup. Steam's rising from the kitchen sink, where Dad must've poured water on a hot pan.

I fly from the house as fast as my short legs will carry me. But Dad's faster. By the time I reach the yard, he's already starting down the steep staircase to the beach.

I keep going. Pump my legs. Swing my arms. Try to control

my breathing so Dad doesn't hear me coming at him like a train down the tracks. Skid to a stop on the top step to keep from careening over the edge and tumbling down the staircase. Then clamber down as quietly as I can.

Dad doesn't look behind him once. As far as I can tell, he has no idea he's being followed. Tripping and stumbling a few times, I stub my toe, bang my knee, and bite back cries of pain—so this can't be because I'm tailing him like a super-stealth silent ninja. It probably has more to do with the fact that he's really determined to reach his destination.

Unfortunately, I don't know what that is. Or if he gets there. Because in trying to pick up the pace, I jump over the last three steps of the steep staircase, land hard in the sand, and twist my ankle. My eyes squeeze shut at the sudden sting. When they open again, Dad's nowhere to be found.

I follow his footsteps, but the Good Samaritans are raking the sand so it's smooth for today's sunbathers. Dad's path disappears halfway across the beach.

"Excuse me?" I ask the closest GS. "Did you just see a man run through here? With a bouncy belly? Wearing penny loafers and a pocket protector?"

"Nope," the GS says. "Sorry."

Looking around, my eyes zero in on the closest path to the beach. It's the one Dad would've come to first, so I head right for it.

A quarter of a mile down, I'm stopped. By a familiar voice. Singing softly. In the arts and crafts building.

Dad doesn't do arts and crafts. Neither does Mom.

So I almost fall over when I go to the building, peek through the open door, and see her surrounded by fabric and ribbon and spools of thread. Grabbing the door frame to steady myself, I watch the scene like I'm watching a really confusing movie.

I'm not just puzzled by the fact that Mom's sewing what appears to be the world's largest blanket. Or that she's singing the lullaby she used to sing to me before bed, but that I haven't heard in years.

It's that she's doing both of these things . . . and crying.

Chapter 21

DEMERITS: 2200
GOLD STARS: 1350

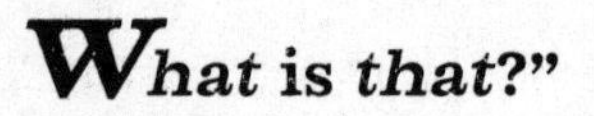

***What** is **that**?"*

"Um, a dress?"

"Why does it have a tail?"

"It doesn't have a tail. It has a sash. The prettiest pink silk sash with sparkly rhinestones ever made! It makes me look like a beauty queen, don't you think?"

"I think it makes you look like a kangaroo in a cotton candy machine."

"A kangaroo? I *love* kangaroos! They're like the cutest,

most adorable animals in the whole *world*! Thanks, Abe!"

"Ugh, please don't—why do you have to—okay. Wow. You're strong."

"Abe," I say, "do I see a smile?"

The corners of his mouth drop. "No, Hinkle. You see a guy struggling to breathe."

Gabby leans down and plants a loud peck on his cheek, which instantly turns red. Then she releases her arms from around his chest, skips over to a mirror on the wall, and plays with her bangs.

The corners of Abe's mouth start to lift again—until he notices me looking at him. Then he frowns and scrubs his tainted cheek with one hand.

"I don't know why you're all making such a big deal about this," he says. "It's just a party."

"Exactly," Gabby says. "It's a *party*. With music and dancing and fireworks! If that's not a good reason to get dressed up, I don't know what is."

Abe starts to say something else, but stops. Probably because no one told him he should wear khakis and a blue plaid button-down shirt, all freshly ironed, and he did anyway. It's obvious he wanted to look nice, too. Maybe even for Gabby, although he'd never admit it.

I'm wearing gray pants, my favorite white polo shirt, and the gray boat shoes Mom bought for me last summer that I brought to Kamp Kilter, just in case. Because I thought maybe I'd want to look nice too. For someone else.

"Our parents will be there," Lemon says, hurrying into the room. "And our brothers and sisters. If *that's* not a good reason to get dressed up, I don't know what is."

Abe's chin drops. So does mine. And Gabby's.

"Dude," Abe finally says. "Is that a tie?"

"And gel in your hair?" Gabby asks, reaching out to pat it.

"And real shoes?" I ask.

Lemon ducks away from Gabby's hand, then nudges her for room in front of the mirror.

"Sorry to keep everyone waiting."

Gabby's chin drops again. So does Abe's. And Lemon's. And mine, furthest of all. We all stare at Elinor, who stands in the living room doorway.

Gabby's the first to recover. She squeals, claps, and beelines toward her friend. "You look *amazing*!"

"Are you sure?" Elinor looks down at her outfit. "It was so nice of you loan me one of your dresses . . . but I don't usually wear them, so I feel a little weird."

"Trust me," Gabby says. "It. Looks. Gorgeous!"

"It's a very nice dress," Lemon says.

"Not bad," Abe says. Coming from him, this is the ultimate compliment.

I'd give her one too if I could talk. But I can't, so all I can do is try not to stare.

Because somehow, wearing the sleeveless turquoise dress she borrowed from Gabby, her long red hair hanging loose past her shoulders, Elinor looks even prettier than I've ever seen her.

If Dad's looking for an angel, here she is. No wings or halo required.

"We should go." Abe jumps up from the couch. "The party's starting soon."

We head for the elevator and gather inside.

"I'm so happy Annika invited us," Gabby says during the ride up. "The party was originally just for our families, right?"

"Right," Abe says. "Until Hinkle convinced her it was a

great chance for us to see our parents in action. Since we haven't really seen them in days."

It turns out my friends are having a hard time gathering information, because their parents have also been leaving the second their kids come to clean. I told Annika this and suggested that watching our families in a casual atmosphere when their guards were down—like at a beach party—might help us learn more. She agreed and sent an e-vite to the rest of the Trouble-makers that night—but asked them not to tell their parents that they planned to attend. She thought the element of surprise could work in our favor.

"Well," Gabby says as the elevator slows to a stop, "I hope this won't be all work and no play. I'm dying to dance!"

The elevator door opens. Gabby skips out. Lemon follows her. Abe follows him.

Elinor and I stay put. She seems to be waiting for me to say or do something. After a few seconds of shy glances and awkward silence, we both speak at once.

"You look really nice."

We laugh.

I smile and motion to the door. "After you."

We hurry from the elevator, out of our fake tent, and to the lake. A boat's waiting for us. It's ten times the size of the canoe we usually take to our parents' beach—and in much better shape. Dozens of Troublemakers are already on board, no one's filling plastic cups and dumping water over the sides, and the ship's staying afloat.

As I follow Elinor up the ramp leading to the boat, I think about how glad I am that Abe made her go with him to his families' cabin the other day. According to the thorough report he gave me that night, he watched her like a hawk, and she did nothing suspicious. That didn't mean he necessarily trusted her, or was ready to invite her to join Capital T, but it at least knocked down his paranoia a few notches.

I also think that I'm with Gabby. I hope tonight's not all work and no play . . . because I wouldn't mind just having fun with my friends. Without worrying about parents, Incriminators, or even making trouble.

The evening has a promising start. Once the last Troublemaker's onboard, we set sail across the lake. The sun starts to set. The sky softens, turning from blue to gold. Waiters pass out glasses of lemonade and iced tea. Other waiters come by with trays of snacks—peanuts and pretzels, chips and dip. Music plays. My friends and I talk and laugh with our classmates.

It's nice. Normal. I almost forget where we're going and why.

But then the boat docks. The music stops. And it all comes back to me.

"Are we really late?" Gabby asks.

"Or really early?" Lemon asks.

"Do we have the right beach?" Abe asks.

"There's the band," Elinor says. "And our teachers."

"But where are our parents?" I ask.

"More food for us!" Chris Fisher declares before bounding down the ramp.

As we disembark, I note that the beach definitely looks ready for a party. There are balloons and streamers. Lit tiki torches. Picnic tables. A dozen Kilter chefs behind grills. Snack and beverage stations. Big speakers playing loud music. But besides camp staff members, our teachers, and the arriving Trouble-makers, there are no guests.

"Hey, hey!" DJ Houdini stands behind a large turntable, holding a microphone in one hand and headphones to his ear in the other. "Welcome to Kamp Kilter's first annual Beach Bash!

Help yourself to some grub, and feel free to cut a rug!" He puts down the microphone, then picks it up again. When he speaks this time, his voice is stern. "But whatever you do, do *not* get into trouble!"

"Was that warning for our parents' benefit?" Abe asks me.

"Probably," I say. "Only they're not around to hear it."

He checks his watch. "The party started at eight. We're fifteen minutes late. Should we split up and check their cabins?"

"Let's ask Annika first," I say. "Maybe she knows something we don't."

"Can you say . . . *conga*?"

Abe winces. "Don't tell me."

I look past him to the sandy dance floor, where Gabby's already skipping and sashaying barefoot. She either doesn't realize or care that no one's joined her.

"She's not bad," I say. "If the singing thing doesn't work out, maybe she has a backup career."

"That'd be *so* much quieter," Abe says, heading her way. "I'll go suggest it. You find Annika."

"Looks like fun."

I turn around and see Elinor standing a few feet behind me.

"Want to join them?" she asks.

"Abe and Gabby?" I ask. "On the dance floor?"

She nods.

"With you?"

She nods again.

"Maybe in a few minutes?" I ask, regretting the words as I say them. "I just have to do one thing first."

"I'll be here."

We exchange smiles. Then I reluctantly leave her and hurry around the beach. Besides Houdini, I see Samara. Wyatt. Devin. Lizzie. They're eating and drinking, talking and laughing. They don't seem concerned that no one from the party's original guest list has made it here. Deciding not to attract attention by asking them if they know where Annika is, I duck behind a tree and take out my K-Pak.

TO: annika@kilteracademy.org
FROM: shinkle@kilteracademy.org
SUBJECT: Beach Bash No-Shows

Hi Annika,

Capital T and the rest of the Troublemakers have made it to tonight's party. Our teachers and the Kamp Kilter staff have really outdone themselves this time—everything looks great!

Just one question. Where are our parents? The party flyer said attendance was mandatory, so I'm just wondering where they are. Did they have another event before this one? That's maybe running late?

If you could let me know as soon as you can, that'd be great. Abe, Lemon, Gabby, Elinor, and I just want to make sure we're doing our jobs!

Thanks!

—Seamus

I hit send. Annika writes back immediately.

TO: shinkle@kilteracademy.org
FROM: annika@kilteracademy.org
SUBJECT: RE: Beach Bash No-Shows

Dear Seamus,

You were right to write. Your parents should be there—and nowhere else.

Stay put. I'll have your teachers find them ASAP.

—Annika

I put away my K-Pak and step out from behind the tree. As I start back toward the dance floor, I see Houdini, Lizzie, Samara, Wyatt, Fern, and Devin all jump and check their K-Paks. Then they casually put down their plates and cups, stroll to the back of the beach—and bolt into the woods.

Fortunately, Houdini hands over DJ duties to a Good Samaritan before leaving. The music keeps going. Which means I'll still get to dance with Elinor.

I wonder if DJ GS takes requests. If so, should I make one? Maybe something a little softer? A little slower? So that Elinor and I can—

"Gotcha!"

Whoever says this is right. One second I'm walking on the beach, looking at Elinor. And the next second, I'm hanging in midair as I look at a giant silver *K*.

"Didn't know that was coming, did you?"

I'm in some kind of net and scrunched up like Play-Doh in a can, but when I hear the familiar voice, my muscles relax.

"I definitely didn't," I say.

Something beeps. The net lowers. When my bottom hits a hard surface, the mesh material loosens and falls away. I look around and see that I'm sitting on the ground in the middle of the woods.

I grin. "Hi, Ike."

"Hey." My tutor grins too. "Hope I didn't interrupt anything."

"Nope." Ducking my head so he can't see my cheeks turn pink, I climb to my feet. "So what's this? I don't think I've seen it before."

There's another beep. The net lifts and lengthens. Strings shoot out from either end and wind around two tree trunks. When it's done, it looks like something that I'd like to hang out in with a book and a glass of lemonade.

"The Kilter Hammock Hauler," Ike says. "Designed to snatch up any unsuspecting snoozer."

"I wasn't snoozing," I say. "I was walking."

"And paying so little attention to your surroundings, you might as well have been sleeping." Before I can disagree he asks, "Ready for a quick lesson?"

"Always."

He holds up a pineapple. A tiny purple umbrella sticks out of the top of the fruit. Ike moves the umbrella right, and the hammock pulls taut. He moves the umbrella left, and the hammock loosens. When he bangs the top of the umbrella, the hammock strings release the tree trunks, the fabric comes together like a sack, and the strings knot at the top. All of this happens in about two seconds. Then Ike hits the top of the umbrella again, and the sack drops to the ground.

"It's pretty straightforward," he says. "And as you just learned, your target doesn't need to actually be in the hammock in order for it to work. That's easiest, of course. And it's always nice when your prey wanders right into your trap. But when that doesn't happen, you just use the pineapple's built-in radar system to aim and fire. The Hammock Hauler does the rest." He looks at me. "Want to try?"

"Definitely."

He hands me the pineapple. I fiddle with the umbrella for a few minutes to get the hang of it.

Ike nods to a nearby rock. "I'll give you twenty demerits for that."

Zeroing in on my target, I press a button on the bottom of

the pineapple. A thin, silver beam of light shoots out. When the light hits the middle of the rock, the pineapple beeps. I press the top of the umbrella. The Hammock Hauler swoops toward the rock, lifts it up, and folds around it. The strings tie together. Now in the makeshift sack, the rock drops back to the ground.

"Nice work," Ike says. "How about thirty demerits for that bush over there?"

"That's, like, rooted in the dirt?"

"Yup."

"No problem," I say more confidently than I feel.

But the Hammock Hauler doesn't disappoint. It takes a few joystick adjustments, but soon the bush is pulled from the dirt and dropped back to the ground.

"I'm going to replant that right away," I say.

Ike gives me a few more targets. I catch them all, each faster than the one before. By the time we're done, I've racked up two hundred demerits.

"Impressive as always," Ike says. "And now you should get back to the party."

The party. Elinor. My parents. I don't think I've been gone that long, but I've been so focused on my lesson it's hard to be sure. Hopefully, I haven't missed anything important.

"That's probably a good idea," I say. "But before I go, can I ask you something?"

"Anything."

I take a big breath. "A few days ago? During our last lesson in the treetops? You said something I've been wondering about ever since."

"How donuts are a better breakfast than fish sticks and maple syrup?"

"No, although I don't get that either." I give him a quick smile. "But I'm talking about the other thing. When you said I should be—"

"Seamus!"

My mouth snaps shut. I look at Ike. He looks at my K-Pak, which is sticking out of my pants pocket.

"Earth to Seamus! Hello? Are you there? Pick up! *Right now!*"

I yank out the K-Pak. The screen's flashing with a v-chat request from Abe, whose loud, anxious voice is the one barking at me.

I accept the request. The video feed turns on. And I instantly forget whatever it was I wanted to ask Ike. All I can do is stare, unblinking, at the screen.

Where Shepherd Bull is staring back at me.

Chapter 22

DEMERITS: 2300
GOLD STARS: 1350

Um, guys? I don't know how much longer I'll last."

"Just a few more minutes, Gabby," I say. "Please. If you can."

"But I haven't blinked in eleven minutes and it's kind of dusty in here and my eyes are starting to wig out."

"Then blink," Abe says. "Give your eyes a half-second break. And keep going."

"Can't. Closing them breaks the bind."

As Gabby keeps her eyes aimed straight ahead, Elinor stands right behind her.

"You're not in a dusty shed," she says near Gabby's ear. "You're in a beautiful, shiny, sparkly shopping mall."

Gabby eyes widen ever so slightly.

"You're strolling past all of your favorite stores," Elinor continues. "When you reach your favorite one—"

"Sassy Threads?" Gabby asks.

"Yes," Elinor confirms. "When you reach that one, you stop. There's an outfit in the window. It's so beautiful, you can't take your eyes off of it."

Still unblinking, Gabby nods slowly. "Yes. Yes, I *see* it. There's a long blue skirt. And a belt made of sapphires. And . . ."

Gabby and Elinor keep talking. So do Abe and I.

"This wasn't part of the plan," I whisper.

"Capturing an Incriminator?" Abe asks. "I know. But he was lurking in the shadows. Carrying that enormous stick. So close to the party. I thought he and his dirty friends had to be up to something, and I didn't want to find out what that was. Especially with so many Troublemakers right there. I mean, if *we* didn't capture *him*, maybe *they* would've captured all of *us*."

I glance at Shepherd Bull. He sits on a stack of three silver inner tubes, the kind we've seen some Troublemaker parents floating around in on the lake. His ankles and wrists are bound together with silver beach towels. A tennis ball's lodged in his mouth.

They're decent constraints. On anyone else they'd be perfect. But on the child-giant, the towels look like ribbon and the tennis ball looks like a piece of bubble gum.

They're working, though, because in the ten minutes I've been here, he hasn't moved an inch. Gabby's icy stare, which no one's immune to, is also helping keep him in place.

"How'd you even do it?" I ask Abe quietly. "He must weigh more than you, Gabby, and Elinor combined."

Abe stands up straighter and squares his shoulders, clearly proud of his accomplishment. "When I first spotted him, I alerted the girls to the situation. Lemon, as usual, was nowhere to be found. I looked for you, too, but you'd totally ditched us."

"Sorry," I say. "Surprise troublemaking training session."

"I figured. Anyway, I told the girls what was up. We scattered for a bigger spy scope. Shepherd Bull snuck around for a little while, staying far enough away from the party that you wouldn't notice him unless you looked for him—but close enough that he could make a split-second attack if he wanted to. He carried that stick the whole time."

I look at the long, skinny stick leaning against one wall of the inner-tube shed. In the hands of anyone else it'd seem like an ordinary tree branch. But in the hands of Shepherd Bull, it was definitely a potential weapon.

"I saw him sneak in here," Abe says. "So I grabbed some towels from the stand by the lake and a stray tennis ball from the beach. Then Gabby, Elinor, and I burst in, locked the door, and tied him up."

"He must've put up some fight," I say.

"Not really—which was weird. He resisted at first, I guess because we caught him by surprise. But when he realized what we were doing, he pretty much let us do it. Except when we tried to take away the stick. He didn't like that."

Shepherd Bull grunts. I'm not sure if this is because he hears us talking about him and agrees that he wanted to hold on to his weapon, or if it's because his eyes, locked on Gabby's, are getting tired too.

"My guess is he's going easy on us so we'll lower our defenses," Abe says. "And the instant he thinks we don't suspect he'll attack—he will. That's why Gabby has him locked in her death stare."

"Good idea," I say. "But you didn't think you should keep watching him instead of tying him up? Like Annika told us to?"

"The situation seemed too risky to just let him and his friends do whatever they came to do."

I scan the shed. Besides us and about a thousand inner tubes arranged in tall stacks, it's empty.

"Where are his friends?" I ask.

"Don't know. No one's come to claim him. And the party's still raging out there."

I follow his nod to a small window. It offers a clear view of the beach, where our classmates are still eating and dancing like they haven't a care in the world. Our teachers are missing, as are our parents.

"I have a theory."

I turn back. Abe's standing so close I can see the small pimple just under his nose.

"About why he didn't resist," he whispers. "Once he realized what we were doing. *And* saw who we were. Want to hear?"

"Not really," I say, since I'm pretty sure this theory has something to do with Elinor's traitor ways. "But I *would* like to know what you think we should do with him. Now that we have him."

Abe eyes his catch. "I think we turn him over to Annika. She might give us a million demerits each for capturing such an important target." He glances at me. "You probably won't get any. Since you didn't help. Sorry."

He doesn't sound apologetic, but it doesn't matter. I don't care about demerits. I do, however, care about pleasing Annika. That's still the best way to keep her from suspecting I don't belong at Kilter—and never did. And staying here, at Kamp Kilter, is still the best way to find out what's wrong with my parents.

Which is why I say, "No." Then I walk away from him and toward our captive. "It's okay, Gabby. You can blink."

"But now we're *inside* Sassy Threads." Gabby's eyes are as wide as Frisbees. "And there's a gorgeous bag with glittery pockets! And—"

"Oops!" Elinor pats Gabby's shoulder. "The mall's closing. We have to go."

Gabby's face falls. "Really? Already? But what about—"

"Wow. Is that my favorite song?" Abe's apparently referring to the muffled music filtering into the shed from the party. "If only I had someone to dance with."

Gabby blinks. Then jumps up from the inner tube she's been sitting on and bounds over to Abe.

I look at Elinor. "Thanks for that."

"No problem."

"You okay?"

She nods. "You?"

I nod.

"Do you have a plan?" she asks quietly, her eyes flicking toward Shepherd Bull.

I don't. Not a well thought-out one, anyway. But I tell Elinor I do. She gives my arm a light squeeze, then retreats to the front of the shed, where Gabby's trying to twirl around Abe, who seems to no longer hear his favorite song as he watches me.

He's just a kid, I tell myself as I slowly lower onto the edge of an inner tube. *A really tall, really big kid . . . but a kid all the same. Just talk to him the way you'd talk to anyone your own age.*

"Hey!" The word sounds like a firecracker in a metal bucket. I take it down a notch. "I mean . . . hey."

Shepherd Bull's eyes are partially hidden by the greasy, stringy hair hanging down his forehead. I know he's looking at me, but

I don't know how. Is he mad? Sad? Bored? He's definitely not feeling chatty, because he doesn't say anything.

Of course, that might be because he can't.

I glance behind me. "Abe? Would you mind . . . ?"

My alliance-mate wriggles away from Gabby, jogs toward me, and slips behind Shepherd Bull. He raises one hand, eyes his target, and makes a face. Then he stoops down, grabs an extra beach towel from the floor, and wraps it around his hand. He gives the back of Shepherd Bull's head a swift smack. Shepherd Bull's head juts forward. The tennis ball pops out of his mouth and bounces across the floor. Abe drops the dirty towel and returns to the front of the shed.

"How's it going?" I ask Shepherd Bull.

Nothing.

"How are the towels? Too tight?"

Nothing.

"Are you thirsty? Can we get you a glass of water?"

Nothing.

I might as well get to the point.

"What are you doing here?"

Behind his shaggy hair, Shepherd Bull's eyes narrow.

I swallow, try again. "What do you want?"

His fat, chapped lips turn down.

"Did you come after us because we came to IncrimiNation? And left with Elinor?"

His fingers curl toward his palms.

"Just talk to me," I say, trying to keep my cool. "Maybe we can reach some kind of understanding."

His fists begin to shake.

"Ogres don't understand English," Abe calls out. "Try grunting."

"He understands English," Gabby says. "When we were at their school we heard him—" She gasps. "Elinor, look! Are those s'mores?"

Abe groans. "Gabby, can you focus? For once? Please? Who cares what our classmates are doing out—"

"Abe," I say, shushing him. "Hang on."

Shepherd Bull cares what our classmates are doing. At least it looks like he does. After being motionless for minutes on end, he suddenly flings back his head, clearing the greasy hair from his eyes. His ankles and wrists push and pull against the restraints. A weird sound comes from his mouth. It's not a word—not one

I've heard before, anyway. It's not a grunt either. It's more like a whine. Or a growl. Or a whine-growl.

"Is he going to explode?" Abe asks.

"He might," I say as our captive begins bouncing up and down on his stack of inner tubes.

"Mmm . . . lll . . . oooooo," Shepherd Bull whine-growls, bouncing faster. "Mmm . . . lll . . . OOOOO!"

"M-L-O?" Gabby asks. "Is that some kind of code?"

"Mellow?" Elinor guesses. "Is that what he wants to be—and we're getting in his way?"

"Milo?" Abe tries. "Is he yelling for one of his friends to come rescue him?"

"MMM . . . LLL . . . OOOOO! MMM . . . LLL . . . OOOOOOO!"

Afraid he's about to charge, I look around for the tennis ball and debate popping it back into his mouth. As I do, I notice that Shepherd Bull's looking around too. But not for the tennis ball.

For his stick. When he sees it leaning on the wall by the door, he bounces so hard and so high, the top inner tube he's been sitting on bursts.

"Wow," Gabby says, noticing him notice the weapon. "That'd be a great tool for roasting—"

She stops, looks at Shepherd Bull. Abe, Elinor, and I look at him too.

"Marshmallow?" I ask in the brief silence between whine-growls.

Shepherd Bull's bouncing slows. His eyes and lips turn down. Looking like he might cry, he nods.

"I'm on it." Abe flings open the door and disappears outside. Seconds later, he bursts back inside and tosses me a bag. "That's the biggest one I could find."

I turn toward Shepherd Bull, holding up the plastic bag of marshmallows. He studies it for a long moment, then turns his head to one side.

"The stick," Gabby says. "Everyone knows marshmallows taste better when you eat them off a stick!"

The three of them work together. Elinor holds the bag while Abe slides marshmallows onto one end of the stick and Gabby slides marshmallows onto the other end. When the tool's entire length is covered in white blobs, Abe hands it to me. I hold it toward Shepherd Bull.

His head still turned to the right, his eyes shift left. One brow arches, and I think he's going to take the bait. But then it lowers and his eyes shift right again.

"Fire," Elinor says.

"Always handy," Abe says, "but unfortunately, Lemon's decided to skip this little alliance meeting too. And now's not the time to—"

"Not to threaten him with." Elinor grabs the stick. "To roast the marshmallows with!"

She disappears outside. Gabby dashes after her.

Abe catches my eye. I know he's asking without asking how Elinor just happened to know that Shepherd Bull may or may not prefer his marshmallows hot and gooey. But we *all* should've known that. I can't name one kid who prefers marshmallows any other way.

While they're gone, I sneak glances at our captive. This close up, he doesn't look quite as gigantic as every other time I've seen him.

"Here!" Elinor bursts back into the shed. She holds the sugar stick like a torch, which it kind of is because bright orange flames still flicker around the top marshmallow.

"And here!" Gabby hurries after Elinor, her arms full. "Chocolate and graham crackers. Just in case our prisoner's in the mood for a s'more. Or in case any of his wardens are!"

Elinor gives me the spear. Gabby dumps the other s'more ingredients at my feet. They both join Abe at the front of the cabin, several feet behind me.

"Is *this* what you want?" I ask.

Shepherd Bull's eye shift left. Both brows lift. His chin drops. His head swivels so fast I think it might snap off his tree trunk of a neck. His wrists still bound together, his two fists become one. He swings the mammoth knot of flesh and bone like it's an iron bowling ball. When it nears the stick, his fingers fly forward like darts.

I yank back the stick. Shepherd Bull lurches forward and nearly topples off the two intact inner tubes he's still sitting on.

"Not so fast," I say. "You must like marshmallows a lot . . . right?"

He nods. Fast.

"Good." I angle the stick toward him until the top end is six inches away from his mouth. "You may take one—and only one."

"Gross," Gabby whispers behind me. "Is he drooling?"

He is. And I'm glad. If he loves marshmallows that much, then we just might have a chance.

As Shepherd Bull shimmies forward on the tubes, his eyes glow in the light of the flickering flames. He takes a deep breath and extinguishes the fire in one blow. He blows again, more gently this time, then tests the marshmallow's temperature with the tip of his tongue. Apparently satisfied, he opens his mouth and guides his top and bottom teeth over and under the marshmallow. Then he chomps down and slides the marshmallow off the stick at the same time.

I yank back the stick. "Next question. You understand English, right?"

He pauses. Nods. I angle the stick so he can take another marshmallow, then pull it back once he has.

"You *speak* English, right?" I ask.

He pauses. Nods. Stares at the next marshmallow.

"Sorry," I say. "That question deserves a better answer."

He sighs, like I'm totally putting him out.

"Gabby," I call over my shoulder. "Would you like a delicious—"

"Okay!"

I turn back.

"Okay," our captive says again, his gruff voice softer. "Of course I understand and speak English. I'm just not supposed to around people who might use what I say against me."

"What's your name?" I ask.

"Shepherd Bull."

"Where are you from?"

"Currently? Black Hole, Arizona. Originally? Miami, Florida."

"How old are you?"

"Thirteen."

Gabby snorts. "Right."

"Why would I lie?" Shepherd Bull asks. "Do you think I like being twice as big as most kids my age?"

"Um, yes," Gabby says.

"Maybe not," I say. I don't like being half as big as most kids my age, so maybe our captive feels the same way about his abnormal size. "Where do you go to school?"

"You know where."

"Remind me," I say.

He rolls his eyes. "IncrimiNation."

"What are you doing here?"

"What were you doing at IncrimiNation?"

"You know what. Getting Elinor. Which we did."

"Well maybe we're here to get her back."

"I don't believe you."

"I don't care."

"Gabby?" I call back. "Our guest doesn't seem to be hungry anymore. How'd you like *all* of these scrumptious—"

"Okay!" Shepherd Bull bursts. "We're here for information."

"About what?" I ask, then give him another marshmallow.

"You guys," he says. "Where you go. What you do. How you do it."

"You mean how we make trouble?" I ask, letting him take another reward.

He nods and chews. The white blob sticks to his teeth and lips.

"Why?" I ask.

"Don't know and didn't ask. I just follow Nadia's orders."

My chest tightens. But if Elinor has any kind of reaction to hearing her mother's name, she keeps it to herself. The group behind me remains silent.

Shepherd Bull continues. "She said we had to come here and investigate. So I gathered the group, and here we are. Nice digs, by the way. A little clean for my taste, but I can see why a certain type would like them."

"A certain type?" I ask.

"People who color in the lines. Think inside the box. Follow the rules."

"We don't—"

I hold up one hand, quieting Abe.

"You follow rules," I point out. "You just said so. Nadia told you to come here, and you did."

"She's the only adult I listen to. Because I don't really think of her as an adult. She's too cool. Plus, after what you guys did, I couldn't pass up the chance to check you out. Mess with you a little."

"By making us see stars?" Gabby asks.

"And turning our hands blue?" Abe asks.

"And attacking us with ping-pong balls?" I ask.

Shepherd Bull's eyes narrow more with each question and statement. But when we're done, he doesn't speak. I let him take another marshmallow.

"I don't know what you're talking about," he says when he's done eating.

I study his face. His expression's blank. His eyes don't twinkle. His lips don't tremble, like he's trying not to smile. He certainly doesn't look like he's trying to hide something. Of course, not looking like he's hiding something when he really is could be part of his Incriminator training. It sounds like a skill the Kilter Dramatists might have.

Deciding I need more time to read him, I recount the events that led my friends, other Troublemakers, and I to the camp infirmary the other day. Every now and then he looks genuinely surprised. A few times, maybe even impressed. But not once does he look proud or like he's about to laugh, the way he should if he and his classmates were behind the attacks.

"Wow," he says when I'm done. "Someone really has it out for you guys. But it's not me. Or any other Incriminator."

"That's not how it looked in the Performance Pavilion a few nights ago," I say.

"You saw that?" Shepherd Bull shrugs. "IncrimiNation kids don't listen very well. That was the third time I told them who we were looking for. We were wasting time, so I turned the lesson into a big thing to get them to pay more attention. It looked worse than anything we actually planned to do."

I try to process this. "So you're saying that you really came here just to gather intel about us—and not to get back at us for breaking into IncrimiNation and kidnapping Elinor?"

He looks at me. I angle the stick toward him. He takes two marshmallows.

"Yup," he says around the white mush. "Elinor's barely a blip on our radar. We have bigger fish to fry."

"Like what kind?" I ask.

"No idea. Nadia hasn't shared specifics."

"But if we're not the fish, and if you didn't want to hurt us . . . what'd you mean when you said you thought it'd be fun to mess with us?"

"Just that if we snuck around enough and let you catch us spying every once in a while, you'd get nervous. Start to freak out. Get sloppy. Show your weaknesses." His eyes meet mine. "As Annika's star you must know that knowing someone's weakness is way more important than knowing his strength."

"I'm not—" I stop myself. He's just trying to take the upper hand by putting me on the defensive. I won't fall for it.

"Still don't believe me?" Shepherd Bull asks. "Just ask Nadia. She told us that, no matter what, we couldn't attack you guys in any way. We could follow and watch you, but that was it. She said we'd mess up the mission if we did anything else."

"And if you didn't listen?" I ask. "And hurled a million ping-pong balls at one of us just because you felt like it?"

His expression turns serious. "Then we'd be kicked out of IncrimiNation. Forever."

Shepherd Bull says this like it's the very worst punishment an Incriminator could receive—and would try to avoid at any cost. And maybe I'm being naive, but I believe him. Enough that I let him take all of the remaining marshmallows from the stick.

As he gobbles and swallows, I turn toward my friends.

"You know what this means," I say.

Abe nods grimly. So does Gabby. And Elinor. We're all thinking the same thing, but it's so hard to believe I say it out loud anyway.

"If the Incriminators aren't after us . . . that means our parents are."

Chapter 23

DEMERITS: 2475
GOLD STARS: 1550

TO: parsippany@wahoo.com
FROM: shinkle@kilteracademy.org
SUBJECT: Bartholomew John

Dear Miss Parsippany,

Thanks for your last note! That was weird about your e-mail address, but I'm glad you figured out what happened and got a new one.

And thanks for everything you said about

honesty and editing the truth. It made a lot of sense. Just so you know, I DID cringe when you said your mom looked like a piñata in her party dress . . . but I DON'T think you're a terrible person. You were just trying to protect her feelings. How's that a bad thing?

Along those lines, I haven't come clean to Annika about what I did or didn't do. There's been a lot going on here so I haven't really had a chance to think about whether I should mention anything. And like you said, sometimes a harmless edited version of the truth is better for everyone. So for now, I'm sticking with that.

By the way, how's your new job? And what is it again?

Oh, and I did hear something about Bartholomew John. I don't have all the details, but my source said she saw him bullying kids on the playground back home. Supposedly there was shoving. And crying. At least one little boy ran to his mom and bawled like a baby. I guess some things—and people—never change, huh?

Well, I should get going! I hope you're having fun wherever you are. Write again when you can!

Sincerely,

Seamus

I'm about to press send without rereading my e-mail, but then think better of it and take another look. Because do I really want to say that about Bartholomew John? It's not a total lie. I did hear (or read) something about him, and my source (Mom) did talk about him bullying a little boy (me). Yes, Miss Parsippany asked for recent Bartholomew John news, and this incident happened a long time ago. But it's still news to her, since she hasn't heard it before. And maybe it'll make her say why she's so curious about him. After all, she hasn't asked about any of the other Cloudview kids she taught . . . so why's he so special?

I press send. Then I start a new message.

TO: loliver@kilteracademy.org
FROM: shinkle@kilteracademy.org
SUBJECT: Emergency Alliance Meeting

Hey, Lemon!

How are you?? Haven't seen you much lately. I won't ask again if everything's okay, because you promised it was . . . but I hope it still is!

Also, I wanted to make sure you knew about our alliance meeting tonight. In case you didn't get the other e-mails I sent or the regular notes I left in your room.

A lot's happened the past few days. There's much to talk about and plan. That's why we'll meet here, at our underground house, at six tonight. Which is in half an hour. I really, REALLY hope you can make it! Capital T is more like Lower-Case T when one of its members is missing. And speaking of missing, I miss my best friend!

Hope to see you soon!

—Seamus

I hit send and start another note.

TO: annika@kilteracademy.org
CC: loliver@kilteracademy.org, ahansen@kilteracademy.org, gryan@kilteracademy.org, enorris@kilteracademy.org
FROM: shinkle@kilteracademy.org
SUBJECT: Update

Hi, Annika!

I just wanted to write and thank you for asking our teachers to look for our parents at the Beach Bash the other night. Their search turned up empty, unfortunately, and not one mom or dad made it to the party, but it was nice of them to try. Those adults sure can be sneaky, can't they? And I'm an only child, but I guess brothers and sisters can be too. We stayed at the party until the bonfire finally went out around midnight, and we didn't see one sibling the entire time.

I also wanted to tell you that there have been some major developments on the Incriminator front. They relate to major developments on the parent front. It's a lot for one e-mail, so maybe we can meet and review everything sometime this week?

Sincerely,

Seamus

I send the message. My K-Pak buzzes. Hoping the new note's from Lemon but figuring it's from Annika, I open it. And I'm surprised to see it's from Miss Parsippany. It usually takes her a few days to get back to me, and it's taken even longer lately.

I'm even more surprised when I see what she wrote.

TO: shinkle@kilteracademy.org
FROM: parsippany@wahoo.com
SUBJECT: RE: Bartholomew John

S—

THANX 4 UPDATE. CAN'T BELIEVE ABOUT BJ. I GUESS LEOPARD + SPOTS = NO CHANGE. WHAT DAY DID THIS HAPPEN? HOW MANY KIDS DID HE MESS WITH? HOW MANY CRIED?

I KNOW U SAID U DIDN'T HAVE ALL DETAILS BUT ANY WOULD BE GR8.

SORRY SO SHORT. ABOUT TO JUMP OUT OF HELICOPTER. HARD TO TYPE. BUT WANTED TO GET BACK TO U RIGHT AWAY.

—MP

Wow. Miss Parsippany *really* wanted to know about Bartholomew John.

My K-Pak buzzes again. I open the new message.

TO: shinkle@kilteracademy.org
FROM: annika@kilteracademy.org
SUBJECT: Role Reverse

Seamus,

Thanks for the update. We'll meet soon. On another note, I've been trying to schedule your Role Reverse session with your parents, but they've been hard to track down, and they're not answering e-mails. Perhaps you can mention the session when next you see them and explain its importance as I have to other parents?

Thanks!

—Annika

"Seamus? Can I come in?"

I toss aside the K-Pak. Jump up from the bed. Wish I'd put on a clean shirt after today's dusting duty as I open the door and smile at Elinor.

"Hi," I say.

"Hi." She smiles too.

"How was your day?"

"Nice. I mean, as nice as scrubbing bathroom tiles with a toothbrush can be, anyway. How was dusting?"

"Not bad. And informative. I thought dust only collected on flat surfaces. Turns out it gets on *every* surface. Including on your nose. And *in* your nose. I've never sneezed so much in my life."

"Did your dad split the second he opened the door?"

"Actually, no. He was there as long as I was. And he followed me around the house. Whenever I changed rooms, so did he. He gave me a few-second head start and then commented on the shifting sun each time he sat down with the book he was pretending to read, like he would've kept moving even if I wasn't there . . . but I knew what he was doing."

"Watching you?"

"Exactly."

"Did he try anything?"

"Not that I noticed."

"That's odd," she says. "How about your mom? Was she home too?"

I shake my head. "Were Abe's parents at his house?"

"At first. But then he asked them so many questions—where they've been, what they've been doing—that they seemed to get uncomfortable. He tried to sound natural, but it was obvious he was digging for information. So they left."

"Smooth," I say. "If one of us had done that—"

"He'd never let us forget it."

We exchange small smiles. When she doesn't say anything else, I try to come up with a new topic. This is hard. Because in the conversation break my brain fixates on the fact that the prettiest girl ever is standing in my room, and I can't think of anything else.

Fortunately, Elinor ends the silence before it gets too awkward.

"So you know today's troublemaking assignment?" she asks. "From Houdini?"

"To swipe something from our parents without leaving their field of vision? Yes. That was tricky."

"I bet. I couldn't find out myself because my parents aren't here. But I still wanted to participate, so at the end of the day I stopped by the arts and crafts cabin." Elinor reaches into her shorts pocket and pulls out two long skinny ropes. "There's a ton of thread in there. Spools and spools of every color in the rainbow, plus about a hundred others. But I only wanted two. Green, which is my favorite color. And blue, which is . . ."

"My favorite color."

She holds one of the ropes toward me. "It's a friendship bracelet. One half's blue, the other half's green. They're braided together. Kind of the way good friends are."

"You made this?" I ask, taking the bracelet. "For me?"

"And for me," she says. "So we each have one."

"That we can wear, like, all the time?"

"If we want . . . ?" She says this like there's a chance I *wouldn't* want to.

"Elinor, that's . . . so nice. Really. Thank you. I can't wait to put it on."

"No need to wait," she says, then helps tie the bracelet around my wrist.

When she's done, I tie her bracelet around her wrist. Then she holds her arm between us, and I hold mine next to hers. We stand like that for a second, comparing bracelets. Then she gives me a shy smile, lowers her arm, and steps back.

"So did you get a chance to swipe something from your dad?" she asks. "Or was he too close to make a move?"

I pause. Then I look at my wrist once more and take my K-Pak from the bed.

"It wasn't easy," I say, "but I did. I was cleaning my parents' dresser while Dad sat in an armchair on the other side of the room. I shook the feather duster really hard, like I was cleaning it off, and then I pretended to sneeze—in Dad's direction—so that the flying dust flew all the way over to him. When he really sneezed, I used my K-Pak camera to take a quick picture. Of this."

I hold the K-Pak toward her. She leans forward for a closer look at the screen.

"It looks like a diary entry," she says.

"It is a diary entry. My mom wrote it a year and a half ago. She's been keeping a journal forever, but I just found out about it last week. I didn't want to take the whole book today—and I already felt a little guilty for reading other entries—so I just snuck one shot."

"Impressive. What does it say?"

"You can read it if you want."

Elinor does. Out loud.

"'Well, it happened again. For the umpteenth time in twelve years, my beloved Seamus has proven his weakness.'" Elinor glances up at me. "Ouch."

"It gets better," I say.

"'The unfortunate incident occurred in the school cafeteria, where Seamus sprinted from his social studies class in order to be first in line for fish sticks. Apparently today was the very first day the cafeteria was offering this lunch special. And apparently my son has been looking forward to this day for months.'"

"It's true," I say.

"'Sadly for him, he wasn't first in line. Bartholomew John, that strapping, confident young man—his mother must be so proud!—beat him to the fried fish. As this was the very first day for fish sticks, the cafeteria staff didn't know how much to make. And they underestimated, because Bartholomew John cleared out their entire prepared supply. I don't know why the lunch ladies didn't limit his serving so others could have some, but I'm guessing Bartholomew John made a very convincing argument.'" Elinor looks up. "Your mom really likes this kid."

"You're telling me," I say.

Elinor continues. "'Anyway, what did my son do? When he found out he wouldn't be having fish sticks after all? I can tell you what he *didn't* do. He didn't tell Bartholomew John to stop hogging them, or snatch some from his tray. He did what he always does. He walked away. He didn't stand up for himself.'" Elinor looks up. "How'd your mom find out what you did?"

I nod to the K-Pak. She keeps reading.

"'When Seamus shared this story at dinner tonight, and his voice actually cracked at the idea of missing out on frozen fish, I wanted to tell him to toughen up, to be the kind of boy other kids respected. But I didn't. There was no point.'" Elinor gives me a sympathetic frown. Continues. "'Which means the time has come. If he can't fix his flaws, then I will.'" Elinor pouts, hands me the K-Pak. "She sounds like my mom."

She does. Of course, she's never tossed me into a pit of snakes and left me there to fend for myself, but maybe that's just because Scales, Slithers, and Sliders, Cloudview's one-stop-shop for all things reptilian, doesn't have enough snakes to fill a sink let alone a swimming pool.

I'd like to talk more about my mom with Elinor. But the mention of her mom reminds of something else I've been meaning to bring up.

"Not to totally change the subject," I say, "but you must be wondering why Abe's been insisting that you help him in his parents' cabin."

She shrugs. "He's Abe. Most of what he does doesn't make sense."

"Right. Only he did have a reason. And I think it's only fair that you know what it is."

"Okay?"

I take a second to think about how to say this. But beating around the bush will probably only raise more questions—and make her even more uncomfortable—than simply stating the truth would.

"He thinks you're working for the Incriminators." The words tumble from my mouth like ice cubes from a glass.

Her face stills. "What do you mean, working for them?"

"Helping them. Feeding them information. By pretending to be one of us." I wait for her to respond. When she doesn't, I add, "He didn't trust me to keep an eye on you. Because of how I—I mean, because he doubts pretty much everything I do. That's why he wanted you with him. So he could watch you himself."

"I don't understand," Elinor says. "After all this time and everything we've been through . . . why would he think I'd do something like that?"

"I'm not sure . . . maybe to make your mom happy?"

She looks at me, her copper eyes worried. "Do *you* think that?"

"Seamus!" Down the hall, the elevator door whooshes open. Fast footsteps pound toward us. "Where are you? We have a lot to discuss! Let's do it!"

"Speak of the devil," I say. "Sorry. We have that emergency alliance meeting."

She looks down. Nods.

"Which you're coming to, right?"

"I'm not in the alliance." She says this so softly, I'm not sure she says it at all.

"Hustle, Hinkle!" Abe shouts.

I take a step toward Elinor. She takes a step away from me. Then she lowers her right hand to her left wrist, covering her bracelet, and hurries from the room.

I should go after her. Apologize. Insist that Abe's completely out of his mind. Reassure her that I'd never think she was capable of doing anything like what he's suggested she is.

But before I can do any of those things, Abe dashes into my room, grabs my arm, and pulls me down the hall.

"Good news!" he says. "Look who decided to show up."

I stop short in the kitchen doorway. "Lemon?"

My elusive best friend is poking around the refrigerator. Now he looks over his shoulder and grins. "Seamus! Hey!"

"And there's more," Abe says. "Lemon, why don't you tell Hinkle what you just told us?"

Lemon grabs a pear from the fridge, stands up straight, and swings the door shut. "No biggie. Abraham just said your parents keep disappearing on you. And I just said I know where they've been going."

My heart skips. "You do? Where?"

"Meetings."

"What kind of meetings?" I ask.

"Secret ones, by the looks of it."

"For?" I prompt.

He takes a bite of pear. Chomps. Swallows. Gives a partial answer. Takes another bite. Chomps. Swallows. Gives a partial answer. Repeats the routine a third time. Until, eventually, his answer's complete.

"The Secret . . . Society . . . of Masterful . . . Angel Makers."

Chapter 24

DEMERITS: 2475
GOLD STARS: 1550

"We're going to die out here."

"No, we're not."

"Yes, we are. It's pitch black. And freezing. And we're walking in circles through an endless forest. It's just like that time we climbed that mountain for history class and Mystery abandoned us at the top and told us to find our way back by ourselves!"

"Gabby," Abe says. "This is nothing like that. Lemon knows exactly where he's going . . . don't you, Lemon?"

Personally, I don't think Gabby's far off. We do seem to

be walking in circles through an endless forest. According to my K-Pak clock we left our underground house an hour ago. Powered by adrenaline, we crossed the lake in our leaky boat in record time and sprinted across our parents' beach like the sand was pavement. But we haven't seen a single light or any other sign of life since ducking into the woods behind the Kamp Kilter beach.

"Almost there!" Lemon calls back.

We're hiking in a line. I glance behind me. It's so dark I can barely see Elinor.

"Doing okay?" I ask.

"Fine," she says.

"Warm enough?"

"Yup."

"Bet you didn't think you'd be doing this today when you woke up this morning, huh? I know I didn't. Nope, when I opened my eyes, there was no way I thought I'd—"

"Seamus?"

"Yeah?"

"I don't really feel like talking. If that's okay."

I frown. "Sure. No problem."

Why *would* she feel like talking? During our alliance meeting, when Lemon said he knew where our parents were, and that they were meeting tonight, we all agreed we needed to see what they were up to—and I said Elinor had to come with us. Abe looked like he was going to refuse, so I asked him a question. That was: Wouldn't he rather know exactly where she is? So he doesn't have to wonder what she's up to when he's not around?

His answer: "Now you're thinking like a Troublemaker, Hinkle."

Elinor didn't hear this conversation. At least I hope she didn't. She's been pretty quiet ever since Gabby pulled her from her room and filled her in, but maybe she's just tired. I know I'd be if I'd spent the day scrubbing floors with a toothbrush.

Or maybe she doesn't feel like talking because she's still hurt from what I told her about Abe and his suspicions. This is probably the likelier reason. I don't want to think about this, though, because it makes me feel terrible. Either way, I promise myself that I'll do everything I can to make her feel better as soon as we're back home.

"Here we are!" Lemon exclaims.

He stops short. Abe runs into him. Gabby runs into Abe. I

run into Gabby. Elinor must have excellent reflexes, because she doesn't run into anyone.

"Where?" Abe asks.

"At the Angel Makers' secret meeting spot," Lemon says.

"Um, no offense," Gabby says, "but we're standing by a rock. A really *big* rock . . . but still. A rock."

"Lemon," Abe says, "if you wasted our time by dragging us all to the middle of nowhere in the middle of the—"

"Aha!" Lemon's been stooped down and rummaging around. Now he straightens and raises one fist. "Found it."

"What?" Gabby asks.

"The spare key."

"Right," Abe scoffs. "Because a secret organization would really leave a key to its top secret meeting place for anyone to just come along and find."

"Of course not." Lemon faces the tall granite wall. "That'd be silly. They bury it. In a different place near the door every night."

"Hon," Gabby says, "I hate to break it to you, but there's no door here. There's only—"

A tunnel. With walls lined by lit torches. Which appears after

Lemon sticks the key into an invisible lock, turns it, and a large chunk of rock slides out and to the left.

"A secret *passage*!" Gabby bursts. "I've always wanted to find one of these! Thanks, Lemon!"

She gives him a quick hug, then darts down the tunnel, taking one of the torches with her. Abe follows her. Lemon follows him. I turn around to ask Elinor if she's okay with this, but she ducks past me and hurries after the others before I can.

Once we're all inside, Lemon presses a button by the opening, and the rock chunk slides back into place.

"Impressive," Abe says as the door's outline disappears. "Unless you knew it was there, you'd never know it was there."

"That's the point," Lemon says cheerfully. "This way!"

We start down the tunnel. Lemon's a confident leader. He walks tall and fast without looking around, like he's traveled this hall many times before. This makes me quicken my pace until I'm hurrying next to him.

"This is amazing," I say. "How'd you even find it?"

He glances behind him, then leans toward me. "Finn."

"Your little brother? What does he have to do with the Angel Makers?"

"Nothing. Except that he's too little to be left alone, so when my parents come here, they bring him with them. Most of the parents do that with their other kids. That's why Kamp Kilter looks like a ghost town so much of the time."

"And Finn told you about this?"

He nods. "I didn't want to come back to Kilter. Not so soon, anyway. I wanted to stay home and spend time with my family. With Finn especially." He slows slightly, looks at me. "Can I tell you a secret?"

"Always," I say.

His eyes darken, his lips turn down. When he speaks, his voice is so soft I have to strain to hear. "One day, many months ago, I was playing with a new lighter and a can of my mom's hair-spray. Together they create the effect of a fire-breathing dragon. That's usually fun."

"Sure."

"Well, it wasn't fun that day. Because when I was done, I accidentally left the lighter on the bathroom counter. The lighter was shaped like a robot, so when Finn went into the bathroom after I left, he picked it right up, not knowing what it really was. And . . . he got hurt. He must've flipped the switch, and the flame got him. Just barely—he dropped the robot as soon as it turned on—but enough that he got a tiny red mark on his thumb. My parents flipped, as they should've. And even though he was totally fine and didn't shed a single tear, it was the last straw."

"That's why your parents sent you to Kilter?" I ask.

"Yes. They knew it was an accident, but they couldn't risk another one. I don't blame them." Lemon shudders, stands up straighter. "So, anyway, when I got Annika's invite and my parents said it sounded like fun, I even tried to talk them out of coming. But they said they thought it'd be a great bonding opportunity for us. And if we stayed home, they would've gone to work the way they always do. But they were willing to take off for Kamp Kilter, so I agreed. Because I thought we'd have even more time to spend together. But then when we got here and were split up right away . . ." He shakes his head. "That wasn't what I signed up for."

"So you started following your little brother?"

"Every chance I got. He was easy to find the first few days, but then they all seemed to spend more and more time away from camp. That's why I bought the Turbo Talkies. I kept one and gave him the other so we could talk no matter where he was. When he started talking about my family's long walks in the woods and his special playtime, I started trailing them. They never take the same route—probably to throw off people like me—but they always end up here."

"Do they meet every day?"

"Sometimes more than once."

As we round a corner and start down another hallway, I try to process this information. On one hand, I'm relieved he's finally opening up. This explanation is what I've been hoping for. But on the other hand, something doesn't make sense.

"Lemon . . . why didn't you say anything? I was getting pretty worried. Since you were gone all the time. If I'd known you were just trying to spend time with your little brother, I would've—"

"What?" he asks. "Encouraged me to go? Told me to have fun?"

"Well—"

"No," Lemon says. "You would've said you understood me wanting to be with my brother, but that I still needed to jump when Annika said to. And do my assignments. And practice with my tutor. And keep our teachers happy."

"You don't know that," I say, even though I probably

would've said something very similar to this. In a much nicer way. But only because I wouldn't want him to be kicked out for underperforming.

"Sure I do," he says. "And if you didn't, Abe would've."

I don't say anything. Because he's right about that.

We round another corner and start down another tunnel. This one's narrower and darker than the others. Lemon walks faster. So do I. When we've put a few more feet between us and Abe, Gabby, and Elinor, I ask another puzzling question.

"If you didn't want to tell me before, why are you telling me now?"

"You're my best friend. I knew you were worried, and I felt bad. You didn't do anything wrong, so I wanted to clear the air. This seemed like a good time to share."

"Thanks," I say. "I'm really glad you did."

"You're welcome. But if you could keep it between us, I'd appreciate it."

"You got it. Can I ask you one other thing, though?"

"Shoot."

"If you wanted your privacy—which I completely understand—why'd you offer to bring us here?"

"Pre-emptive strike. Abe was bound to start making my life difficult very soon. So I thought I'd buy some time and throw him a bone."

"Smart. Abe would approve."

"What's that?" Abe calls out from behind us. "Did I just hear my name? You better not be—"

He stops. Because Lemon stops. The rest of us do the same. Our secret-passage leader motions for us to come closer. We do.

"We're about to pass the daycare rooms," he says. "The kids get to stay up later on meeting nights. They should be too busy to notice us, but move fast and duck past the doors just in case. And don't talk. Got it?"

We exchange looks. Nod. Lemon brings one finger to his lips, then creeps around another corner. We creep too.

"It's so quiet in here," Gabby whispers right away. "Are you sure—"

She's cut off. By Abe's hand over her mouth.

As we make our way down this tunnel, I see that Lemon was right. The kids, who must be the brothers and sisters of other Troublemakers, are definitely too busy to notice us. We pass by a series of rooms—or small caves. In one, a few kids color at a table. In another, they nap on blankets laid out on the ground. In another, they read books around a large TV, which is off. In another, they seem to practice cleaning dishes, making beds, taking out the trash, and other chores on various household props.

Halfway down the tunnel, Gabby stops. She faces one cave, eyes wide and chin near the ground. When we gather behind her to see what's so shocking, she points into the cave.

"My sister," she mouths.

Flora sits on a chair behind another chair holding a mannequin. The mannequin's dressed like an ordinary mom in pressed khakis, a red cardigan, and gleaming white sneakers. She has long brown-and-gray hair, which Flora's brushing. She shares the room with three other teenagers, and they do the same thing the same way with their mannequins.

Gabby steps forward. Abe grabs her hand and pulls her back.

"This way," Lemon mouths. And we move on.

We turn down another tunnel. And another. And another. They grow even narrower, darker. The ceiling slants lower. Soon I wonder if the Angel Makers caught wind of a rat and relocated. I'm sure of it once we reach a dead end. And there are no more tunnels to turn down.

But then Lemon whispers, "Ready?"

We nod. He reaches one finger into a small crevice in the rock. There must be a button in there, because the wall begins to lift.

"Holy . . ."

"Cow," Gabby says, finishing Abe's stunned sentence.

It's an appropriate reaction. Because when the wall stops moving, we're standing in the mouth of another cave. Only this one's huge—and it doesn't have a ceiling. A million stars shimmer overhead. There's a turquoise waterfall. It falls into a natural turquoise pool. Dozens of large rocks rim the pool. Sitting on the rocks are dozens of Troublemaker parents. They're still. Silent. Transfixed.

The scene before us is hard to believe. But one thing isn't.

Perched on a tall rock in the center of it all . . . is Mystery.

Chapter 25

DEMERITS: 2475
GOLD STARS: 1550

What's he doing?" Gabby asks.

"Why does everyone look hypnotized?" Abe asks.

"I see my mom and dad," Lemon says. "I think I'll go say hi."

"Are you crazy?" Abe asks. "If Mystery sees you he'll shut this thing down in the blink of an eye."

"But—"

Lemon's cut off by an explosion. I can't tell what or where it is, but the force shakes the ground and makes us stumble and knock into one another.

"Wonderful! Spectacular! Amazing!"

When I'm steady enough to look away from my feet, I look toward Mystery's mini island. Wearing the same white shorts and T-shirt I saw him in earlier today, he punches the air with one fist. The repeated action is like an exclamation point after each word.

"Splendid! Awesome! Glorious! You! Are! The! Best!"

"Whoa," Abe says, "Is that . . . me?"

He's staring straight ahead. I can't see what he's talking about. This is because I'm short, but also because the parents sitting on rocks fifty feet away jump and cheer, blocking my view.

"Over there!" Gabby calls out over the noise. She points to a nearby boulder.

Crouching down, we dash over to the rock. I glance behind me once to make sure Elinor and Lemon are following. Given how they've both been acting, I wouldn't be surprised if they ditched the rest of us. But for better or worse the weird scene must be weird enough that they want to see more. They look sideways, toward Mystery and the explosion's source, but they keep running forward.

Reaching the boulder, we use grooves as handholds and footholds and scramble to the top.

"It *is* me!" Abe exclaims. "What on earth is my dad doing?"

"Totally messing with your masterpiece," Gabby says.

She's right. From this high up, we have a clear view of Mystery—and everything else. His island is a stone's throw away from a long, flat slab of rock. It seems to be some kind of stage, because that's where Mr. Hansen is standing behind Abe. Or someone Abe's shape and size wearing a mask of Abe's face. The Abe impersonator is standing at an easel, painting a very abstract picture of a cat. As we watch, Mystery raises one hand. The crowd quiets and sits down. Mr. Hansen reaches into a box at his feet. Takes out a balloon. And throws it at the Abe impersonator.

At least that's what it looks like. It's not until the balloon hits the easel, pops, and releases black paint, completely covering the painted cat, that I realize the artwork was really the intended target.

Fireworks boom overhead.

"Superb!" Mystery punches the air again. "Exactly! What! This kid! Needed!"

Impersonator Abe's shoulders slump. Mr. Hansen leans toward him and seems to say something.

The fireworks stop.

"What are you doing?" Mystery demands into a megaphone.

Mr. Hansen faces our history teacher. "Apologizing for ruining his picture?"

"Why?" Mystery asks.

"Because he's my son? Or is pretending to be my son? And I—"

"Who cares about his feelings?" Mystery demands.

Mr. Hansen steps back. "I do," he says meekly.

"Thanks, Dad," Abe whispers.

Mystery aims the megaphone toward the crowd. "You're all good parents! You love your kids and want nothing but the best for them! You feed them! Give them shelter! Wash their snotty, smelly clothes! Wipe their tears! Make their needs and wants *your* needs and wants, forever sacrificing the things that made you happy before they did!" Mystery pauses. His dark eyes shift around the cave-room. "But I ask you this. What have you gotten in return?"

The crowd's silent.

"Um, our adorable faces?" Abe says quietly.

"And beautiful singing voices?" Gabby says.

"And overall enjoyable company?" I say.

Mr. Hansen puts one fist on his hip, scratches his head.

"Are you kidding?" Abe asks. "He can't think of one nice thing he's gotten from being my dad?"

Mr. Hansen stops scratching his head. Snaps. "A paperweight."

"A paperweight," Mystery says.

"Yes," Mr. Hansen says.

"Did you *ask* for a paperweight?"

"No, but—"

"Did you *need* a paperweight?"

"No, but—"

"Does a paperweight compare in any way, shape, or form, to anything you've given him?"

"It's a different kind of—"

"Wrong answer!" Mystery shouts. "*No.* It does not!"

"But . . . but . . . he made it himself!" Mr. Hansen exclaims. "When he was five!"

Mystery lowers the megaphone. Lowers his head. Walks from one end of the rock island to the other and back again.

"Mr. Hansen," he says, still pacing. "Has your son made you other things recently?"

Now Mr. Hansen's head lowers. "Yes."

"Please tell us more."

Mr. Hansen sighs. Then he lifts his head, turns toward the crowd, and raises his voice. "Two years ago, Abe gave me a tie. That he supposedly sewed himself. I'm a lawyer and wear ties all the time in the courtroom, so I thought this was a wonderful gift. Unfortunately, it was no ordinary tie. It was somehow programmed so that whenever I said 'Your Honor,' which I can do countless times an hour in my line of work, the long part of the tie flew up, right into my face."

"Nice," Gabby says to Abe.

"Thanks." He grins.

"Do you believe your son knew what his gift was capable of?" Mystery asks Mr. Hansen.

"I do," Mr. Hansen says.

"And why is that?"

"Because I demonstrated it at home. Abe looked shocked. And apologized for the obvious malfunction." Mr. Hansen hangs his head. "But before he did either of those things . . . he laughed."

Mystery continues with the line of questioning. "Why do you think your son would do such a thing? And intentionally, repeatedly embarrass you?"

Mr. Hansen shrugs. "Because he could?"

Mystery snaps the megaphone to his mouth. "Because . . . he . . . *could*! And why could he?"

Mr. Hansen mumbles something.

"I can't hear you!" Mystery sings.

"Because I let him!" Mr. Hansen declares, like he's making a great confession.

"Exactly," Mystery says, his voice closer to normal. "Thank you, Mr. Hansen. You may take your seat."

Abe's dad lowers his head and returns to the crowd.

Mystery continues. "As Mr. Hansen has just reminded you all, your children aren't the kind, sweet, faultless creatures you think they are. Sure, they have their moments. Like when they hug you. And on the rare occasions that they thank you. And when their chubby cheeks and cute little dimples make you forget every bad thing they've said and done. But even these moments are selfish. Why do they hug and thank you? Usually because you've done something for them. When they're very young they might not realize the powers their chubby cheeks and cute little dimples possess—but they learn. And fast. By and large children are much smarter than they look. And it doesn't take long for them to figure out what they can do . . . and how."

As we watch, another man takes the stage.

"Now," Mystery says, "your babies didn't drop from the stork with hearts made of stone. The transformation happened gradually. Isn't that right . . . Mr. Hinkle?"

"Dad?" I say.

Just as he says, "Yes."

I feel the heat of eight eyes on my skin as my friends look at me and I look at the stage. I want to tell them not to worry. That I'm totally fine. Because until recently, Dad and I have gone together like peanut butter and jelly, Christmas and carols, addition and subtraction. Unlike Mom, he loves me exactly as I am—and always has. So there's no way he'll say anything now to suggest that he's disappointed in me.

But then I picture the weird closet filled with parent guides and fluffy wings . . . and I realize I have no idea what my dad is about to say.

"My son Seamus is the best!"

I smile.

"Until he wasn't."

And frown.

"A few months ago," Dad continues, "there was an altercation in the cafeteria of my son's former middle school. Seamus, being the well-behaved boy he is—or was—tried to break up the fight between several students by taking the apple he was about to eat and throwing it across the room. He intended to hit the instigator of the fight. Instead, he hit his substitute teacher, who fell to the floor."

Murmurs and gasps fill the cave-room.

Please don't . . . please don't . . . please don't . . .

The plea cycles through my head. Once upon a time I would've been scared that Dad would say I killed Miss Parsippany in front of all these people. Now I'm scared that he'll say she lived. At this point the last thing I need is for word of my innocence to spread back to Annika.

"This incident," Dad says as my heart pounds faster, "changed Seamus. In many ways he hasn't been the same since. And I have to say . . ."

His voice trails off. I try to swallow the knot in my throat but can't.

"I miss him."

The knot goes down. The breath that was stuck rushes from my mouth.

And then the relief I feel for his not telling the truth about the Unfortunate Apple Incident gives way to something else. Maybe regret? Guilt? Sadness? Because after he says he misses me, Dad looks unhappier than I've ever seen him.

"Anyhoo!" He shakes his head and claps his hands together once. "That's why we're all here, right? To get back our sons and daughters?"

"And back *at* them!" another parent shouts, making others chuckle.

"Now, now," Dad says. "Let's not—"

"Thank you for the touching tale, Mr. Hinkle," Mystery barks into the megaphone. "But I think we're all eager to see your demonstration."

"Right," Dad says. "Of course. My apologies."

"Harrison!" Mystery shouts.

Impersonator Abe yanks off Abe's facemask and replaces it with another. Before his real face is covered, I notice that he's young. Maybe twelve or thirteen, like my friends and me.

"Look at that, Hinkle," real Abe whispers. "You've grown, like, a whole foot!"

Because Harrison, who must be Mystery's assistant, is about

twelve inches taller than I am. And my two-dimensional face is now on top of his neck.

"The other tricks have been fun." Dad stoops down and picks up a long bag I didn't notice before. "Startling Seamus with ping-pong balls, confusing him by moving objects around with my gym socks and chewed gum, rearranging the interesting wall mural he made for us in our living room."

Us. For the first time since we got here, I think of Mom. She has to be here. I still can't believe Dad would've ever gotten involved in this—whatever this is—on his own. But scanning the audience, I don't see her.

"Who here enjoys a rousing game of miniature golf?" Dad asks the crowd.

Two-thirds of the gathered parents raise their hands. Gabby starts to raise hers, but Abe yanks it back down.

"So do I!" Dad exclaims. "Seamus does too. In fact, playing miniature golf is one of our very favorite father-son activities. That's why I'm especially excited about this trick. I think it'll be more effective than all the others combined."

The parents watch, mesmerized. Dad takes two mini-golf putters from the bag. One he gives to Harrison, the other he keeps for himself. He takes out a bucket of rainbow-colored golf balls and places it by his feet. Then he pulls out a plastic cooler, opens that, and lifts out a snow cone. Just like the one I ate on the drive home from our last miniature golf game.

Dad gives Harrison the snow cone. Harrison thanks him. This is super weird to see since Harrison's wearing my face.

What happens next seems to happen in fast-forward and slow motion at the same time. Harrison swings the putter back and forth and eats the snow cone, like the rock stage is a course at the Cloudview Putt-n-Play and he's waiting for his turn. Dad stands a few feet behind him. He swings his putter too, the way he does when practicing for his next hit. And then, one by one by one, with barely a second between each, he drops golf balls to the floor and hits them toward Harrison's feet.

Harrison drops the putter and snow cone. He jumps around as he tries to dodge the balls. But Dad's too fast. His aim's too good. And before long Harrison slips on a ball and joins the club and frozen dessert on the ground.

Dad raises his club overhead in victory. The crowd cheers. Mystery punches the air.

"Marvelous! Fantastic! A real! Sight! To! Behold!"

Dad takes a bow then heads for his seat. He pauses by Harrison, who's still on the ground. His smile fades and I know that, in this moment, he feels bad about what he just did. But then he turns away, continues down the stage, and sits down.

"Impressive demonstration, Mr. Hinkle!" Mystery says. "And another fine example of just how successfully parents can teach a lesson if they only think like kids a little more. Your training options go far beyond sending a child to his room or taking away computer and TV privileges!"

"I don't get it," Abe whispers. "Is he teaching our parents how to freak us out?"

"That's what it looks like," I whisper back.

"Why?" he asks.

Then, as if Abe shouted this question for everyone in the cave to hear, Mystery explains.

"When I contacted you all several weeks ago, I was very clear about our organization's purpose. I wanted to help you help your children. I knew they were giving you problems—and that you were running out of solutions. That's why, when they were invited to apply for admission to the Kilter Academy for Troubled Youth, the very best, most exclusive reform school for the country's worst children, you jumped at the chance to send them away. And let someone else do what you couldn't, no matter how hard you tried."

At this, my friends exchange frowns and glances. I can tell that thinking about whatever their parents did to try to keep them in line makes them uncomfortable.

"I don't blame you for that," Mystery says. "In fact, I applaud you! Not many parents would recognize the severity of their children's behavioral issues. Most would ignore it. Pretend it doesn't exist, that their kids are as sweet as honey. You didn't. And you're to be commended for it." He pauses. "However. As good a reform school as Kilter might be, it's not foolproof. Your children went wayward once, and they'll likely go wayward again. That's why I reached out to you. To make sure you're as prepared as possible. To keep the power where it belongs: with *you*, the parents. And, I hope, to teach you how to prevent future troublemaking tragedies."

At this, Harrison, still wearing a mask of my face, jumps up. He rushes to the front of the stage.

"WHAT DO WE DO?" he yells.

"Give them a taste! Of their own! Medicine! Give them a

taste! Of their own! Medicine! Give them a taste! Of their own! Medicine!"

The parents chant this, over and over and over. They punch their fists in the air, just like Mystery. And they do both in perfect unison, like they've done so many times before.

"WHY DO WE DO IT?" Harrison shouts.

"For! Their! Own! Good! For! Their! Own! Good! For! Their! Own! Good!"

"WHO ARE WE?"

"MR. TEMPEST'S! ANGEL MAKERS! MR. TEMPEST'S! ANGEL MAKERS! MR. TEMPEST'S! ANGEL MAKERS!"

This chant lasts longer than the others. Harrison asks no further questions.

While our parents are still yelling, the cave darkens. Then the walls begin to glow.

"There's me!" Gabby exclaims.

"And me!" Abe exclaims.

"And me!" Lemon exclaims.

And me. And every other Troublemaker in our class, minus Elinor. Enlarged pictures of our faces are plastered all over the jagged rock. As I watch, the faces change. First they're happy and smiling. Then they're grumpy and frowning. The expressions switch back and forth like holograms. When the faces are happy, white electric halos shine above them. When they're grumpy, the halos turn off and red devil horns turn on.

Eventually the chanting dies down. A spotlight shines on Mystery, who stands tall on his rock island as he brings the megaphone to his mouth.

"I've been very impressed with your performance so far. Tricking your children is a very new concept to most, if not all, of you. Yet day after day you take the skills you've just learned and implement them in real-life situations, successfully catching your kids off guard. And there's more work to be done! Before we get to tonight's lessons, I must implore you not to speak a word to anyone outside these cavern walls. As I explained in my initial invitation several weeks ago, Angel Makers is a top secret program. It must stay that way in order for it to be successful. That means no one can know about it . . . especially not *Annika Kilter.*"

Mystery spits out Annika's name like it's poison.

"And I must say again," Mystery continues, his voice lighter, "kudos for contacting me right away about Kamp Kilter! I thought we'd have to be in touch electronically for a while, so to be able to work with you all together, in person, is a real dream come true!"

The parents cheer like it's their dream come true too.

Abe leans toward me and shouts over the noise. "This is great!"

I look at him. "It is?"

He nods. "They're asking for trouble—and that's what they're going to get! Better than they've ever gotten before!"

I try to smile. I want to be excited for this reason to show our parents that they're no match for us, not with our Kilter training.

But I can't. Because I'm not excited.

I'm sad.

Chapter 26

DEMERITS: 2600
GOLD STARS: 1650

First I'm going to sing 'Silent Night.' That's my favorite Christmas song, so Flora hates it. Then I'm going to do 'Happy Birthday' for Mom. She doesn't like when people sing that to her, because it means she's another year older."

Gabby bursts into the living room. Abe follows close behind. They carry Kommissary shopping bags, which are filled to the brim.

"I'm not sure about Dad yet." Gabby plops her bags onto the coffee table, then drops onto the couch. "He's not a fan of country music so probably wouldn't enjoy something with twang . . . but I could also rip apart one of his favorite show tunes. What do you think?"

Abe takes his purchases to the beanbag chair. "Neon."

"Huh?" Gabby asks.

"You should see our place back home," he says, reaching into a plastic bag. "Mom's favorite color is cream. Dad's is tan. So everything—the walls, furniture, carpet—is some shade of those two sort-of colors." He holds up a pack of bright markers in one hand and a set of even brighter paints in the other. "So I'm going to assault their sight. With neon."

"By drawing on the walls?" Gabby asks.

"And everywhere else." Abe pulls out a small jug. "See this?"

Gabby leans forward, reads the jug's label. "FluorEssence?"

"It's a cleaning solution. Only whatever you wash it with, like dishes or clothes, turns fluorescent yellow. The Kommissary just got it in. I can't wait to try it."

"Your parents are going to be so surprised!" Gabby says appreciatively. "Mine will be too. As long as I get the songs right. And sing them into this amazing new microphone!" She takes a short, skinny wand from one of her shopping bags. "Can you hear me?" she whispers.

Abe drops his supplies, claps his hands to his ears.

"The Kilter Voice Enhancer." She smiles, switching off the device. "Guaranteed to turn up the volume ten times louder than your normal shouting voice. I guess it works!"

"This stuff is awesome," Abe says, reaching into another bag. "And when we use it, we will be too. Our parents don't stand a chance."

They try out a few more supplies. They're so excited I'm not even sure they notice me sitting in the lounge chair in the corner of the room. Of course, it's not like I've made my presence known. I haven't even said hello . . . let alone do what I've been working up the nerve to do since last night.

"Hey!" Lemon dashes into the room. "Sorry I'm late."

"Late?" Abe says. "For what?"

"Seamus's news." My best friend drops onto the couch and puts his feet on the coffee table.

"What news?" Abe asks.

"Whatever it is, you're not late," Gabby says. "Seamus isn't here. We haven't seen him in—oh! Seamus! Where'd you come from? That kind of sneakiness will really come in handy when you get your parents. Speaking of, you just missed out on the. Best. Shopping. Spree. Ever!"

"You both did," Abe says, looking from me to Lemon. "I expected Lemon to skip it. He couldn't even make it to our emergency alliance meeting last night."

"I told you," Lemon says. "I was tired."

"But I thought *you'd* come." Abe looks at me again. "I had to pull strings to get GS George to open the Kommissary for us again. I doubt we'll get another chance to shop before Troublemaking Tuesday."

"That's next week," Gabby adds. "When we're going to cure our parents by giving them a huge dose of troublemaker medicine! So that they freak out, give up—and stop their silly Angel Maker attacks, once and for all."

"I know," I say. "I was at the emergency meeting."

"Were you?" Abe asks. "I mean, I saw you sitting in that same chair . . . but you didn't say much. Half the time it seemed like you were on another planet."

He's right. I didn't say much. That's because I didn't know what to say. Not when he and Gabby were going on and on about all the ways they planned to thwart our parents, and Mystery, before the Angel Makers could do any more damage. And when I was thinking that I'd rather let Mom and Dad get it out of their systems so we could call it even for good.

I've always had a hunch, but after reading Mom's journal I'm now positive that I haven't been the son she wishes I were. But Dad? For him, I've always felt like the right amount of everything. Good. Smart. Fun. Tough. Not-so-tough. So to know that he's been so worried about me he thought teaming up with Mystery was necessary . . . that's not okay. And it's time to right what's gotten so wrong.

That means it's also time for something else.

The truth.

"I hope you didn't think we'd pick up stuff for you," Abe says. "It's not like I have tons of extra credits to be—"

"I didn't," I say.

"Good." Abe relaxes slightly. "So what's your news?" He sits up straight and leans forward. "Is it about Mystery? Or the Angel Makers? Did Ike tell you something?"

Gabby gasps. "Is it about Elinor? Did you two finally profess your—"

"No," I say quickly. "We didn't." I haven't even seen Elinor since we got back from the secret cave last night and she excused herself to her room. I e-mailed this morning and said I had something to share with her, Lemon, Gabby, and Abe this afternoon, and that I'd love it if she'd come to the living room at four o'clock, but she didn't answer. She skipped today's Kamp Kilter chores, and she's not here now, so she must still be too upset over what I told her about Abe to talk.

Or listen. Since I'm the one who should be talking.

"We're all ears," Lemon says, as if reading my mind.

I take a deep breath, trying to remember everything I want to say. I had a whole speech prepared, but now that the time has finally come, I can think of only one word.

"Liar."

Gabby gasps again. "So it *is* about Elinor."

"It isn't." Eager to prove her wrong, I somehow find the words. "It's about me. And who I am. Or more importantly . . . who I'm not."

They look at me. Quiet. Curious.

"Do you remember Parents' Day?" I ask. "Our first semester, when we had that barbecue after the campus tour?"

They nod.

"Do you remember what my mom told your parents that day?" I swallow. "About what I did that made them send me to Kilter?"

Gabby and Abe exchange looks.

"It was an accident," Lemon says, already jumping to my defense. "We were a little freaked out at first, but then you explained, and we understood. You were trying to do something good, and something bad happened instead."

"It was the worst kind of accident," Abe says.

"But it was still an accident," Gabby finishes.

My heart swells. That my friends have been so accepting makes it even harder to tell them they've been so for no reason.

"The thing is," I say, reminding myself that it's good news I'm about to share, "is that Mom lied. Because I didn't kill my substitute teacher after all. Miss Parsippany . . . is alive."

The room falls silent. I make myself keep going.

"I didn't know at first. I didn't see Miss Parsippany get up from the cafeteria floor, and then I was sent to Kilter right away. But Mom knew. She sent me here anyway, and then let me believe I did this terrible thing for months."

"But . . . why?" Gabby asks.

"I'm still trying to figure that out," I say. "But I think part of it is because she wanted me to be tougher. And that was another thing she didn't tell me: When she sent me to Kilter, she knew it wasn't a reform school. She knew what it really trains kids to do."

"But Annika's so careful about keeping it a secret," Abe says.

"I know. Somehow, Mom found out."

"When did you find out that you didn't do what you thought you did?" Gabby asks.

"A few months ago."

Abe scoffs.

"I'm really sorry I didn't tell you," I say quickly. "That was wrong. You're my friends, and you deserved to know the truth. It's just . . . I was afraid."

"To tell us you weren't a murderer after all?" Abe asks. "That makes sense."

"It doesn't, I know. And I was *so* happy that Miss Parsippany was okay. But by the time I found out, things were going really great. I was having fun at Kilter. More importantly, I was having fun at Kilter with you guys. And I knew that if Annika knew the truth, she'd make me leave. I didn't want that. I couldn't leave the best friends I've ever had."

They're quiet again. I wonder if they can hear my heart banging in my chest.

"Why are you telling us now?" Lemon asks a long moment later.

With the hardest part over, the words come easier. "Because I can't do it anymore. I can't lie. Things are too complicated. And I miss my dad. When I saw him at the Angel Makers meeting last night, I could tell he was sad. I think he misses me, too. And Abe, even though part of me thinks it'd be a lot of fun to prank our parents and teach them a lesson they'll never forget . . . another part thinks it'd only make things worse." I pause and take a deep breath. "Anyway, I decided to come clean to Annika. But I wanted to tell you guys the truth first. You're way more important to me than she is . . . and also, she might have a Kilter helicopter whisk me away the second I tell her. And take my K-Pak so I can't e-mail you anymore."

Abe frowns. Gabby pouts. Lemon stares at his lap. I try not to be disappointed when nobody says anything else. I definitely don't want to part on bad terms, but I can't blame them for being mad.

"Well," I say, starting to stand. "I should go pack."

"Wait," Abe says.

I stop. He gets up and goes over to Gabby. He motions for Lemon to join them, and they form a small huddle. After a lot of whispering and nodding, they split up and face me. Looking serious, Abe starts to speak.

"You can't leave!" Gabby blurts out.

Abe rolls his eyes.

"Sorry," she says. "I couldn't help it!"

"Do you *want* to leave?" Abe asks me.

"And never see us again?" Gabby asks.

"Of course not," I say. "But I just can't lie anymore."

"What if there was a way to do both?" Lemon asks. "To come clean—and still stay at Kilter?"

"That'd be amazing," I say. "But it's impossible."

"Not necessarily," Abe says.

Apparently worried the walls have ears, he waves for me to come closer. They huddle again, and when I join them, Abe and Gabby share their potential plan. Which is: to use what we learned in the Angel Makers' secret cave last night to prove to Annika that I deserve to be at Kilter. Even if Miss Parsippany's alive.

"That sounds great," I say when they're done. "But I really don't want to prank my parents anymore."

"You don't have to," Abe says. "If you do everything else right, Annika won't even notice your parents were left out."

I think about this, then look at Lemon. "You're onboard?"

"I'm onboard with keeping my best friend," he says, "so I'll do what I can."

My chest warms. I want to hug them all, but since I don't want Abe to run away when there's so much to plan, I resist.

Still huddled, we discuss the next steps. When we break after several minutes, Gabby and Abe take their shopping bags and go to their rooms to test their purchases. Lemon goes to his room to take a nap.

When they leave, I sit on the couch. I'm about to take notes on my K-Pak when I notice a green ribbon on the coffee table. It's Elinor's ribbon, for her hair.

Grateful for the reason to pay her a visit, and eager to tell her the truth too, I grab the ribbon and hurry from the room. Stopping outside her bedroom door, I take a second to catch my breath. Then I knock lightly.

"Elinor? It's Seamus. Can I come in?"

There's a long pause. Then, "Okay."

I inch open the door. Elinor's sitting cross-legged on her bed. A book's open in her lap.

I smile. "Hi."

She sort of smiles. "Hi."

"How are you?"

"Okay. You?"

"Okay too." I try to think of what to say next. Then I remember the reason for my visit and thrust one fist toward her. "I found your ribbon."

Her eyes lift from the book in her lap to the satin strand hanging from my hand. "Oh. Thanks."

"You're welcome. Should I . . . ? Where would you like me to . . . ?

"On the desk is fine."

I walk over and place the ribbon on a closed notebook. Before turning away I notice her friendship bracelet, the one that matches the braided string currently wound around my wrist, lying on top of a different notebook.

I force my feet away from the desk. "So that was pretty

crazy last night, huh? In the cave? With Mystery? And the Angel Makers?"

Still looking down at her book, she nods. "Yup."

"Elinor, I'm really sorry if—"

"Seamus, I'm kind of in the middle of a chapter. Can we talk some other time?"

My heart sinks. "Sure."

I lower my head and shuffle back to the door. I stop with one hand on the knob, hoping she'll say something, anything to suggest that she's not as mad at me as she seems to be . . . but she turns a page instead. And I leave the room, closing the door quietly behind me.

Back in my room, I picture the friendship bracelet on her desk. Did she take it off after I hurt her feelings last night? Or was she wearing it today and just removed it before changing into her pajamas? Most importantly, what can I say or do to make her want to put it back on?

After everything that's happened in the past twenty-four hours, my chest feels empty. Like a shell without a turtle. Unable to do anything else, I flop onto my bed and stare at the ceiling a while. Eventually my K-Pak buzzes with a new message. I open it.

> **TO:** shinkle@kilteracademy.org
> **FROM:** annika@kilteracademy.org
> **SUBJECT:** Your Parents
>
> Your father's ignoring my Role Reverse e-vites. Your mother wrote back and thanked me, but she failed to say whether she accepted. They're the only parents I have yet to meet with, and I'm curious as to why they're being so elusive.
>
> Any ideas?
>
> —Annika

I reread the note. She sounds annoyed, like she thinks I have something to do with my parents' poor social skills.

Not in the mood to try to make her feel better when I'm feeling bad myself, I exit that message and start a new one.

TO: ike@kilteracademy.org
FROM: shinkle@kilteracademy.org
SUBJECT: Careful?

Hi, Ike! How are you? I hope you're having fun doing whatever it is you do at Kamp Kilter!

Thanks again for that super-fun Hammock Hauler lesson. I can't wait to try it out on moving targets, and not just rocks and bushes!

On another note, I've been wondering something. When we were talking about Annika the other day and you told me to be careful . . . what did you mean? I have some guesses, but I'd love to know the truth.

Thanks!
—Seamus

I send the note. My tutor's response comes two minutes later.

TO: shinkle@kilteracademy.org
FROM: ike@kilteracademy.org
SUBJECT: RE: Careful?

Hey, Seamus,

Glad you enjoyed the lesson. We'll have to have another one soon.

As for Annika and being careful, I'll just say this. A few years ago, I was you. A skilled marksman. Top Troublemaker in my class. Teacher's pet. Annika's favorite. Destined to get the real-world assignment of my choice after graduation.

Then I got a peek at our director's true colors. And feeling like I could, I called her out on it.

Now I am me. Tutor eternal. With no hope of doing anything more than teaching great kids like you what they could teach themselves with the help of online demos.

Don't get me wrong, I like my job. I just thought I'd be doing more. Better. Good. For so many people who needed it.

But it turns out Annika's only concerned about the good of one person. Herself. And when you get in her way, she'll get in yours. Forever.

And that, my friend, is the truth.

—Ike

I read Ike's note three times. Then I get another message.

TO: shinkle@kilteracademy.org
FROM: annika@kilteracademy.org
SUBJECT: Meeting

Seamus,

So sorry I wrote without mentioning your meeting request from the other day. I'd love to get together ASAP. Am dying to hear all about this exciting development on the parental front!

How's tomorrow morning, before you head across the lake? I'll send a cart.

Hugs!

Annika

I press reply. Without even thinking about what I'll say, I start typing.

TO: annika@kilteracademy.org
FROM: shinkle@kilteracademy.org
SUBJECT: RE: Meeting

That's okay, Annika. Was a false alarm. Will let you know if anything changes.

—Seamus

Chapter 27

DEMERITS: 5200
GOLD STARS: 2950

My friends and I spend the next few days gathering information for Troublemaking Tuesday. When we report for cleaning duty in our families' cabins, we observe our parents' behavior, let them act out the way Mystery tells them to, and note their strengths and weaknesses. This helps us plan our retaliation. I still don't want to prank my parents, but watching them—or watching Dad, since Mom's still mostly MIA—is useful. Or it will be, when the time comes.

I feel more prepared, and confident, every day. But I'm still caught off guard when, on the Monday before Troublemaking Tuesday, Dad throws a curveball.

Dear Seamus,

Your mother and I would like to invite you to dinner at our cabin tonight. Seven p.m. Bring your appetite!

Love,

Dad

I found the note taped to our tent flap early this morning. Standing on my parents' front porch now, I read it for the hundredth time, searching between the lines for hints of a hidden agenda. Because it's been five days since my friends and I spied on the Angel Makers meeting. Nine days since we all arrived at Kamp Kilter. According to Annika, my parents have been ignoring her Role Reverse invitations. And this is the first time since we got here that they've wanted to spend time with me.

So I can't help but wonder . . . why?

There's only one way to find out, so I raise a fist. The door swings open.

"Hello, Seamus."

"Mom?" I ask. Because the woman before me kind of resembles the one I've known as my mother for thirteen years. Her hair's still brown. Her eyes are still green. She's wearing her favorite red sundress and matching red sandals. But something's different.

"Oh, it hasn't been that long, has it?" Mom opens the door wider. "Won't you come in?"

Still trying to pinpoint what's off, I step into the living room. She closes the door behind me.

"These are for you." I hold out the bouquet of wildflowers I picked from the woods behind our underground house. Mom and Dad always bring flowers whenever they're invited to someone else's house for dinner, so it seemed like the thing to do.

Mom gasps. Brings both palms to her heart. Smiles.

That's it! Her smile. It's totally different. Usually her lips press tightly together. The corners of her mouth barely lift. Her cheeks, chin, and forehead are tense, as if it's taking every bit of her facial muscle strength to hold the expression.

But now her lips actually part. The corners of her mouth lift

up her cheeks, which are totally relaxed. Instead of being frozen in place, her face looks warm. Open.

Happy.

"They're *beautiful*!" she exclaims, taking the flowers. "Thank you. Come into the kitchen with me while I find a vase." She turns, stops, and turns back. "I mean, would you *like* to come into the kitchen with me while I find a vase?"

I shrug. "Sure."

She beams. As I follow her across the room, I note the lit fireplace. Soft light coming from a dozen candles set on the coffee and side tables. Jazz music playing from several round wall speakers.

"The place looks great," I say once we're in the kitchen.

"All thanks to you." Mom opens a cabinet and takes out a tall glass cylinder. "You're doing great with your chores. I've never seen a house so immaculate day in and day out."

"What about our house? Back home? You always make it look it perfect."

She stops arranging the flowers in the vase and looks at me. I think her eyes might start to water.

"Do you really think so?" she asks.

"Of course. The only reason I know how this house should look when I'm done is because you've shown me a million times."

She sniffs. Blinks. Continues arranging the flowers.

"It smells great too," I say. "What's for dinner?"

Her face brightens. "Baked ziti!"

This throws me off for two reasons. The first is that she didn't say fish sticks. The second is that I can't recall baked ziti in my internal dinner database.

"Is that filled with tofu?" I ask.

"Nope," she says, placing the flowers on the table.

"Broccoli?" I ask.

"Not a spear." She hurries to the stove and puts on quilted oven mitts.

"Soy cheese?"

She opens the oven door, pulls out a deep dish, and places it on the counter before me. My nostrils tickle as all sorts of yummy smells—garlic, tomato sauce, more garlic—float up with the steam.

"Nope," Mom says. "*Real* cheese."

Smiling wider, she reaches back into the oven and pulls out a long, skinny slab wrapped in tinfoil. She places that next to the baked ziti and peels back the tinfoil so I can see what's inside.

"Garlic bread?" I ask. "Made with . . . ?"

"Real butter? Yup."

Practically drooling, I reach one hand toward the loaf. Then I stop.

"Go ahead," Mom says. "Have a piece."

"But we're not seated at the table." She's scolded me for pre-meal munching countless times before.

She peels back the tinfoil some more. Then she tears off two pieces of bread, hands one to me, and keeps the other for herself.

"I won't tell if you don't," she says, and takes a big bite.

I smile. Take a bite. And another. And another. The bread's hot and moist and salty. I don't know if I've ever tasted anything so delicious in my entire life.

"Well, well! Look who's here!"

I turn around. "Hi, Dad."

He's standing in the kitchen doorway. His eyes shift from me, to the counter, to the floor, to the ceiling, to each wall, and back to me.

"Thanks for coming," he finally says.

"Thanks for inviting me," I say.

"Dinner's ready," Mom says. "Shall we?"

Dad comes all the way into the room. Cautiously. Like he's afraid the floor's booby-trapped. I stay where I am so he can give me a hug before sitting down.

But he doesn't give me a hug. He breezes past and sits down.

"Isn't this nice?" Mom motions for me to take the chair across from Dad. "The whole family, together again."

"It is." I glance at Dad.

"Indeed." Dad glances at me.

Mom scoops the gooey pasta onto our plates. We start eating.

"This is great," I say. "Thanks for making it."

"You're very welcome." Mom beams for about the fourteenth time since my arrival. "I was hoping you'd like it. I thought it'd be fun to cook something none of us has ever eaten before. As a way to . . . kind of . . . I don't know. Start over?"

Dad and I stop chewing. Our forks hover over our plates.

"From what?" I ask.

"Yes," Dad says. "From what?"

"Oh, come now. We all know it's been a difficult few months. A lot's happened. Changes have been made. Our whole world was turned upside down."

I shove another forkful of gooey noodles into my mouth to stifle the question that wants to pop out.

Whose fault was that?

"Anyway," Mom continues. "Now we're here. It's summer vacation. Which is for recharging. Preparing for whatever comes next. And I thought, even though we're not spending every second together, that we could still try to do all those things. As a family."

"It was a very nice thought," Dad says, and pats Mom's hand.

It *was* a very nice thought? Does he think starting over as a family is impossible? Or that it's simply too late?

This reminds me of Annika's last e-mail.

"By the way," I say casually, "how come you didn't get back to Annika about her Role Reverse invitation?"

"I got back to her," Mom says.

"With an answer?" I ask.

"Well . . ." Mom avoids eye contact. "We need parmesan!" She jumps up and heads for the refrigerator.

I look at Dad. "She said she wrote you, too. And didn't hear anything."

Dad becomes very busy spearing noodles with his fork. "Yes.

Ah, I did get those notes. And I've been meaning to respond. There's just so much to do! We've been so busy!"

"Too busy to type yes or no and hit send?" I ask.

Dad shoves the noodles into his mouth. Chews. Shrugs.

"Everyone else's families have already role-played. Annika says it helps kids understand parents and parents understand kids. Which helps them become better families. Don't you want our family to be better?"

"Water!" Dad gulps, then jumps and heads for the kitchen sink.

Mom comes back to the table with the grated cheese. Dad fills and empties the same glass three times. They must have their reasons for avoiding Annika's role-playing request, and they're clearly not about to share them.

I've been here all of fifteen minutes and I'm way more confused than I was before I walked through the door. Deciding I'll need to control the situation better if I'm going to figure out what this night's really about, I ask another question I've been holding back.

"So how'd you swing this?"

"Swing what?" Mom asks.

"Dinner. Here. With me. None of my friends' parents invited

them over tonight, so this can't be an Annika-approved event. That means you got special permission."

"We don't need Annika's permission," Dad says quickly.

Mom and I look at him. A second later, they continue eating. I watch his hands. He holds a fork in one hand, a piece of garlic bread in the other. The fork's shaking. The garlic bread keeps slipping and dropping onto the gooey noodles.

He's nervous.

Mom, on the other hand, seems perfectly at ease. Despite getting a little emotional before, when I said how nice she keeps our house back home, and jumping up for cheese when I brought up role playing, now she looks as if she hasn't a care in the world. She sits back. Eats slowly. Offers me more bread. Gives me more teeth-revealing smiles.

And when Dad's done talking, she asks a very unexpected question.

"How are you?"

I stop chewing. "Fine?"

"Good," she says. "Your teachers seem to be keeping you very busy."

I swallow. "They are."

"But I hope it's not all work and no play." Now Mom sounds concerned. "This is your summer too. I understand you have certain . . . lessons . . . that need to be learned, but I hope you're being appropriately rewarded for your efforts."

"Like how?" I ask, genuinely curious to know what she thinks that I deserve.

"With the kinds of things all kids enjoy at sleepaway camp. Dances. Pool parties. Movie nights. Free time."

"Free time's for good kids. And if I wanted to be treated like a good kid, maybe I should've acted like one."

Which is what she said to me right before she and Dad left me at Kilter nine months ago. I've replayed this sentence in my head so many times it must be permanently etched in my brain tissue. But Mom doesn't seem to remember it all. And I have to admit, she's being so nice now, it doesn't sound quite as bad as it used to.

"You *are* a good kid!" she exclaims, and my heart warms. "You're the *best* kid! All parents should be so lucky to have such—"

She stops talking. Probably because a butter knife just sailed past her face, nearly taking her nose with it.

"Nice catch," Dad says.

"Thanks." I reach across the table to hand him the utensil.

"Hang on tight to that. Real butter's slippery."

"As I was saying," Mom continues, "Seamus, you're—"

"Whoopsie!" Dad cringes. "Sorry, son. Don't know what happened there!"

I do. He took a fistful of ice cubes from his water glass and chucked them right at me. I then picked up my water glass and quickly moved it up, down, left, and right to catch the flying cubes.

"No problem." I place the glass back on the table. "Frozen water's slippery too."

Mom tries again. "Seamus, you should never—"

Take my eyes off of Dad. Because next he flicks gooey noodles from his plate. Before they can splatter across my face, I pick up my plate and angle it down so that his noodles land on top of mine.

"Thanks," I say when he's done. "I am pretty hungry."

Dad frowns. Stares at my hands. Holds the edge of his plate with both of his.

"Eliot, are you feeling okay?" Mom asks.

"What? Of course! Never better!"

As if to prove his point, he scoops more pasta onto his plate and starts shoveling forkfuls into his mouth.

"May I be excused?" I ask, trying not to smile. "I need to use the restroom."

"Of course," Mom says.

Now trying not to laugh, I dart down the hallway and into the bathroom. I quickly close the door, then crack up into a towel for a few seconds. When that's out of my system, I take out my K-Pak. Imagining how fun it'd be to trade tricks with Dad at home, especially if we both knew that's what we were doing, I start a new e-mail.

TO: loliver@kilteracademy.org, ahansen@kilteracademy.org, gryan@kilteracademy.org, enorris@kilteracademy.org
FROM: shinkle@kilteracademy.org
SUBJECT: Tomorrow

Hi, guys!

Just wanted to check in. Everything's fine here so far, although my parents are acting really weird. I expected it from Dad, who keeps trying to pull pranks, like, right in front of me, but I didn't expect it from Mom. Why would I? She's being super nice, which she never is. And she seems to really care about making me happy. That's also a first.

We know why Dad's acting up, so I'm not worried about him. In fact, stopping his table tricks is kind of hilarious. Between that and Mom being so nice, it's turning out to be a great night.

So now I'm wondering . . . are we sure we want to go through with Troublemaking Tuesday tomorrow? Maybe there's another way to stop the Angel Makers without misbehaving. It might sound crazy, but what if we tried just talking to our parents? During Role Reverse it seemed like grown-ups and kids had very different ideas about what went down pre-Kilter, and talking stuff out helped clear things up. So maybe we all just need to communicate with our parents more, in general? And get on the same page? I could talk to my parents tonight, and you could talk to yours during chores tomorrow. After that, no one would have to trick anyone.

Of course, I'd still tell Annika the truth about

me. And if coming clean after all this time—and reminding her of my stellar troublemaking record at Kilter—doesn't convince her I deserve to be here, well . . . there are always school vacations. I can visit you when you're home, and you can visit me, too. We'll work it out. That's what friends do.

What do you think?

—Seamus

I press send. Not surprisingly, Abe's the first one to write back.

TO: shinkle@kilteracademy.org, gryan@kilteracademy.org, loliver@kilteracademy.org, enorris@kilteracademy.org
FROM: ahansen@kilteracademy.org
SUBJECT: RE: Tomorrow

Hinkle, whatever your parents are feeding you, STOP EATING IT. Something in there is messing with your head.

Lemon writes next.

> **TO:** shinkle@kilteracademy.org, ahansen@kilteracademy.org, gryan@kilteracademy.org, enorris@kilteracademy.org
> **FROM:** loliver@kilteracademy.org
> **SUBJECT:** RE: RE: Tomorrow
>
> Abraham, chill.
>
> Seamus, I think this is an interesting idea. But maybe you should wait to talk to your parents until we discuss in person?
>
> —L

I close my K-Mail and put my K-Pak in my jacket pocket. I'm sure my friends will have much more to say about this, but their input can wait. Right now I want to hang out with my parents—even if they are acting a little like strangers.

I open the bathroom door and step into the hallway. Mom and Dad are talking in the dining room. I hear Dad compliment Mom on the ziti. Mom thanks him, then starts reciting the recipe.

It sounds like a perfectly normal, pleasant conversation—one I'd like to be a part of. But instead of going right, toward my parents, my feet turn left.

Toward their bedroom.

"What are you doing?" I whisper once I'm standing before the dresser.

Looking for answers. Despite the new plan I just suggested to my friends, I must still have some trust issues. As in, I don't fully buy Mom and her new behavior. It'd be really helpful to find some sort of rock-solid evidence—like a recent entry detailing her change of heart—that the new attitude isn't an act.

Why else would I want to snoop through her journal now?

This is it, I tell myself. *The last time. For the good of us all.*

I take the book from the coupon folder and flip toward the back, where the newer entries should be. Mom thought I was too weak in the past. Does she think I'm stronger now? Is that why she's decided to be nicer? Because she doesn't think she has to be as hard on me?

I have many other questions for her, like how she knew about Kilter, and what she's been doing at camp while Dad's been chucking ping-pong balls and going to Angel Makers meetings.

We'll get to those. I hope when the answers no longer matter, because we've all turned the page—and gotten on the same one. Just like I suggested to my friends.

Then again, maybe we won't.

As I'm flipping through the book, a small card slips out from between the pages. When it lands on the floor, the handwriting is facing up.

My eyes fix on two words near the bottom of the card.

Then my heart stops. And I read the rest.

Dear Mrs. Hinkle,

Thanks for the present. Messing with Seamus is fun, so you definitely didn't have to give me video games and homemade cookies, but I'm glad you did. Those chocolate chips were YUM-O.

We should be good now that he's gone, but if you ever need my help again, just let me know. I'm always happy to tease the little fish face. Keeps me sharp.

From,

Bartholomew John

P.S. Looks like Miss Parsippany's going to make a full recovery. Whew!

Down the hall, my parents laugh. I barely hear them as I pick up the card, stick it in the journal, and put the journal back in the coupon folder.

Then I take out my K-Pak and type so hard, so fast, my fingertips burn.

TO: loliver@kilteracademy.org, ahansen@kilteracademy.org, gryan@kilteracademy.org, enorris@kilteracademy.org
FROM: shinkle@kilteracademy.org
SUBJECT: Troublemaking Tuesday

Forget what I said.
It's ON.

Chapter 28

DEMERITS: 5200
GOLD STARS: 3050

Good morning?" I whisper. "Hello? This is Seamus. From your class? I'm really sorry to bother you, but—"

Abe yanks the K-Pak from my hands. "We're trying to wake them up, Hinkle, not put them back to sleep."

He nods to Gabby, who holds up the stereo remote. Then he takes my K-Pak across the living room and raises it toward a silver speaker. Gabby presses a button. Rock music shakes the floor and rattles the fake windows.

I cover my ears. The pounding, shrieking, and squealing

lasts five seconds. Then Abe nods to Gabby. She presses another button on the remote. The room falls silent.

Abe grins at the K-Pak screen. "That's more like it."

Uncovering my ears, I hear moans and groans coming from the small computer. The noises get louder as Abe crosses the room.

"You have their undivided attention," he says, and hands me the K-Pak.

I take the computer and scan the small squares displayed on the screen. After sending out a mass v-chat blast to reach all of our classmates at once, my K-Pak screen divided into thirty miniscreens showing thirty individual Troublemakers. Now some of them are getting up from the floor, where they fell when the music burst through their K-Paks. The ones who managed to stay in bed are pulling pillows away from their heads. Many are trying to turn off their K-Paks—and get rid of the horrible source of their rude awakening.

"Wait!" I exclaim. "Please. It's Seamus Hinkle, from your class." I wait for Troublemakers to register my voice, stop freaking out, and look at their computer screens. "I'm sorry for all the noise, but I really have to talk to you."

"And you couldn't wait until we were all above ground?" Chris Fisher asks.

"Unfortunately, no," I say. "We couldn't risk anyone overhearing. The situation is too sensitive. And we need as much time as possible to prepare."

"What situation?" Alison Parker asks.

"Prepare for what?" Carter Montgomery asks.

I glance at Abe. He nods. I take a breath and fill in our classmates.

"By now you probably know that something's up with your parents. Maybe they've been sneaking around while you're cleaning their cabins. Or performing practical jokes. Or setting silly booby traps. I saw a lot of you at the infirmary the other day, when we were supposed to send our moms and dads there, so I know their tricks have been working."

"*Their* tricks?" Alison asks. "You're saying the reason I walked into the screen door I knew I left open—"

"Was because one of your parents closed it when you weren't looking," I said. "Exactly." She frowns. I keep going. "Listen. Our parents love us. They would never hurt us. But they're afraid of us hurting ourselves—by being bad kids and missing out on all the things that being good can bring. So their job is to get us back on track. That's why they sent us to Kilter. And it's also why, when they had the chance to do more, they took it."

"You mean by dropping everything and coming to Kamp Kilter?" Chris asks. "So we could have even more time at our pretend reform school?"

"That," I say. "And . . . joining The Secret Society of Masterful Angel Makers."

There's a long pause as Troublemakers stare blankly at their K-Paks.

"Huh?" Carter finally asks.

"Let's cut to the chase," Abe takes my K-Pak and talks to the small camera. "Mr. Tempest brainwashed our parents. He formed some sort of weird club, invited them to join, and convinced them that playing tricks is the best way to get us to be good. A few days ago, they put ink in a soap dispenser that turned my hands blue. They never would've done that at home, but here? Under Mr. Tempest's watch? That's another story. And your parents have been doing the same kinds of things to you."

"I don't believe that," Alison says.

"It's true!" Gabby declares over Abe's shoulder. "We saw them practicing at their secret meeting spot. They're up to no good!"

"That's why they need to be taught a lesson," Abe says. "Today."

"What kind of lesson?" Eric asks.

"The kind that'll remind them who's really in charge." Abe points to himself.

"They're our parents," Alison says. "They're always the bosses—even if we make their jobs difficult sometimes."

"Right," Abe agrees. "So they don't need to prank us on top of it. And *we* have to remind *them* that trying to won't help anything."

"I don't know," Eric says. "My parents have been through a lot with me. If they want to prove some kind of point, maybe I should let them?"

"If we tell them we get it, who's to say they'll stop?" Abe asks. "What if they take Mystery's twisted tricks home? And keep practicing and trying new things until they're totally out of control?"

Our classmates are quiet. I motion for the K-Pak. Abe hands it over. I look into the camera.

"Our parents thought joining the Angel Makers was a good opportunity. And we think launching a surprise sneak attack today will show just how much we've really learned at Kilter."

It'll also really impress Annika. That was the original reason I agreed to this when my friends suggested it the other day. They thought as long as I rallied the troops and led the charge, it wouldn't matter that my parents weren't among the targets. I could leave them alone, the way I'd wanted to, and Annika would still be awed by my participation. Enough that, once I told her the truth about Miss Parsippany and me, she'd let me stay at Kilter.

Of course, that was before last night. When I discovered Mom had been in cahoots with my ultimate enemy. Pleasing Annika now is just icing on the cake.

"How'd you find out about the Angel Makers?" Alison asks.

"We have our ways," Abe says.

"When did you find out our parents were in the club?" Carter asks.

"Last week," Gabby says.

"And you're just telling us now?" Chris asks.

"We wanted to be sure of what was going on before saying anything," I explain.

"Okay," Reed says, "but now that we know, we need at least a few days to prepare."

"We don't have that kind of time," Abe says.

"Why not?" Liam asks.

"Because they could launch a sneak attack on us any second!" Gabby says.

"Then you guys should've given us more notice," Natalie says.

"You don't need it," I say. "You've been training for this since you got to Kilter. You know what to do, and you have the skills and weapons to do it. If you had more time, you'd overthink. And get nervous. Then you'd get sloppy. And maybe even accidentally spill the beans to your parents. Right?"

Nobody disagrees.

"So what's the plan?" Chris asks.

I hand the K-Pak to Abe. He fills in our classmates.

"Our families are attending a special breakfast in the Kamp

Kilter cafeteria this morning. Unlike the mandatory beach party they skipped, this is an event they won't want to miss. If they do, they'll also miss out on a chance to win a million dollars."

Our classmates gasp.

"Annika's giving away a million dollars?" Eric asks.

"Nope," Abe says. "But thanks to flyers we plastered all over camp last night, they'll think she is. That means they'll be really excited—and not worrying at all about trying to get us. They won't even think we're around, since we always go right to their cabins every morning. Their guards will be totally down. Troublemaking conditions don't get any better."

"Will we go after them as a group?" Alison asks.

"We'll be there together," Abe says, "but we'll act individually. Each Troublemaker will teach his or her parents a lesson they'll never forget."

"What if they see us?" Carter asks.

"They won't!" Gabby chimes in. "Not if you're doing your job!"

Abe hands me the K-Pak, and I field a few more questions,

like what our teachers will do when we don't show for assignments, what the Good Samaritans might do if anyone reports us, what we'll do if we're caught. I wait until my classmates are done asking, and then I give one answer.

"I don't know."

"What?" Eric asks.

"How could I?" I ask. "We've never done this before. But I do know one thing: Annika will *love* it. And she'll probably reward us better than she ever has."

This does it. At the idea of credits and Kommissary shopping sprees, I can tell all doubts have been erased.

Just to be sure, I ask, "Are you in?"

"YES!" they shout.

"Great," I say. "We'll meet on the beach in an hour. See you then!"

I hang up. Gabby and Abe dash to their rooms to get ready. I check in on Lemon, who's just getting up and promises he'll be ready in time. He also reminds me that he won't be attacking anyone, least of all his parents, but that he'll station himself outside the cafeteria and be on the lookout for potential surprises.

Then I go to Elinor's door, which is closed. When we told her about the plan, she said she had no reason to participate, since her mom's not here. Gabby's the only one she's really been talking to ever since I told her about Abe suspecting she was working for the Incriminators, and she tried to convince her to play long anyway, but Elinor refused.

Now, feeling a little bolder after rallying the troublemaking troops, I knock gently on her door.

No answer.

"Elinor?" I ask. "Are you up?"

Nothing.

I'm about to knock again when my K-Pak buzzes. Reminding myself I'm not the happiest when someone wakes me up from a sound sleep, I reluctantly leave Elinor alone. Then I return to the living room to read the new message.

TO: shinkle@kilteracademy.org
FROM: ike@kilteracademy.org
SUBJECT: Training Session?

Hey, Seamus!

Any interest in a quick prebreakfast lesson today?

—Ike

I press reply and start typing.

TO: ike@kilteracademy.org

FROM: shinkle@kilteracademy.org

SUBJECT: RE: Training Session

Hi, Ike!

I'm always interested in hanging out with you, but I kind of have plans this morning. Big ones. I'll tell you all about them ASAP!

Also, I wanted to thank you for getting back to me the other day. I'm really sorry to hear that your Kilter career hasn't gone the way you wanted it to. Whoever you hoped to help is really missing out. I know if I were in trouble, you'd be the first guy I called.

And thanks for the warning about Annika. She's been a hard one to figure out, so I definitely appreciate the feedback. I'll proceed with caution and tell my friends to do the same!

Can we meet later today? Let me know!

—Seamus

I send that note, then remember I owe another.

TO: parsippany@wahoo.com

FROM: shinkle@kilteracademy.org

SUBJECT: Spots

Dear Miss Parsippany,

Thanks for your e-mail. I've thought a lot about what you said about leopards not changing their spots. Mostly I've thought about if I think that's true. Or if I want it to be.

Take me, for example. For years, I was a really good kid. Then, on the day of the Unfortunate Apple Incident, I suddenly became a bad kid. It was like a switch flipped from off to on. I've been getting into trouble ever since.

My parents are other examples. For the longest

time, Dad was nice and Mom was . . . well, Mom. Not mean, but definitely not warm and caring like Dad. But recently their switches flipped too. Now Mom's nice and Dad's not. I never could have imagined them acting the way they've been acting lately if I hadn't actually witnessed the weirdness with my own eyes.

So if a leopard CAN change his spots, then I can be a good kid again. And my parents can go back to normal. But if a leopard CAN'T change his spots, then maybe I was never really a bad kid, and Mom and Dad's new behavior is just a strange phase. BUT, what if a leopard can do both? Like, change his spots once, and then never again? What if my parents and I are stuck in these new roles forever? Is that good? Bad?

I don't know . . . but I might be about to find out.

Will keep you posted!

Sincerely,

Seamus

P.S. There's no question about Bartholomew

> John. When it comes to him, once a bad leopard, always a bad leopard!

I send the note. Then I finish gathering my stuff. A half an hour later, Lemon, Abe, Gabby, and I meet at the elevator.

"Ready?" I ask.

"Absolutely!" Gabby sings into her megamicrophone.

Abe winces. "Always."

"If I have to be," Lemon says.

We head aboveground. Once outside, I'm struck by how normal everything seems. The sun shines. The turquoise lake sparkles. Our classmates talk and laugh as they head for their boats. It's a morning just like any other we've experienced since arriving at Kamp Kilter.

Until, a few minutes later, it isn't.

My friends and I still climb into our boat. Lemon still pulls us while swimming. The boat still leaks. Abe, Gabby, and I still fill plastic cups with water to keep from sinking. All across the lake, our fellow Troublemakers do the same.

But then, when we reach the other side of the lake, something changes.

Instead of sprinting down the beach, my classmates stop. At first I think something's wrong, or that they've changed their minds about the plan. After all, we told them we're surprising our parents in the cafeteria. I assumed they'd run right there.

But then I step out of the boat. And I realize they've stopped . . . because they're waiting for me.

"No." The word pops from my mouth. I stand up a little straighter, speak a little louder as I address the group. "We left early. The Good Samaritans and our teachers are probably on their way. We need to get off the beach before they see us."

"Our teachers teach us how to make trouble," Alison points out. "If they knew what we were about to do, why would they stop us?"

"They work for Annika," I say. "This wasn't her idea. At the very least they'd hold us up while they tried to reach her and ask what was going on. Who knows how long that could take? Our parents could be gone by then."

"My parents would wait at least a week for a million dollars," Carter says.

"Not if Annika or our teachers got there before we did and told them they're waiting for no reason," I say.

"Good point," Carter says.

"Any other questions?" I ask.

My classmates, holding backpacks and duffel bags of troublemaking supplies, are silent. A few of them look nervous. Most look anxious to get to work. I try to figure out how I feel as I press one finger to my lips, reminding everyone to be quiet, point to the woods behind the beach, and start walking.

Chapter 29

DEMERITS: 5200
GOLD STARS: 3050

My last name starts with an H. That's the eighth letter in the alphabet. Whenever my class back at Cloudview Middle School traveled the halls together, there were always nine people ahead of me. I was never a line leader. I was never *any* kind of leader.

"Seamus?" Gabby whispers.

"Hinkle?" Abe hisses.

"If we're hanging out awhile," Lemon says, "I'm going to grab a nap on that beach chair over—"

Excited. Halfway to the cafeteria, I decide that's how I feel. I'm nervous, too, and a little uncertain . . . but I'm mostly excited. But not because we're about to launch a sneak attack on our parents. On Dad, who might have fun battling back. And on Mom, who deserves whatever she gets for conspiring with Bartholomew John, the son she wishes she'd gotten instead.

No. I have butterflies in my stomach and a smile on my face because my classmates listened to me. When I started across the beach, they followed. Even Abe, the most competitive Trouble-maker I know. And I'm not on some sort of power trip. It's just nice to be taken seriously by my peers. That never happened at Cloudview Middle School.

If she could see me now, Mom might even be proud.

But she won't. Invisibility is key when it comes to trouble-making. That's why, when we reach the large cabin housing the Kamp Kilter cafeteria, I duck down, dart to the back of the building, and wave my classmates closer.

"Okay," I whisper. "They're in there. Do what you can, and remember: Don't let them see you! As soon as they do, our jobs get a lot harder. And the longer we last, the more fun we'll have, the more impressed Annika will be—and the more credits she'll give us!"

Eyes light up. A few girls clap quietly. A few boys exchange silent high fives.

"Ready?" I ask.

Their heads bob up and down.

"Let's go!"

Troublemakers bolt left. Right. Around the sides of the building. In front of the building. A few even scale walls and climb onto the roof.

I stay where I am. Ike loaned me his Kilter Katcher, which folds up for easy storage. I take that from my backpack, assemble it quickly, and step onto a large rock beneath a cafeteria window.

"You sure about this?" Lemon asks.

He's standing next to me. His hands are empty. His face is serious.

"It was partly your idea," I remind him. "So that I might be able to stay at Kilter after telling Annika the truth."

"I know, but now that we're here, I'm wondering . . . what if *none* of us stayed at Kilter?"

I grab the wall to keep from falling off the rock. "You want to go home? Like, for good? And never see each other again?"

"We'd see each other," he says. "Friends make it work. You said that yourself."

"ACK!"

Now I fall off the rock. Then I jump back up, stand on tiptoes, and peer inside the cafeteria. That's where the shriek came from.

"Abe," I report. "When his dad wasn't looking, he turned his pancakes, eggs, and bacon into a 3-D head. Like a breakfast snowman. That looks like Abe." I smile. "Mr. Hansen's totally freaking."

"Do you see my family?" Lemon asks.

I scan the large room. As predicted, no parent wanted to miss out on a million bucks, so it's packed. Mr. and Mrs. Hansen are sitting at a table near the back. Mr. Ryan, Mrs. Ryan, and Flora are sharing a table with another family I don't recognize. Dozens of other moms, dads, brothers, and sisters fill their plates at the long buffet, pour coffee and orange juice at the beverage stand—and hardly eat or drink as they talk and check their Kamp Kilter computers. My guess is they're awaiting news or instructions related to this morning's imaginary prize. They don't seem to mind the wait, though. There's a lot of smiling and laughing. Even by Mr. Hansen, who, after recovering from the shock, seems to think edible Abe is a sign of good things to come.

Until edible Abe explodes, sending butter, syrup, and bacon flying.

The Hansens squeal, leap from their seats, and wipe the goo from their faces. In his hiding spot under their table, Abe grins.

"Silent, happy niiiight . . . holy birthday briiiight . . ."

"Gabby," I announce.

"I hear her," Lemon says.

Thanks to her special microphone, so does everyone else. As our musical alliance-mate belts out "Silent Night" mixed with "Happy Birthday" in a country twang, Mr. Ryan clamps his hands over his ears. Flora stuffs napkins into hers. Mrs. Ryan looks all around the room, searching for the song's source.

"She's behind a Kilter cook," I say. "Moving when he does so no one sees her."

"She's not bad," Lemon says. "I wonder why her family doesn't like her singing?"

"Maybe too much of a good thing?" I guess.

"Maybe. How about my parents? And Finn?"

I scan the rest of the room. "They're here. Having muffins and tea."

"Are they okay?"

"I think they're better than that. Your mom's dancing in her seat while she eats. She must like Gabby's entertainment."

"Can you watch them while I'm out here? And make sure Troublemakers leave them alone?"

"You got it," I say.

"Thanks. Keep your K-Pak on. I'll let you know if—"

Lemon's cut off by a long, loud whistle. It comes from Carter Montgomery, who's just launched a Kilter Kanary at his parents' table. That's a remote-controlled robot bird that releases an ear-piercing warble each time it zings past its target. Peering through the window I see Mr. and Mrs. Montgomery jump up and swat at the small metal creature swooping down and around their heads. I also see Carter off to the side, wearing the same gray shorts, shirt, and apron the cafeteria employees wear. He must've found an extra outfit somewhere. And it's working; he's standing ten feet away from his parents, in broad view, but he blends in so well no one gives him a second glance.

"Nice. Do you want to—"

Have a look? That's what I'm about to ask Lemon, but when I glance down, he's gone.

Assuming he's manning his station near the cafeteria entrance, I look through the window again. I have to give my classmates credit—they're not wasting time. Abe, Gabby, and Carter aren't the only ones already acting up. Alison bounds from one trash can to the next, hiding behind each as she sprays waffle whipped cream at her parents. Reed balances on the blades of a ceiling fan, hangs down a rope with a hook attached to one end, and, whenever his parents turn around or return to the buffet, rearranges their plates and utensils. I don't see her do it so have no idea *how* she does it, but when her family goes up for seconds, Natalie places four live chickens on their table. By the time her parents and little brothers get back, their new breakfast guests are clucking and pecking at the crumbs they left behind.

For the first few minutes, the scene remains fairly calm. Adults are definitely confused, but they seem to think these surprises are related to the ultimate one—a million dollars—that got them out of bed. So puzzled looks and head scratching are followed by smiles and laughter.

Eventually I think of Annika—and Ike's warning. And for a second, I'm torn. From what I know and from what my tutor has said, it's obvious our director's up to something. That makes me not want to try very hard to make her happy. But after what I learned at my parents' cabin last night, I need to be able to stay at Kilter now more than ever. As much as I'd miss Dad—and already do—I can't imagine living with Mom again, or seeing Bartholomew John at school every day.

But I can't keep lying about Miss Parsippany. I must tell the truth.

And that means I need to keep Annika happy.

I take out my K-Pak and fire off a quick e-mail.

TO: year2troublemakers@kilteracademy.org
FROM: shinkle@kilteracademy.org
SUBJECT: Crank it up!

Hi, guys! Great job so far! Your parents are TOTALLY surprised.

But what do you say we kick it up a notch? And show them what trouble REALLY looks like?

You know you want to! (And that Annika would want you to too!)

—Seamus

I press send, then peer through the window again. I can't see every Troublemaker because many of them have really good hiding spots, but the ones I can see whip out their K-Paks and read my message.

After that, the chaos starts. Abe makes bigger breakfast sculptures, faster. Their explosions are stronger and send food flying higher. I didn't think Gabby could sing any louder, but thanks to her megamicrophone, she can. As the volume goes up, so does the number of singers; there must be a special setting that multiplies her voice so it sounds like an entire Gabby chorus has entered the room. At the same time, whipped cream streams by. Plates and utensils zip through the air. A dozen chickens appear out of nowhere. They're soon joined by a pig and a goat. So much happens so fast, the scene begins to blur. Like I'm inside a speeding car, and the other Troublemakers and their families are acting crazy on the side of the road.

But two things are crystal clear.

The first is that it's getting to be too much. Parents are starting to lose it. Adults aren't laughing anymore. A few of the younger siblings, uncomfortable in the noise and confusion, are whimpering.

The second . . . is Mom.

She's standing at the far end of the room. Her back and spread-eagled limbs cling to the wall like fabric softener sheets to flannel. She's watching the commotion like she can't believe what she's seeing. But, hello—she knowingly sent me to a school for professional Troublemakers—how is any of this a surprise?

Dad stands next to her. His fists are raised, as if he plans to give a quick one-two to any whipped cream or robot bird that comes his way.

The noise is getting louder. It's only a matter of time before Good Samaritans hear the ruckus—and our teachers realize we're not coming for our cleaning assignments. Then they'll investi-gate, and they'll stop us.

Now's my chance. I raise the Kilter Katcher to the open window. Use the reel to zero in on Mom. Aim for the belt buckle at her waist.

And fire.

The hook releases. Watching the Katcher's screen and jerking its lever, I guide the hook through the labyrinth of Troublemakers, parents, and other moving obstacles. Fortunately, Mom's so stunned that she stays as still as a statue. After clearing the crowd, the hook zips toward her. The plan is to snag her belt buckle, then harmlessly tug her around the room until she resembles a Cloudview Community Center modern dancer. When she's as dizzy as I've often felt from everything that's happened since last October, I'll let go and watch her spin.

"Um, Seamus?" Lemon's voice comes from my K-Pak, which is in my shorts pocket. "We have company."

"Okay!" I call out, still guiding the Kilter Katcher. "Hang on. I'm about to—"

"LOSE?"

I turn toward the loud, low voice—just in time to see a man in white bolt inside the cafeteria's side entrance.

Mystery.

A smaller version of our cranky history teacher, also decked out in white, races after him.

Harrison. His assistant.

Before I can figure out what's happening, it's already happened.

Mystery and his sidekick charge into the cafeteria. Holding two enormous sacks each, they jump onto a table in the middle of the room, scattering chickens and sending feathers flying. Mystery brings two fingers to his mouth and whistles for the adults' attention. Once he has it, he and Harrison reach into their bags and start chucking things into the crowd. Like brooms. Mops. Garden hoses. Fly swatters. Watering cans. Pots and pans. Other various household items that, outside of Kamp Kilter, only parents use.

And because they've had years of practice, our parents know what to do with them now. When they see Mystery, they must realize the chaos isn't related to the imaginary million dollars they're waiting for—and they switch into battle mode. They catch the items easily, then start defending themselves. The broom diverts whipped-cream streams to the floor. Garden hoses are hooked up and water sprayed toward the ceiling, where several Troublemakers hide in eaves. Wooden spoons clang pots and pans, drowning out Gabby's singing.

I snatch my K-Pak from my pocket, connect to my entire class, and shout into the speaker.

"Troublemakers! Stay focused! Don't panic! Hold your ground! Remember: These are your parents! You've fought this battle before. The only difference now is that you're better prepared!"

Anxious to get in there and help, I jump off the rock—and fall to the ground. When I try to get up, I can't.

The Kilter Katcher. I forgot about it in all the excitement and never caught what I meant to. So instead of grabbing Mom's belt, the unguided line flew back toward the reel. And because I didn't wind it back up, it tangled around my arms and legs.

I wiggle and squirm against the plastic restraints. My K-Pak's back in my pocket, but I can't move my arms enough to reach it. The Kilter Katcher rod is on the ground a few feet away. I can't reach that, either.

I'm stuck. While, by the sounds of it, the biggest trouble-making battle ever waged gets even bigger.

"Lemon!" I shout. "Abe! Gabby! Alison! Carter! Anybody! HELP!"

Under other circumstances I wouldn't be so loud, because I wouldn't want the wrong person to hear me. But under these, I have no choice. If Mystery finds me before my classmates free me, who knows what he'll do?

"Well, what do we have here?"

My heart stops. My limbs freeze.

"I guess what goes around comes around, huh?" a familiar voice asks.

Somehow my head turns. I see Shepherd Bull squatting next to me. Eight dirty Incriminators are gathered behind him.

I force a smile. "Hey, Shepherd! Great to see you! Funny thing happened. I was playing with that fishing pole over there and—"

He clamps one dirty hand to my mouth. Grins. "Did I ask what you were doing? Do I look like I care what—"

"My mom wouldn't be very happy about this."

Now Shepherd Bull freezes.

"Elinor?" I mumble against his palm.

She steps out from behind the gang of misfits. Shepherd

Bull removes his hand, jumps up, and steps back. He actually looks nervous as she passes him. I feel that way as she walks around me, picks up the Kilter Katcher, and presses the release button.

The plastic line unwinds. In half a second, my arms and legs are free again.

"Thanks!" I scramble to my feet. "That was amazing timing. I was just—"

"Inside," Elinor barks. "Now."

I spin toward the building.

"Not you," she says, her voice softer.

I turn back as the Incriminators sprint to the cafeteria entrance.

"I thought you might need some help," she says. "And that taking charge of the Incriminators, on my own, might help my mom see I can be the daughter she wants me to be. I'm not working with them," she adds quickly. "I really didn't know they were here before you found out they were. But since they are, we might as well work together. There are two parents to every Troublemaker, after all. We could use the backup."

I'm so happy to see her here, and to know that she's not so mad that she'd leave me tangled up, I almost laugh.

But I don't. Because I'm trapped again.

By Annika. Who zips up in a golf cart, pulls me inside, and slams the gas pedal. Before I can ask what's going on, we jerk to a stop. Annika takes a pouch from the backseat, tosses it to me, and jumps out of the cart.

"Um—"

"Act now, talk later!" Annika yells, then disappears into the cafeteria.

Where did she come from? How did she know we were here? Does she know what's going on inside?

These are just a few of the many questions bouncing around my head. But I forget them all when I open the pouch and see what's inside.

The Kilter Academy Faculty Handbook.

Everything You Need to Know to Train Tomorrow's Trouble-makers Today.

Houdini has one of these. So do Samara, Wyatt, Fern, Devin, and Lizzie. Our teachers don't go anywhere without their copies. Flipping through the book, I see chapters on maintaining decorum. Keeping lessons fun yet informative. How to make know-it-all students realize they have much to learn. There's also a campus map featuring secret passages and underground tunnels, and a long list of hidden troublemaking tools that teachers can access anytime they need them.

A handwritten note is at the back of the book.

Seamus (or should I say, Professor Hinkle?),

You help me. I help you. Together, there's nothing we can't do.

Deal?

-Annika

This book contains top secret information. The fact that Annika has given it to me must mean one thing: She wants me to be a teacher. Not even a tutor, which is the next step in the professional Troublemaker's career. That means I can stay at Kilter. Teach kids my own age things that I think are important. Never have to worry about having fish sticks taken from me again.

Because I'll be in charge.

I don't know what made Annika decide to promote me—at all, let alone now—but we can talk about that later. Already imagining the fun I'll have, especially after I convince Annika that Lemon, Abe, Gabby, and Elinor should also be on the Kilter staff, I put the handbook back in the pouch and race toward the cafeteria. Before I can get too excited, I have to do two things.

Finish what we started today.

And tell Annika the truth.

"Seamus! Hurry!"

I've just burst through the back door. Annika's standing on top of the nearby buffet table, ankle-deep in home fries. When she sees me, she points at my feet. I look down—and see a barrel of shiny red apples. Early this morning they were meant to be eaten. Now they're meant to be thrown.

"You know what to do with them!" she shouts. "So do it already!"

"Hinkle!"

"Seamus!"

"This is out of control!"

My head snaps to the left, right, and left again as I look in the direction of the familiar voices. The room is jam-packed with people running, standing, and crawling, but I see Abe, Gabby, and Elinor. Along with the rest of our classmates and the Incriminators, they've switched from pranking parents to defending themselves as moms and dads zoom around the room, following Mystery's housekeeping orders. As they duck behind chairs and behind dirty breakfast plates, they look confused. Tired. And something I've never seen them be before.

Scared.

"Seamus!" Annika hollers. *"Now!"*

I jump up, stoop down, and grab an apple. As I scan the crowd, Annika shouts some more.

"HE! MUST! NOT! WIN!"

He? Not they?

I look at Annika. Her eyes are on fire as she stares across the cafeteria. My head snaps left again, and I know who he is.

Mystery. He's standing on a table on the other side of the room. He shouts commands into a megaphone as Harrison, who stands next to him, continues to arm parents.

"Son! There you are!"

My head snaps to the right once more—just as Dad dives under a flying sack of potatoes. He must decide that lower is safer, because he starts crawling toward me. I hurry over to him, reach out one hand to help him up.

"Seamus! My dear, dear boy! Thank goodness!"

My head snaps back to the left—just as Mom opens an enormous red net. Only a few feet away from me, she lowers her head and charges.

One of the first things I learned at Kilter was that too much thinking can get you into trouble—and make it harder to make trouble. So I don't think now. When I see Mom coming at me, prepared to catch me in her big red net, I stand up straight. Pull back my arm.

And collapse to the floor.

Chapter 30

DEMERITS: 0
GOLD STARS: 0

Enough!"

Lying flat on my back, I blink.

"Do you see yourselves?"

I can't see anything.

"You're all acting like children! And half of you are grown-ups!"

I wipe my eyes. My fingers come away wet.

"How is it raining inside?" a woman yells.

"When it's sunny outside?" a man shouts.

I smell smoke. Where there's smoke, there's fire. And once upon a time, where there was fire . . . there was usually Lemon.

Moving carefully to keep from slipping on the slick floor again, I climb to my feet. I take a plastic cafeteria tray from the table behind me and hold it over my head. Now protected from the water falling from the ceiling, I wipe my eyes dry and look up.

Lemon is here. He's standing on a table and holding a fistful of long, large matches toward the ceiling. The matches aren't lit now, but they were. The heat and smoke from their flames must've set off the sprinklers, which are still dousing—and confusing—parents, Troublemakers, and Incriminators.

"What is going on?" Lemon asks.

"Yes." Annika steps onto a chair, hops onto the table next to Lemon, and pushes him aside. "That's exactly what I'd like to know! Who's going to fill me in?"

The room falls silent. All I can hear is water dripping from wet furniture, hair, and clothes.

"Nobody?" Annika asks. "Really?"

Abe's standing ten feet away. I catch his eye. He shakes his head.

Personally, I don't want to confess to planning this attack in front of the entire camp. In addition to our families, Annika, Mystery, and the cafeteria staff, the Good Samaritans, Nurse Marla, and our teachers are here. They must've heard the noise and come running. I want to tell Annika everything, but not like this. I assume my fellow Troublemakers stay silent because they're trained not to tattle. As for our parents, they seem embarrassed, although I'm not sure if that's because of their behavior, or because they were caught. They may also have been trained not to tattle on Mystery.

Now Annika's trying to break our silence. And she seems to have her work cut out for her.

Or maybe not.

"Abe," she says. "Spill the beans and I'll give you a thousand Kommissary credits. You'll need them, since after that episode, when it was impossible to keep track of who was doing what, I have no choice but to reset your current demerit and gold-star tallies to zero."

"Two thousand credits," Abe says.

"Done," she says.

"We were teaching our parents an important lesson!" Abe declares.

I look at him. Gabby gasps.

"And what lesson would that be?" Annika asks.

"That Angel Makers are no match for Troublemakers."

Annika pauses. "Angel Makers?"

"That's a secret club," Abe explains. "For our parents. It teaches them tricks and pranks so that they can give us a taste of our own medicine, which is what they've been trying to do since we got here."

Annika's eyes narrow. "Every club needs a leader."

"That'd be Mr. Tempest," Abe says. "Or Mystery, as we call him."

"Stop right there!" Annika's arm flies forward, her pointer finger aiming at the back of the room.

We all turn around—just as GS George steps in front of the exit, blocking Mystery's escape. When Mystery tries to push past him, the tall Good Samaritan grabs him by the shoulder and pushes him down into a chair. Then he picks up the pig that's still roaming around the room, snacking on fallen food, and places it in Mystery's lap, locking him in place.

Annika frowns at Mystery, then at Abe. "How do you know about this club?"

"We spied on one of their meetings," Abe says.

"In a cool cave!" Gabby chimes in from across the cafeteria. "With a real secret passage!"

"When?" Annika asks.

Abe shrugs. "A few days ago?"

"And you're just bringing it to my attention now?"

Abe's mouth opens. Nothing comes out.

"We wanted to learn more first," I offer, heart thudding. "So we could tell you as much as possible."

Annika's head snaps toward me. "You knew about this too?"

I gulp. Nod.

"You did?" a familiar voice whispers.

Dad. He's standing somewhere behind me. I'm afraid to look away from Annika to look at him, so I nod again.

"Is this what your parents were up to?" Annika asks coolly. "When they were acting so strangely at home?"

"Yup," Abe says. "Mystery mailed them pamphlets and training materials. Then when you invited everyone to Kamp Kilter, he jumped at the chance to work with them in person. Whatever they learned during their secret meetings, they tried out on us when we were cleaning their cabins."

"And why would they do that?" Annika asks.

"To weird us out," Abe says. "So we'd stop acting up. And maybe even think we need them again. That's our best guess, anyway."

"You *do* need us!" Mrs. Hansen exclaims.

"*All* children need their parents!" Mr. Ryan adds.

"Not true!" Annika shouts. Then, as if realizing just how loud she was, she lowers her head and is quiet for a second. When she looks up and speaks again, her voice is back to its normal volume. "Well. I have much to discuss with many different people—you know who you are, and I'll get to you all. But for now, I must say I'm extremely disappointed. This is the thanks I get? For giving your families a fun-filled, free, luxurious vacation to enjoy while we continued working with your terrible kids—"

"They're not terrible!"

My chin falls.

Mom, who landed somewhere behind me when the sprinklers turned on, now steps forward. She's clutching the big red net she was about to capture me with before the sprinklers turned on.

"Really, Mrs. Hinkle?" Annika asks, now sounding almost amused. "Is that why you sent Seamus to Kilter Academy for Troubled Youth? The most exclusive reform school in the world? That accepts only the worst kids in the world?"

"Our kids aren't the worst!" Mom insists. "They're the best! They just have good days and bad days, like we all do. Seamus, my son . . ." When she turns and looks at me, she has tears in her eyes. "He's perfect! He doesn't have a bad bone in his body!"

"Mrs. Hinkle," Annika says, "most of us know why Seamus is here. You announced it yourself months ago, during Parents' Day lunch."

"I know. But I was wrong. I lied! Seamus didn't do it. His substitute teacher? She's alive! The apple he threw left a bump, and that was it! Just like I told you in an e-mail last—"

"She's right!" I chime in. Mom was about to tell Annika about the e-mail she sent her last semester—the one I deleted from Annika's K-Pak before she could read it, because I didn't want her to know the truth then. It's hard enough telling her the truth now, let alone the lengths I went to to keep it from her. "I didn't do what you thought I did. I know I should've told you way sooner, but—"

Annika holds up her hand. Everyone is silent. Feeling dozens of curious eyes on me, I'm tempted to crawl under Mom's big red net.

But then I feel a little better. Because Elinor weaves through the crowd and stands next to me. Her fingers find mine. Our arms brush together, and I feel the braided rope around her wrist.

She's wearing her friendship bracelet again.

"It's our fault!" Mom cries out, shattering the silence.

"Mrs. Hinkle," Annika says, "you'll need to—"

"No! I won't be quiet. I can't! Because it's my fault that Seamus is here. He didn't start down the wrong path on his own. I pushed him there!"

"Judith," Dad hisses. "This isn't the time to—"

"Yes! It is!" Mom faces me and turns me so I face her. Then she drops to her knees and holds my face between her palms. "It's my fault, Seamus. All my fault."

Still seated under a pig at the back of the room, Mystery snorts. Mom ignores him and continues.

"You see, when I was a little girl, I was painfully shy. Kids picked on me. I never stood up for myself. My parents, fearing

I'd break under the negative attention, were incredibly over-protective. They never taught me how to fight back and be strong. So when you were really little, and Bartholomew John walked all over you, and you came to me instead of defending yourself . . . well, I panicked. I didn't want you to live in fear the way I always had. So I pushed you to become harder. Tougher. So you could take care of yourself. And I admit, when you threw that apple in the school cafeteria—I was overjoyed! I thought finally, *finally*, my son has proven that he has that confidence, that *fire*, to take a stand and hold his own against whatever and whoever comes at him! I really believed I was doing my job the way it was meant to be done." Her eyes water more. She blinks quickly, sending tears down her face. "But then everything got so . . . messy. And you went away to Kilter, and I missed you. At first I was so proud to send you to a place that would nurture your natural troublemaking—"

"Who's cold?" Annika shouts suddenly.

Parents exchange looks. Shivering, most raise their hands.

"Let's towel off and warm up in the sun. Staff members, please escort our families and other guests"—she shoots a look at Shepherd Bull, who stands with a dozen Incriminators—"to the beach. We'll resume our group discussion shortly."

Scattered throughout the room, Houdini, Fern, Lizzie and my other teachers lead everyone toward the nearest exits. Still on her knees, Mom watches them go. Dad continues staring straight ahead. My friends and I exchange waves as they leave.

"Mr. and Mrs. Hinkle," Annika says, "you may join the others."

"But—" Mom and Dad say at the same time.

"I'd like a word with your son. Alone."

Mom looks at me. Dad looks at her, then at me. I'm about to reassure them that it's fine—even though I have no idea if it is—when Dad drops to his knees too. They both throw their arms around me and squeeze tighter than they ever have.

"I'm sorry, Seamus," Dad whispers near my ear. "I was just trying to help. I wanted everything to go back to normal. So when Mr. Tempest sent the Angel Makers information, I thought it was worth a shot. I know I went overboard, but—"

"Mr. Hinkle!" Annika barks. "We'll have plenty of time for heart-to-hearts later. Please join the others. Now."

As Annika picks up her K-Pak and starts typing—probably an e-mail to our teachers to make sure they don't lose sight of

Mystery—my parents' arms tighten around me even more. Then Mom kisses my right cheek. Dad kisses my left cheek. They both stand and start to leave.

Annika and I are having a staring contest that I'm about to let her win when Mom spins around and sprints back to me. She pulls me into another hug and talks fast.

"We won't go back to normal. Okay? When we get home, I won't push you to do anything you don't want to do. I'll cancel my Kommissary subscription so they never send another weapon. I've been nice to Bartholomew John because I thought he was helping toughen you up, but I won't talk to him again. And you never have to be tough again. If you feel like crying, cry. If you're scared, don't try to be brave. If you want me to sit next to you until you fall asleep every night, the way you asked me to when you were just a little boy, I will. And I'll tuck you in every night with this." She opens up the red net she's been carrying, then shakes it out and holds it up for me to see. Different images are sewn into the fabric, which isn't a net, after all. It's a blanket.

"Is that our house?" I ask.

"Yes. And you, Daddy, and me. One happy family." She

pauses, sniffs. "I started making this quilt for you when you were a baby . . . but I never finished. My own silliness got in the way. But ever since we got here I've been holed up in the arts and crafts cabin day and night. I wanted to finish it before we went home." She looks to Annika. "That's why I didn't want to role play. I couldn't bear to hear what Seamus thought I was thinking about the Unfortunate Apple Incident. Not until I finished this, and presented it to him, and told him how much I love him, how much I've *always* loved him." She looks at me again, her eyes watering. "I can't change the past, but—"

"Mrs. Hinkle!"

Mom jumps. So do I.

"You need to join the others!" Annika yells into her megaphone. "Immediately!"

Now *I* hug *Mom*. "It's okay. Neither of us has been on our best behavior, but it's not too late. We can fix it. As soon as we're home."

She kisses my head and hurries away. When she's gone, Annika climbs down from the table she's been standing on, then leans against it.

"Your parents love you," she says.

My lips start to lift automatically. I force them back down. "Yes. I guess they do."

"Abe's parents love him. Gabby's parents love her. Lemon's parents are so crazy about him they couldn't bring themselves to prank him while at camp."

"How do you know that?" I ask, since she just found out about Mystery's secret group.

"Silly Seamus," she says. "You must know by now that I see everything. Didn't the fact that the Kommissary mysteriously continued monitoring your troublemaking while you were home convince you of that?"

So that's how that happened. She must've installed some sort of trackers on our K-Paks before we left school for the summer.

"Then how'd you miss the secret meetings taking place under your nose?" I ask.

One of her eyebrows lifts into a high arch. "Do I sense . . . *tone*, Seamus? That's very unlike you."

I start to defend myself, but stop. Because what's to defend?

"You're right. It is unlike me. And you know why? Because

I'm a good kid. Up until a few months ago, all I did was what everyone asked of me. I did my homework and got great grades. I made my bed and took out the trash. I tried to make my teachers and parents happy." I pause and take a deep breath. "What I did *not* do . . . was kill Miss Parsippany. She's alive. I've talked to her. Which means I'm not a murderer. I've been lying about what I did and who I am for months."

And there it is. The truth. Finally. Considering how mad she seems now, Annika will kick me out of Kilter instead of making me a teacher, but that's okay. Mom, Dad, and I will go home. Start over. Maybe not forget all of this ever happened if it brings us to a better place than we were before, but at least let it become the past so we can get started on the future.

Annika folds her arms over her chest. "You've been lying."

"Yes. A lot."

"You're very good at it."

For a Troublemaker, this is a compliment. For a good kid, it's the opposite. So I don't thank her the way I would've before now.

"Well, if we're sharing secrets, I suppose it's my turn." Annika pauses. "I knew."

"What?"

"About Miss Parsippany. And about you. Not right away, of course. You wouldn't have been accepted into Kilter if I'd known the truth immediately. Once I did, I considered letting you go and ending your troublemaking career before it started. But by then, it was too late. Your career had already taken off. It was clear you possessed raw talent, the likes of which I'd never seen before."

I stare at her, trying to make sense of what she's saying. "But . . . when? How? Did you get my mom's e-mail? The one that I deleted from your K-Pak?"

"You deleted an e-mail from my K-Pak?"

"The day we got back from IncrimiNation. You left the room—and your computer. I saw the message and erased it before you could read it and send me away."

I expect her to yell at me, but she smiles instead.

"I never saw your mother's e-mail. Nice work."

Again, for a Troublemaker, this is a compliment. For me, it's not. So I don't say anything.

"As for how I learned the truth," Annika continues, "let's just say I have my ways. As I do with so many things." At this, she stands up and begins walking across the room, her hands clasped behind her back. "You're very lucky, you know. To have parents who love you so. Not all children are as fortunate." She turns and walks back the other way. "Do you recall the video I showed you and your classmates before announcing your first Ultimate Troublemaking Task?"

"Yes." In it, a young Annika sat by a window, waiting for someone to come home. While she was watching snowflakes fall, she got a phone call. Whatever the caller said made her cry. The video ended right after that.

"When that video was taken, I was waiting for my father. He'd been away on business but promised to be home for Christmas. An hour after his scheduled arrival, he called to say that he wouldn't be coming home after all. That was the story of my childhood. My father cared so little for my sister and me, he saw us only when it was convenient for him. On the few occasions that we were together, he showered us with gifts and other meaningless tokens of affection."

"Like Annika's Apex?" I ask.

"Precisely. Many wouldn't find an amusement park made just for them a meaningless gift, but I did. I knew my father gave it only to make up for his perpetual absence and inattention. I'd have enjoyed it more if he'd spent time there with me. If we'd gone on rides together, and if he'd won me a stuffed animal from one of the game booths . . . but we didn't. It was just another grand yet empty gesture to distract me from the fact that he didn't love me enough to want to simply *be* with me."

This is a lot to take in. I do my best. "So . . . that's why you were happy when Capital T set the carousel on fire? Because it reminded you of bad times you had as a kid?"

"Indeed. Especially since the bad times only got worse when my mother was no longer with us."

I recall the newspaper clipping I accidentally saw in Annika's childhood bedroom several months ago. It announced Mrs. Kilter's passing away from a mysterious illness when Annika was twelve years old.

"I'm sorry about that," I say.

"Thank you." She takes a big breath, then releases it. "I am too. I was devastated when it happened. The only thing that kept me going was that I believed my father would be home after that. He'd have to be. But he wasn't. He was around just long enough to wipe a few tears away, but then it was back to business as usual.

In fact, he was around even less. He hired two live-in nannies to care for Nadia and me."

"Didn't he love your mother?" I ask, shocked that any parent would leave his or her children in such awful circumstances.

"Yes, I believe he did. And it's possible that he left as quickly as he did to try to escape the pain. It's also possible that Nadia and I were excruciating reminders of his loss. But that doesn't excuse what he did."

"No," I agree, "it doesn't."

"I tried to earn his love. I wrote him letters. I drew him pictures. When he was home, I cleaned and cooked and brought him his slippers, even though we had staff to do all those things. I did whatever I could think of to be the best daughter possible."

"What happened?"

"It didn't work. So I was forced to try another approach."

"Troublemaking?" I guess.

"You got it. Tricks. Pranks. Lies. Everything you've been taught at Kilter I tested on my father decades ago."

"What happened then?"

"I definitely got his attention."

"But not his love?"

She stops walking and faces me. "No. That continues to elude me to this very day."

This very day? As in today? "Do you still see him?"

"All the time. He's my prisoner."

My heart stops. Annika laughs.

"Don't look so alarmed. He's not locked up in a windowless cell. He can have all the sunshine and fresh air he wants. So long as he plays by my rules."

"What kind of rules?"

She shrugs. "I ask that he stays where I can see him, within reason. And that he doesn't try to escape. And . . . that he teaches the Troublemakers of tomorrow about the Troublemakers of yesterday."

She falls silent. Waits. Inside my head, fragments of information click together like puzzle pieces.

"Is your dad . . . Mr. Tempest?"

She winks. "And that, Seamus, is why I've kept you around."

She resumes pacing. A million questions bounce around my brain. I ask the one that bounces harder and faster than the rest.

"Does Elinor know? That Mr. Tempest is her grandfather?"

"Probably not. My sister stopped speaking to him long ago, before Elinor was born. And I never told her he was working for me, so she didn't have this information to share with her daughter."

"And you didn't tell Elinor that her grandpa was here? That she was seeing him every day?"

"I really don't see how that was my responsibility."

"You're her *aunt*."

Annika stills. With her back to me, she speaks slowly. Quietly. "True. But being related doesn't automatically make two people family. Telling Elinor about her grandfather wouldn't have been enough. It wouldn't have made up for everything else I did—and didn't do for her." Annika pauses, then shakes her head. When she continues, her voice is normal. Sharp. "Besides. As you saw for yourself, my father isn't exactly good grandpa material. It's quite possible I did Elinor a favor by keeping them apart."

I hate to say it, but this *is* possible. Still, shouldn't Elinor have at least known that she and Mr. Tempest were related? So she could've decided for herself if she wanted him to be family?

"Is that why his last name is different from yours and Nadia's?" I ask. "To help keep his real identity a secret from Elinor?"

"And everyone else. Plus, 'Tempest' is an excellent name for my father. It means severe disturbance. And that's what he's always been." Annika faces me. "Getting back to our history, when I was older and more experienced, I really got his attention. I pretended to be his secretary and canceled important business meetings around the world while he was still traveling to them. I infiltrated his financial accounts and drained every penny. I hacked his e-mail, wrote preposterous notes on his behalf, and blasted them to everyone in his address book. Soon his business, which had been everything to him, was gone. He had nothing."

"Except you."

"And Nadia. Who, by the way, only started IncrimiNation when she saw how successful Kilter had become. She was jealous. She still is. And she's been fighting to catch up for years."

"Is that why Incriminators are so bad?" I ask. "Because she thinks the worse they are, the more attention she'll get?"

"Exactly. She's trying to outdo what I've done so well."

I pick another question from the swirling mass inside my head. "And you started Kilter to try to help other kids with bad parents?"

She pauses. "Correct."

"Will you ever let Mr. Tempest go?"

"He's free to leave anytime. All he has to do . . . is love me. Truly. Unconditionally. The way any parent should love his child." Annika's voice has grown softer. When she speaks again, it's harder than I've ever heard it. "But he'd rather start a secret organization of parents. Form an army. Try to get back at me."

For a moment, we're quiet. Annika stares off at nothing. I try to keep my head from exploding.

"Well," I finally say. "Good luck with everything. I'll be thinking of you guys. When I'm home."

Annika looks at me. "You're not going home."

I swallow. "But Miss Parsippany's alive. I lied."

"Better than any Troublemaker ever has."

"But—"

"Seamus. You have great power. You're capable of doing so much good for countless kids around the world."

I shake my head. "Thanks, but I don't think so. I know I've made a lot of trouble, but I'm just . . . not a Troublemaker. I don't have that kind of power."

"Yes. You do. Right now you're wielding it more than you ever have." She smiles. "Don't you see? No one else knows what you do. I've told you all my secrets. That's how much I want you to stay. *That's* how powerful you are. And together we can change the world!"

I have to admit, when she puts it like this . . . I do feel a little like a superhero. But then I glimpse Mom's quilt draped across the back of the chair. I remember Ike's warning. I remind myself that even though Annika claims to want to assist countless kids with bad parents, the only person she really cares about is herself.

"I'm sorry," I say, backing away. "But I can't help you. Not anymore. My parents and I have made a lot of mistakes. And we might not have the best relationship, but it can get better. So we're going to work on it. At home."

As I'm talking, Annika walks toward me, matching my pace step for step. When my feet move faster, so do hers. When I bump into something and stop, she does too.

"Whoopsie!" Dad exclaims. "Sorry about that, son. Your mother and I are all dry and ready to go when you are."

I turn around and see him and Mom standing by the cafeteria's main entrance.

"Yoo-hoo!" A familiar female voice sings somewhere nearby. "Annika! I'm here! I made it! And you'll never guess who I brought with—"

"Miss Parsippany?" I ask as a woman who looks a lot like my former substitute teacher and current pen pal bursts through the cafeteria's back door.

Miss Parsippany freezes. She looks from me, to my parents, to Annika, and back to me.

"Seamus! What a surprise! I had no idea—"

"Seamus?" Another voice calls out. This one's also familiar, but male. "You mean Hinkle? What's *he*—"

"Bartholomew John?" I stare at my archnemesis. He can't really be standing next to Miss Parsippany . . . can he?

"Bartholomew John?" A third familiar voice asks. This one belongs to Lemon. He, Elinor, Abe, and Gabby, have come back to the cafeteria. "As in the kid who took your fish sticks? And made your life miserable?"

"Whoa." Dad holds both hands before him, like he's trying to stop the crazy scene from getting crazier. "Does anyone know what's going on here?"

"Of course," Annika says easily. "We're waiting."

"For what?" Mom asks.

Annika looks at me. Her eyes glitter. "For Seamus to decide."

"Decide what?" Elinor asks nervously.

Annika shrugs. "Who he can trust. The grown-up with whom he's shared his innermost thoughts of the past nine months, never suspecting that she was really working for me as a Kilter Academy recruiter. . . ."

My head snaps toward Miss Parsippany. She bites her lip and looks away.

"Myself, who only wants what's best for him—and for countless children around the globe. . . ."

My eyes meet Annika's. She winks again.

"Or his parents. Who, when he made a single mistake, couldn't ship him off fast enough. Especially once his mother learned about Kilter's true purpose from my best recruiter, who divulged top secret information while half-conscious and recovering from a concussion in the hospital. *And* whose mother not only wanted him to get into trouble, but then befriended his ultimate enemy, Bartholomew John, once her son was gone."

"Only because I thought he'd helped you toughen up!" Mom whispers urgently near my ear.

I step away from her. When no one says anything else, I turn slowly. I look at Annika. My friends. Miss Parsippany. Bartholomew John. I think of the past nine months. What happened before them, and what might happen after.

And then, heart racing, I go to my parents. I take Mom's hand in one hand and Dad's in the other, the way I used to when I was a little boy. And I ask the only question I can think of.

"Can we go home now?"

Chapter 31

And then we went swimming. And snorkeling. And after that we went for a walk on the beach. And after that we went to a drive-in movie where you'll never. Guess. What. Happened! We shared a bucket of popcorn! Just the two of us! That was the first time we ever shared anything just because we wanted to! It. Was. Amazing!"

"What about the movie?" Abe asks.

"What about it?" Gabby asks.

"Was it any good?"

"No idea! I was so happy I couldn't even pay attention." Gabby looks away and waves. A second later, Flora, her older sister, appears. Gabby hooks one arm around her neck and kisses her cheek. "We're not just sisters. We're best friends! Right?"

"We're definitely not enemies," Flora says. "But if you don't mind, I want to get back to this." She holds up a book and disappears.

"I recommended that!" Gabby declares. "She's been suggesting fun activities to do together, and I've been suggesting books for her to read!"

"That's great, Gabby," I say. "I'm so glad you and your sister are getting along better."

"The whole family is," Gabby says. "We've been spending so much time together since we got home three weeks ago. As crazy as Kamp Kilter was, it actually worked. Who knew?"

"Not me," I say.

"Or me," Abe says.

"Or me," Lemon says.

"Or me," Elinor says.

I look at Elinor on my laptop screen and smile. We're talking with the help of an online video chat program—on regular computers, not K-Paks. Annika confiscated those before kicking us all out of camp, which she did as soon as I said I wanted to leave. At first it was hard not being able to reach my friends anytime I felt like it, but a few days after we got home Dad gave me his old laptop. My friends and I had exchanged phone numbers and called each other to exchange e-mail addresses. Now we're in touch as easily as we were before—and without any Kilter-related distractions.

"How about you, Abe?" I ask. "Any change on the home front?"

"'Change' is an understatement," he says. "The second we walked in the door Dad started chucking sports equipment. Baseballs, basketballs, footballs, anything you could throw or hit, he shoved into big black garbage bags. He promised he'd never try to get me to do anything I didn't want to do."

"Aw!" Gabby says. "That's so nice!"

"It is," Abe agrees. "Only after he threw everything out, I started to feel bad. I thought if playing catch every now and then would really make my dad that happy, then I could throw him a bone—or a softball—every now and then. So each night after dinner, we talk while we play catch. When we're done, we go inside and hang out with Mom. Sometimes I teach them something about art, and we all draw or paint. And sometimes they watch TV while I work on my latest project. Either way, we're in the same room. Together." He shrugs. "And it's kind of fun."

"Sounds it," I say. "Lemon? How are things with your family?"

He smiles. "Better than ever. My parents and I talked a lot after we got back, and agreed that Finn and I could both keep playing with fire—but *only* on family camping trips. Then we build campfires—safely and in a controlled environment—like my dad and I used to." He picks up his laptop and turns it around so we have a view of Finn and his parents holding frying pans over a small campfire. A large tent is behind them. A long strand of origami stars is looped across the front of the tent. Lemon turns the laptop back around. "And everyone's taken up my newer hobby. Turns out folding paper is fun for the whole family."

"What about you, Hinkle?" Abe asks. "Anything different with your family?"

"Definitely," I say. "For a few days we all tiptoed around each other and were really careful about what we said and did.

We were extra polite, almost like we didn't know each other. But we're loosening up a little bit now. Tonight we're even going to a carnival in town. With rides and games and junk food."

"And a fish-stick booth?" Gabby asks.

I shudder. "I hope not. After everything that's happened, I'm kind of done with frozen fried seafood."

"What about cotton candy?" Mom calls out from the hallway as she walks past my bedroom.

"And buttery popcorn?" Dad adds, following after her with a laundry basket.

"Nope!" I call back. "I'm all over those!"

"Me too!" Mom exclaims.

"Your veggie-loving mom is going to down straight-up sugar?" Abe shakes his head. "Talk about change."

I grin. Then I look at Elinor, and the expression fades slightly. Besides a brief phone call, during which I got her e-mail address just before she said she couldn't really talk, we haven't been in touch. I have no idea where or how she's been.

As if sensing my concern, Elinor picks up her laptop and turns it so we can see the room behind her. The room appears to be in a restaurant. It's empty except for one table, where two women and one elderly man sit, picking at their dishes and not speaking.

I bring the laptop screen closer to my face and squint. Abe, Lemon, and Gabby do the same. "Is that . . . ?"

"My mom?" Elinor finishes. "And Annika? And Mr. Tempest—a.k.a. Mystery, a.k.a. Grandpa? Yup."

She sounds pleased. That makes me happy.

"Where are you?" I ask. The dining room doesn't look like any I've seen at Kilter or IncrimiNation.

"Kansas." Elinor turns her laptop back around. "It was the weirdest thing. After everyone left Kamp Kilter, Annika asked me to stay behind. Then she actually apologized for not being a better aunt and said she'd like to make it up to me."

"Wow," Gabby says.

"I know," Elinor says. "She was like a different person. She even asked *how* she could make it up to me. I said I wanted her and Mom to stop fighting, and I asked if we could all have dinner together in a neutral zone. Somewhere between Kilter and IncrimiNation. That's how we ended up here. And somehow she convinced my mom to come too."

"And Mystery?" Abe asks.

Elinor glances behind her, then faces the laptop and holds up a porcelain doll. "He gave me this," she whispers. "Once Annika told me we were related. His whole body seemed to get smaller, like he'd been possessed by an evil old man until the second he found out that he was my grandfather. Then he left the camp cafeteria, where we'd been talking, and came back twenty minutes later with this. I think he got it from that creepy oversize dollhouse in the woods."

I picture the small cottage. That's where Mystery once chased after me with an ax. How times have changed.

"Anyway," Elinor continues, "they're not exactly best friends yet. Or even really talking. But at least they're here. *We're* here. Together. It's a start."

She hugs the doll close. As she does, I notice she's wearing her friendship bracelet. The one that matches mine, which I haven't taken off since the day she tied it around my wrist.

"What about trouble?" Abe asks, moving on. "Has anyone made any?"

"Nope," Gabby says.

"Never," Elinor says.

"Don't want to," Lemon says.

"Ditto," I say.

"Same here," Abe says. "So . . . what does that mean? Do we all go back to our regular schools in the fall?"

"I guess so," I say.

"But then we can't see each other every day!" Gabby pouts.

"Sure we can," I say. "On our computers. Just like this."

"It's not the same." Gabby's pout turns into a frown.

"We can still get together," Lemon offers. "Like during breaks and vacations."

"Right," Abe says. "We'll have rotating alliance meetings. At each of our houses. And instead of talking about trouble, we'll just talk. Hang out. Have fun."

"That sounds great," I say.

"Perfect!" Gabby smiles.

"Oh, and Elinor?" Abe asks.

Her eyes meet his on her laptop screen. "Yeah?"

"That means you, too. Welcome to Capital T."

Her face lights up. "Thanks."

"Hey, little sis." Flora appears next to Gabby. "I'm going go-karting with some friends. Want to come?"

Gabby's eyes grow wide. "Do I!" She blows us a kiss. "Miss and love you guys! Call you later!"

"I should go too," Lemon says. "Dinner will be ready soon."

"Dad and I are about to toss around the football," Abe says.

"I need to try to get Mom, Annika, and Grandpa talking," Elinor says.

"And I need to eat some cotton candy," I say. "Check in tomorrow?"

"Tomorrow," everyone agrees, and signs off.

I'm about to close my laptop when I have an idea. I sign into my e-mail and start a new message.

TO: parsippany@wahoo.com
FROM: goodkid@wahoo.com
SUBJECT: Thanks?

Dear Miss Parsippany,

Since we didn't get to talk at Kamp Kilter a few weeks ago, I just wanted to send a quick (last) note.

You probably don't need me to tell you that I was really surprised to see you that day. At all, let alone with Bartholomew John. I was also really surprised to learn that not only did you know about Kilter's true purpose all along, you helped recruit me. And at first that made me mad. The past year hasn't been easy, and it wouldn't have happened if I hadn't gotten involved with a top secret trouble-making school.

But guess what? Even despite all the weirdness and confusion, things are way better now than they were that day I accidentally knocked you over (still sorry about that, by the way!). Mom, Dad, and I are really getting along for the first time ever. I have a great group of friends. And I learned that if ever I have to defend myself or anyone I care about, all I need is a piece of fruit and a second to aim. So now I wonder if I should be thanking you.

Either way, I want you to know that I don't think you're a terrible person for recruiting Troublemakers. Annika's hard to say no to. And besides, in the end, Kilter did what the best reform school in the country should do. It made kids behave, and it brought families closer together.

That's the truth.

Sincerely,

Seamus

I send the e-mail and close my laptop. Then I hop off the bed and start toward the door. Just as I'm about to leave the room, I glimpse something out of the corner of my eye.

A shiny red apple. Just like the one I threw across the Cloudview Middle School cafeteria all those months ago. I'd grabbed it from the fridge earlier and brought it up here to snack on. Then I got the chat request from Abe, left it on my desk, and forgot about it.

Now I go to the desk and pick it up. Turning it over in my hand, I think about everything that's happened since I aimed for Bartholomew John and hit Miss Parsippany instead. I think of my first trip to Kilter, and standing by the chain-link fence topped with barbed wire. Annika holding a water gun to my neck. Meeting Elinor, Lemon, Abe, and Gabby. Getting to know Ike, Houdini, and my other teachers. Dodging the Good

Samaritans. Calling Ms. Marla. E-mailing my former substitute teacher. Stealing a helicopter and sneaking off to the desert. Making mischief. Having fun.

When I picture the chaos in the Kamp Kilter cafeteria, one question comes to mind.

Who knew a single apple could make so much trouble?

And then I grin, take a big bite, and hurry from the room to find my parents.